Pursuit of
the Prodigal

BOOKS BY
LOUIS AUCHINCLOSS

The Indifferent Children

The Injustice Collectors

Sybil

A Law for the Lion

The Romantic Egoists

The Great World and Timothy Colt

Venus in Sparta

Pursuit of the Prodigal

by Louis Auchincloss

Pursuit of
the Prodigal

HOUGHTON MIFFLIN COMPANY BOSTON

The Riverside Press Cambridge

1959

126586

FOR JAMES OLIVER BROWN

CONTENTS

Parmelee Cove

PART I

Parmelee
Cove

REESE PARMELEE had always promised himself that when he grew up and married, he would never live at Parmelee Cove. And when he *had* grown up and married, Esther had at least professed to agree with him. But that had been back in 1941, and by the time the war was over and he had returned from the Pacific to be a law clerk in Clark, Day & Parmelee on Broad Street, he had succumbed, rather inertly and much to his own disgust, to the usual flood of arguments: that children could not be brought up in New York City, that Granny Parmelee was offering him for nothing a home of his own and, finally, the clinching point, that it would actually *help* Granny, the hitherto so grand and unhelpable, if the whole family would stick together to keep the old place in Northfield going. For the money — and here the voices were lowered — was not what it had been. The money, the unmentionable money, had to be mentioned at last. Grandpa, it seemed, had left things in rather a mess. It was only another proof of what Reese had long suspected: that all the Parmelee zest for life, all the Parmelee love of adventure, all the Parmelee superiority to the crass and worldly and mundane, depended, and had always depended, on the now dwindling pile of Granny Parmelee's fortune.

When Parmelee Cove had first been purchased in 1895, on what had then seemed like a remote and unsociable part of Long Island's north shore, it had represented the determination of Reese's grandfather to underline the difference between himself and the Hubbells. Indeed, Grandpa Parmelee had been apt to speak of his own father-in-law, the president of a great railway, as a duke might have spoken of a brakeman. "Surely," he had said to his friends in the Century or the Knickerbocker, "there are better ways to spend one's money than rearing Florentine palazzos in Newport and filling them with bad Corots." And the big house at the Cove survived to Reese's day as a monument to the eclecticism of his grandfather's taste. Shorn of one wing in the nineteen-thirties (though, as Granny always said, it looked as if it might grow it back) the great gabled shingled hulk still presented forty windows to the lawn that ran down to the sound. Within, the cavernous dark rooms were heaped with good and bad, irretrievably intermixed. There were the marks, of course, of late Victorianism: enormous jardinieres and bronze deer and elephants, Bouguereau nudes and Gérôme bazaars, Greek chairs designed by Alma-Tadema and unexpected little conservatories with rather dirty, plopping fountains. But there was also the gleaming refulgence of Tiffany glass, the small, oblong, reflective portraits of John La Farge, two matchless Houdon busts of George Parmelee, an ancestral ambassador and his lady, a whole dining hall of Duncan Phyfe and in the main parlor a magnificent set of rose-red Louis XV furniture made for Madame de Pompadour herself. Mrs. Parmelee, now well in her eighties, lived here with her aging and faithful household. The subsidiary buildings on the place had all been constructed in the same gabled shingle style: the barn, the garage, the gatehouse, the superintendent's cottage, even that massive, unheated wooden cube, the indoor tennis court. It was the kind of place one visualized as the abandoned relic of a grander era; a passing boy might have assumed that he could hurl a pebble through the gatehouse window with impunity. But if he had ever dared, he would have soon discovered how quickly the police from Northfield would have tracked him down. For Parmelee Cove was very far from a crumbling ruin. It had become, like many of its neighbors, a kind of small development, but a development limited to Parmelees, to the children and grandchildren of the dowager in the big house. The Alfred Parmelees, Reese's parents, lived in a sober red brick house which they had built near the main road, planting out of sight all the shingle on the place. Fanny Parmelee Talcott, Reese's aunt, had erected a low white modern house on the beach in full sight of and in startling contrast to her mother's mansion, while Vera Parmelee Reid, the youngest of the second generation, who had married a professor at Columbia, occupied the white farmhouse, the oldest structure on the place, which she had remodeled and expanded. Each of the old lady's children was convinced that he or she had the perfect habitat and indulgently smiled on the others'. All were agreed that their mother's house was a lovable monstrosity.

The married grandchildren occupied more humble quarters. The Talcott twins had remodeled the barn into a two-family house, one of Reese's sisters had an apartment over the garage and the oldest Reid girl had dragged in a prefabricated house which her grandmother had made her hide out of sight behind the indoor court. Reese, as the eldest grandchild and sole male Parmelee of his generation, had been awarded the gatehouse. It was the best built structure on the place, and as the huge wrought iron gates attached to it were now permanently locked, the service drive having been converted into the main entrance, there was no crunching of gravel to disturb the sleepers at night. From the other side, indeed, where the twin gables overlooked a small English garden, only the raised wings of the eagle on top of the nearer gatepost were visible. It was generally agreed that Reese and Esther were lucky.

The gatehouse, indeed, was so far from the rest of the buildings that it was "practically independent." But Reese, for all his love of the land itself, every foot of which he had known since boyhood, could never quite get over his sense that these locked gates, whose huge rusting grillwork he could see in the morning from his bathroom window as he shaved, were doing their superannuated best to keep him in. Time was a great leveler, and Reese refused to see any valid distinction between what his grandfather had created on Long Island and what the old man had sought to avoid in Newport.

On a particularly hot morning in late June, almost four years after the Japanese surrender, Reese was having breakfast with Esther before driving to the station. There was a faint aching in the back of his head from the whiskey that he had drunk the night before — his sister, Joan, and his brother-in-law had come for dinner, and they always stayed too late — and Reese resented as usual his wife's unquenchable good spirits. Esther even hummed as she strode back and forth between the kitchen and dining room, as big and brown-eyed as a farm girl, keeping her square chin in line with her broad shoulders, always half smiling, seeming to have stepped down from the colored eighteenth century world of the "season" engravings on the walls, where youth was always healthy, poverty patient and old age benign. Reese had the feeling that morning that he and the humid weather were to her a rather laughable pair of twins which, like everything else in a Long Island summer, had to be "made the best of." If he hadn't shaved as closely as he might have, if he hadn't properly combed the high standing shock of his absurdly blond hair, if he hoped that his blue eyes were more sullen than usual, it was to dispel in his own mind the idea of how neatly he matched Esther physically, to obliterate the picture, as described by one of his aunts, of "two great big handsome overgrown youngsters." As he felt that morning, he would have rather had the hundred and ninety pounds of his hulky figure turn into soft fat than continue to justify the family legend of young Reese, a latter-day Billy Budd in the wicked sophistication of Long Island's north shore.

Esther came back and sat down at the table. She was wearing her "Can I have *two* minutes for business?" look, with the smile of a nurse who raises the needle to a bared arm. But then, as always with Esther, she sensed his disapproval of the look and puckered her brow. The vanished smile, however, hovered about her features like the ghost of an apology to which she felt he was not entitled. "Will you talk to Alfred tonight? About his summer homework? Honestly, Reese, he hasn't done a thing."

"Why should he? Why can't he enjoy his summer?"

"Oh, darling, you know perfectly well that if he doesn't pick up his grades, he's *never* going to get into St. Lawrence's!"

Reese stared at her almost with admiration. He could never cease to wonder at women's reputation for subtlety. Actually they obtained their ends by the crudest kind of stubbornness. For years he had made clear to her his reluctance to have Alfred go to St. Lawrence's, and for as many years she had pretended not to hear him. It annoyed him intensely that she should so take for granted that his talk was simply talk, "men's talk," never meant to have any relation to the practicalities of daily life. "Why must you always assume that we're going to send him to St. Lawrence's?"

Her clear brown eyes met his, and he waited to see how he would be "coped with."

"Because if he goes there, Granny Parmelee will pay his tuition," she answered mildly.

"I never heard there was any tuition at the Northfield Public School."

"Oh, he's to go there, is he?"

"Why not?"

"Won't he feel just a bit different when the rest of the boys at Woodbury Day go off to Choate and Exeter and St. Lawrence's?"

"Good. I want him to feel different."

"Oh, Reese!" Her tone was suddenly impatient, and she looked away, as if he were pushing a game beyond the boundaries of taste. "I know it's fun to say: 'To hell with everything.' I'd often like to do it myself. But unhappily somebody in the family has to be practical."

"And we always have to admire the practical one, don't we?" He did not look up as he said this because he knew that she was staring at him now with her fixed, quizzical stare. His tone would have suggested that this was something more than a morning mood.

"Reese, we needn't go on with this, you know," she said unexpectedly.

He looked up, startled. Had she heard about Cynthia? "Go on with what?"

"With our whole way of living. If you don't like your job and living here at the Cove, we can pull up stakes. There's no law that says we have to stay here."

Oh, but there was! There was a law in that bright smile, in the undaunted cheerfulness of that manner. There was a law in her courage, in her challenge to him to provide a better life if he could. And if he ever should provide it, with what deft fingers would she speedily transform it into another Parmelee Cove!

"You think I'm saying this only for effect," she continued. "But I'm not. I mean it."

"I'm sure you mean it," he mumbled. How could those eyes *not* know about Cynthia?

"Of course, it would be difficult for you to get as good a

job. And it would obviously be impossible for us to get another free house. And there's the question of Al's school. But these are only problems, and problems can always be solved. *If* you make up your mind that what you really and truly want is a change!"

He stared, fascinated, as she put him firmly back in his place. But was he being fair? She had made him an offer. What had he made her?

"Esther," he said, troubled, "if I knew what I really and truly wanted, even if it was only a change, I'd be further along than I am. It's hard to describe." He passed a hand over his brow. Was there *any* use talking? "It's as if . . . well, as if I'd lost my sense of the function of things. When I had that fever in Guam in the war, I can remember looking at an orange and wanting it, but not having any idea how to take it into me. It didn't seem to have any relation to my hands or nose or mouth. It's a bit how I feel now when I think of a school like St. Lawrence's or a brief at the office. I know what it is, but I don't know how to absorb it. Does that make *any* sense?"

Her look of steadfast sympathy had gradually clouded over as he talked. "You don't suppose you should see a doctor?"

"Oh, no . . . no. It's nothing that bad."

"It doesn't really sound like anything a change of scene would cure, does it?"

"No."

"You're sleeping all right?"

"Like the dead."

"And eating properly?"

"As you see."

Her eye suddenly took in the clock, and she gave a little cry. "Then perhaps it can wait till this evening, darling. You'll miss your train!"

How many thousands of suburban discussions had ended on that note! As Reese drove to the station, too fast and too jerkily, he had ample time to reflect that Esther was justified in her assurance. She was bound to win. For there never seemed to be any clear-cut arguments any more. Everybody was so damnably reasonable; his parents and uncles and aunts were constantly braying in his ears that they *knew* these were changing times, that they realized they weren't living in the "dark ages." Old Dr. Avery, the headmaster of St. Lawrence's in Reese's own day would have simply given him hell. Reese wondered if Dr. Avery wasn't, in the long run, the easier type to deal with. At least one had known where one stood.

Which was precisely what he had never been sure of, from his earliest childhood, at Parmelee Cove. It had always been represented to him as a haven of happiness where Grandpa and Granny had been able to preserve for their descendants an atmosphere of kindliness and rather whooping enthusiasm amid a great deal of physical exercise. Outside the gates lurked the envious wolves of worldliness and snobbishness, but that was why one had gates. "What a wonderful place to bring up children" was what Reese always heard his mother's friends say, and his mother would smile in agreement, for she had long accepted the Parmelee ways. If she had ever thought it was not a wonderful thing to live so surrounded by her husband's family, she had never said so. Like a foreign princess imported to wed the heir apparent, she seemed to have left all reminders of her own upbringing with her dresses and undergarments at the border. And as her husband, at least so far as his children could make out, always deferred to his own parents, it was natural for Reese and his sisters to look up to the old couple in the big house, with whom they always lunched on Sunday, as the true arbiters of their destiny. The

second and third generations of Parmelee Cove had seemed
to merge in the row of attentive faces at the family board
while Grandpa held forth, with a roar, pounding the table as
he switched the discussion from excavations in Crete to tribal
customs in Borneo. For there was no matriarchy at Parmelee
Cove while Grandpa lived; he made Granny an allowance out
of her own fortune and coolly criticized her for extravagance.

The thing about Grandpa was that he was supposed to be
admired. People were always saying things like "Now, of
course, if your grandfather had been there" or "I wish you
could have heard your grandfather the other night." Life at
the Cove both indoors and out was dominated by the tall,
spry, bony figure of this chuckling and goateed old man, in-
cessantly talking and gesticulating, the ribbon of his pince-
nez floating out behind him, inspecting, probing, judging,
hurrying from house to house, from house to barn, picking up
a tennis racket to hit a few balls, despite his business suit and
stiff collar, with the grandchildren, changing activities like an
agile bullfrog leaping from lily pad to lily pad, as in the city
he leaped from committee to committee, pounding his gavel,
addressing ladies' groups for better government, for more
kindness to animals, for lower tariffs, excitable, dogmatic,
emotional, sentimental, caustic, brilliant, a shrill parody of the
Theodore Roosevelt whom he had so passionately admired
ever since he had followed him in the great charge up San
Juan Hill. It was not until Reese had grown up that he found
out that others shared the persistent, guilt-ridden suspicion of
his childhood, never imparted to anyone, that his grandfather
was a bit of a phony.

There had been other secrets that Reese as a boy had kept
from the happy families of Parmelee Cove. But the feeling
about Grandpa had been the most important because it had
been the first. Reese had felt from the beginning that, unlike

Grandpa, he was a creature of great coarseness in a world that at least professed itself the contrary. It might have been that the world, like Grandpa, was a hypocrite. But it was not a boy's duty, or even a boy's concern, to correct this. It was an established world and suspicious of the only son of Grandpa's only son. Those loving voices were also inquiring, penetrating voices. The only hope was to be silent, for silence was simple enough, and then one was left, more or less, to oneself.

Yet even this was harder as one grew up. The world of Grandpa Parmelee seemed to grow more rapidly than oneself. When Reese went off at twelve to St. Lawrence's it was to be greeted by a gaunt white-haired Dr. Avery, who spoke of his old friendship with Grandpa, and to sit in the great Elizabethan dining hall with three hundred boys under a line of portraits of trustees, in various academic robes, one of whom, wearing a monocle, looking like Otis Skinner in *The Honor of the Family*, was, of course, his father's ubiquitous progenitor. The school itself might have been founded by Grandpa, for he always said that austerity was essential to the subsequent appreciation of luxury, that a gentleman had to start amid the ripe smell of fresh varnish, tin washbasins, bare cubicles and a heavy program of athletics in order to emerge multilingual, a connoisseur of wines and a member of the Knickerbocker Club. But Reese at school continued to dwell in his interior castle. He had none of the troubles, fortunately, of the non-athletic; he could defend his privacy with a strength that was early and widely respected. He was easily the strongest boy in his class, and he was liable to fits of a murderous anger. But he always shied away from the violent spirit of social competition in the school. He resisted hazing and he refused to haze, and his friends were drawn from the social dregs of the class. It pleased some of the masters to see this handsome, blond, hulking silent boy, the first of his class

to play on the varsity football team, the school boxing champion, the stroke of the crew, walking to the village on Saturday afternoons with the pimpled son of the printing teacher
who had a scholarship and a withered arm. But it was a lack
of discrimination which commended him more to the faculty
than to the boys. Reese's refusal to join in the gossip, the gig-
gles, the snobbishness of the smaller boys and later in the
cliquiness of the older ones kept him from the popularity
that his looks and athletic ability would have otherwise ac-
corded him. He was trusted and respected by the boys even
more than they realized or would allow, but he had about
him too much the air of an adult to be invited to any intimacy
that he refused to seek himself. Reese was not "fun." Yet he
was so little known that on the very day of graduation, when
his grandfather made the commencement address and spoke of
his pride in "dear Reese," nodding before everyone in his
grandson's direction, it was viewed with astonishment that
Reese should turn so sullen a red and fail to appear at the
gala lunch that followed the exercises.

At Harvard he gave up organized athletics and spent his
time after classes drinking whiskey and visiting women of the
town. He did it quietly enough, though without particular
effort to conceal, and his family had the impression that if his
career was disappointing, it was not drastically different from
that of his cousins. In point of fact it was. Indeed, they would
have been horror-stricken had they had any real conception of
it. The only person who knew was Esther Means. She was an
old friend, having been brought up in Northfield on the place
adjoining Parmelee Cove, and had been the first person to understand, or to claim to understand, the distinction in Reese's
emotional prejudices between the girls of his Boston evenings
and the girls at home. The latter must have seemed to him
like so many delicate creatures in white, sister figures who,

however clever and designing, were essentially destroyable by someone of his own crude strength. The others were fair game. At least such was Esther's theory as she cheerfully expounded it to Reese himself, a theory as firm in her mind as her theory that she was the one person capable of bridging the gap between his two kinds of women. He was not unaware of the hint of fatuity implicit in this; he could even be irritated by the inexhaustibility of her understanding, but she was as persistent and undaunted as she was handsome, and she succeeded in marrying him when he was a first-year law student despite the unanimity of both their families' approval. Reese had "settled down," it was jubilantly agreed; he had taken his place with dignity in the Parmelee world. Only in the excitement of the general congratulation could he sense how deep and real their smothered doubts had been.

And then had come the war. It had been coming, of course, for some time; its very imminence had helped Reese to take the matrimonial step which might have otherwise received more extensive consideration. He had gone off immediately as an ensign in a sub chaser and after a year in the Atlantic had been transferred to the amphibious navy. Thereafter he had taken part in seven Pacific invasions: in small boats, in LCI's, in LST's, eventually as skipper of a rocket ship. He had been on the beach in Tarawa in charge of an advance supply base and had fought hand to hand with the Japanese. Afterwards he had shot with a revolver a prisoner who had spat in the face of an American corpse. It would be too much to say that Reese had enjoyed the war, but the violence and brutality of those Pacific landings had conformed more closely to what he regarded as the essential nature of the universe than anything he had experienced before. If life was to be fighting, well, at least he could fight. The fancy dress had been discarded, and there was a grim, proverbial kind of truth in sweat and blood.

When he read one night in Guam in a letter from his father of
Grandpa Parmelee's death, after a speech at a Madison Square
Garden war bond rally where he had praised his grandson for
carrying on the family tradition of San Juan Hill, he could
shed a tear at last for the old man who seemed, like everything else, a casualty in the holocaust of a false civilization.
There was no reason not to feel close to Grandpa if the same
war was to dig their graves.

And then, suddenly, one survived. Suddenly one was back
in the gatehouse at Parmelee Cove with a wife whose radiant
smile at cocktail parties seemed to imply that one had won the
war singlehanded, a job in Clark, Day & Parmelee, a son
whom one barely knew and a daily commute. It took a couple
of years before the shock of the war was entirely over, but
then the realization began to bite more and more deeply into
Reese that change was a thing of the past, that he had been
somehow committed to an irrevocable way of life without a
chance to make up his own mind. Life so far had been a series
of not necessarily related compartments; one could stay in
any one of them for the allotted period without bothering to
articulate a protest, because one knew that one was bound
eventually to move on to the next. Woodbury Day and
Parmelee Cove were followed by St. Lawrence's and Harvard
and Harvard Law School and marriage and paternity and
then the presumably final explosion of war, but what he had
avoided facing was just what had now happened, that he was
committed, irretrievably committed, with no end, no relief in
sight. Of course, it was quite an ordinary problem, a favorite
subject of current plays and novels, of self-pitying conversations in bars, but what he had never believed, like the average
soldier and the whine of the bullet, was that it could be
destined for him. It seemed strange that Parmelee Cove, un-
conscious of his lifetime's rebellion, should have so easily won

the game. Parmelee Cove, or was it Esther? Hadn't she
tricked him into the whole thing? And hadn't he deserved
it? It was as if he had dozed off to sleep on a train and awakened with a sense of hard beating sunlight, of its being almost
noon and a porter bending over him and pointing out the window at an infinite prairie slipping by them to say: "You see,
we got there, sir. This is life."

2

WHEN he arrived at his office that morning he found by a red slip on his desk that Mr. Stillman wanted to see him. He hated seeing partners in the first hour of the day; it was not until ten that the irritability of his early morning moods was under control. Stillman was in charge of the anti-trust suit against a group of manufacturers on one small aspect of which Reese had been working for a year. He was a small, bustling, affable man, well-tweeded, a fountain of little smiles and quick ideas beneath the popping and plashing of which moved the well-oiled gears of a first-class legal mind. He believed in big law and big law firms with the passionate naïveté of a freshman cheering the varsity team.

"I trust you had a pleasant weekend?" he asked as Reese came in.

"Oh yes. Thank you."

"Blue Monday." Stillman smiled as people do who use such phrases. "But I'm happy to report that I have a prospect that may dissolve the blue or at least dye it a bit. Could you take time off to lunch uptown today?"

"*Could* I?" Reese repeated flatly. He would never go along with Stillman's concept of the firm as a group of independent professional souls. He had been in the Navy, and he knew organization when he saw it.

"Well, here's the proposition," Stillman answered with his

persistent smile. "Claude Bonham has asked me to meet him uptown today. He used to know your grandfather. I thought it would be a good thing to introduce you, as you may have to be working in his files when we get to that part of the case."

"Well, actually I have a luncheon engagement."

Stillman's eyebrows were raised the least bit.

"One you can't break?"

"Well, let's say one I'd rather not break."

"I see, I see." Stillman spun away from him in his swivel chair. His voice was hard and loud, and he coughed repeatedly. "Well, I'm sorry. It seemed such a good chance to have you meet him."

"Is that all, sir?"

"That's all."

Reese had turned to go when he heard the chair swing violently back.

"Oh, Reese!"

"Yes, sir?"

"Tell me something." Stillman's eyes peered up at him intently. "Do you like working here?"

"Well enough."

"I wonder if 'well enough' is quite enough?"

"Isn't my work satisfactory?"

"I have no complaint about your work, except that I sometimes feel you might do more." Stillman smiled now more affably. "Sit down, my boy, sit down. I realize, of course, that you have more distractions than I had at your age. And then, too, you've had a war which I didn't. You come of a distinguished family, and the city is full of your friends and relatives. There are many calls on your time. When I came to New York I didn't know a soul, and I didn't have a dime to my name. If I sat up all night to put an extra shine on a brief that could have got by without it, I wasn't giving up anything. But a successful legal career is made up of just those extra shines. That's what I want you to bear in mind."

Well, he was trying to be friendly. And there was truth in what he said. And Reese knew, too, that Stillman had admired his grandfather and would have been flattered and pleased to have had a younger Parmelee seek his counsel and guidance. One appeal to Stillman's wisdom, indeed, would have helped him more than ten briefs. But for this very reason, perhaps, the appeal could not be made. "I'm sorry about lunch," was as far as Reese would go.

"It's quite all right," Stillman said dryly, and the interview was over. As Reese walked down the long corridor to his own office, the closed doors on either side acted as a mute chorus to pick up and swell the sense of his senior's pursuing disapproval.

Closed doors were a feature of Clark, Day & Parmelee. It was unique in this respect, as in many others, among the big firms downtown; it gloried with a fierce pride in the "Clark, Day" legend of industriousness as Sparta had gloried among the Greek cities in its legend of fortitude. A handsomely bound biography of the late Mr. Clark, written by one of his partners and privately printed, was given to each new clerk who entered the office. It abounded in stories of his prodigious energy, of how even as an old man, coming home from the opera in a white tie and flowing evening cape, he would work to the small hours of the morning with the clerk on duty, a perpetual sentinel in his library. There was none of the expensive décor of a modern office about Clark, Day. A walnut-paneled reception room with a portrait of Mr. Clark in the robes of a doctor of law darkly greeted the visitor, beyond which spread a labyrinth of long grey corridors without pictures and with closed doors. Some of the offices of the partners, no doubt, were more luxurious, but these were hidden away; to the initially inspecting eye it was a vast, austere monastery, a kind of legal Escorial, where even the secretaries were male.

Reese would not have been employed by Clark, Day on his own merits; his marks at Harvard Law had been middling, and the firm drew only from *Law Review* men. But Grandpa Parmelee had been a "name" partner; such had been his reward, fifty years earlier, for bringing his father-in-law, Abram Hubbell, into the roster of the Clark, Day clients. For the rest of his life he had used his great paneled office as the base of his various civic activities, developing to an almost comic degree the staccato crescendo of the distinguished lawyer's speaking voice and allowing it to be widely believed that his revenue was derived from his portion of the firm's profits rather than his wife's dividends. Reese as a law clerk had his first moment of posthumous admiration for his grandfather when he considered the magnificent chicanery of such daring to pose as a leader of the bar from the great black mahogany frame of this firm of dedicated souls.

His own role in Clark, Day was far humbler. He had wanted to be a trial lawyer and had spent two years in the library writing memoranda of law. Then he had been assigned to Stillman's anti-trust suit and had spent the past fourteen months collating and assessing correspondence between the various defendant companies. He worked less hard than the other clerks, for he lacked their ambition, but he still worked a good deal harder than he found agreeable, and it seemed increasingly odd to him to be competing so intensely for a partnership that he was not even sure he wanted. What bothered him, however, still more was the widening gulf between his own and the firm's attitude towards the practice of law. In the anti-trust suit, for example, Reese had no doubt that the conspiracy charged by the government had, in fact existed, but had existed in so tenuous and subtle a form that it probably could not be proved. This in no way concerned him. It was up to the Department of Justice to prove its case, and it was up to him to make the Department's job as difficult as possible. That was his profession. What concerned him more deeply was that the other lawyers working on the case, both partners and clerks, had a conviction in the rightness of their cause which seemed to spring from an emotional need within them that they should be not only on the winning but on the holy side. It was as if they saw themselves as priests in the inner sanctum of the capitalist system whose privilege it was to supervise the unveiling of the ultimate corporate mysteries. Or it seemed this way, at any rate, in their solemn moments; at other times they were like schoolboys at St. Lawrence's, cheering with actual tears in their eyes for their team to go in and win. There were moments when the whole fantastic paraphernalia of the case, the special office space rented to hold the file cabinets filled with its documents alone, the teams of lawyers working far into the night to complete the picture in their brief of a system of free competition that would have appalled even their clients, the weeks of hearings, the dozens of carefully coached witnesses, struck him as a grotesque parody of life itself, a conspiracy to prove there was no conspiracy, a gigantic hoax in which the hoaxers themselves were the most passionate believers.

Back in his office, he closed the door and telephoned to Cynthia Fearing. She was Esther's oldest friend, and the wife of his own oldest friend, and she had been, for the past two months, his mistress. This was a sufficient commentary in itself, he thought a bit grimly, on the childhood idylls of Northfield. He and Cynthia met twice a week in the middle of the day in a small walk-up apartment in the East Forties that Cynthia had sublet from an unmarried girl friend. He usually went to their rendezvous during his lunch hour, but today, in more defiant mood, he decided to meet her first in a restaurant. Since breakfast that morning, it seemed, he had been pulling away at the wrappings of his existence with something more than his usual sporadic, almost perfunctory tugs. It was as if part of the tough brown paper had suddenly begun to peel and his fingers were now itching with an irrational, damn-the-consequences impulse to tear off the rest.

"I feel extravagant today," he said when Cynthia answered. "I want to take you to lunch. At the Tasse d'Or."

There was a guarded pause. "Do you think we need be quite so conspicuous?"

"I *feel* conspicuous."

"But all my friends go there!"

"You can tell them I'm drawing your will."

"At the Tasse d'Or?"

"It's as good a place to die as any."

"For me? Or my reputation?"

But she met him there and punctually. She looked very urban in a black velvet hat that bulged up over her high forehead, very unlike the Cynthia of Northfield picnics, in slacks with a Mexican shirt, stroking her long blond hair as she nervously talked. At table, where they sat side by side, he was conscious of her eyes darting discreetly to each corner in turn of the darkened amber-colored room. "Are you looking for someone?"

"I'm looking *out* for someone."

"Who?"

"Well, Mummy, for example. She often lunches here."

"Which would you least like to see walk in here now? Your mother or Andy?"

"Oh, Mummy, of course. I can always explain things to Andy."

He gave a little snort of laughter. "I don't suppose anyone even knows the name of Desdemona's mother," he speculated. "But today Iago would be working on her instead of Othello. What have we men become? Mere pawns in the game of adultery!"

"Please don't use words like that."

"Like adultery?"

"*Don't!*"

"Why not? It's an exact term. A true one."

"Oh *true!*" She sniffed contemptuously as she turned to her menu. "How like a man. To think that truth excuses anything."

Cynthia had been just old enough to be the junior of the children's athletic class that had assembled on summer mornings at Parmelee Cove. When Reese had been fifteen she had been twelve, a bony, long-legged, uncoordinated girl with stringy blond hair and a loud, rasping voice who would do anything, even jump backwards off the high dive, on a dare. Since then she had been through different stages, including an arty, Bennington, hate-the-family pose (the Coits were very rich and owned a furniture business) which had ended in her marrying Andy Fearing, a naïve and amiable young man who had put all his money in a small, liberal newspaper and had the dubious advantage of being despised by her parents. They had not been married two years before the newspaper had collapsed, and he had accepted a job, to her disgust but in the absence of other offers, in the Coit business. To the Coits young Andy had simply "come to his senses"; they began now to appreciate the sunny benignity of his unrufflable disposition. Not so his wife. Cynthia, insufficiently occupied with one small daughter, of whom Andy's old nurse took jealous care, grew bored and beautiful. Her figure filled out, her long, oval face developed color and animation, her restless, green-grey eyes took on a sparkle, and the stringy hair became tawny. Reese and she saw each other suddenly with different eyes; their affair started with equal suddenness one night at a picnic, down the dark beach almost within earshot of their unsuspecting spouses and friends. It was his first infidelity since the war, and it created a curious relationship. Neither he nor Cynthia had ever thought much of the other during the long years of their adolescent acquaintance. Now a violent physical intimacy took the place of their old indifference. When they met face to face in a crowded room, there was a nervous constraint between them. They had so much and so little in common.

"You know what I thought?" Cynthia asked, putting down the menu and turning to him deliberately. "When you suggested that we lunch here? I thought perhaps you wanted to get people accustomed to the idea."

"What idea?"

"The idea of *us.*" When he still failed to respond, she continued, less assured, with a touch of asperity: "Well, is it madly vain of me to suppose you may not want things to go on this way forever?"

"On the contrary, it's very modest. I *do* want things to go on this way forever."

"*Just* this way?"

"Just this way."

"Well, you're more thick-skinned than I am, then," she said, frowning as she lit a cigarette. "Don't you ever get tired of this furtive sneaking in and out? Don't you ever feel *ashamed?*"

"Never."

"I mean about Esther and Andy."

"Why should I? They don't know. And, anyway, it would give Esther a chance to feel hurt and noble."

"You're just saying that. You pretend to be such a *free* soul. It's all a big bluff!"

Just then she recognized somebody and nodded across the room. He was surprised at the easy assurance of that nod. There was a sophistication about it that had not existed a few weeks before. Or at least, if it had existed, he had not been aware of it.

"I wish we were out of here," he murmured, trying to regain her attention by squeezing her hand. "I'm sorry we came now."

"Oh, I'm glad," she said unexpectedly, pulling her hand away. "It gives me a chance to ask you something. Something I wouldn't dare ask if we were alone." She gazed at him for a searching moment. "Have you no idea what I mean?"

"Not a clue."

"I'm trying to get you to say that you want to marry me."

He kept his expression fixed as he continued to stare across the room. What *did* he want? He wanted to go on meeting Cynthia twice a week as they had been doing. That gave him all he needed for the present. And what had there ever been but the present? The future — well, the future was for women.

"There are complications."

"None that are insurmountable."

"Would Andy let you go?" he asked.

"In time. With sobs. And then send me roses to Reno." This kind of remark was new to her; she had always been kind, even a bit fatuous about her husband. But she sensed his surprise and flushed slightly. "I know that sounds catty, but I can't help it. I'm so *sick* of him! Girls shouldn't be allowed to marry as young as I was! I'm a nice girl, Reese. Or as least I was before *you* came along. But does being a nice girl mean I've got to be tied forever to a man whose sweetness is killing me?"

"Of course it does."

"Oh, Reese!" There was anguish in her exclamation. "You *want* me to?"

"No. But then I never wanted you to be a nice girl."

She looked at him dubiously, not sure in what spirit to take this. Then she returned to the attack. "Do you think Esther would give you a divorce? If you ever decided you wanted one?"

"She doesn't believe in it."

"But she's not a Catholic! How can any woman with an inch of pride want to cling to a husband who's tired of her!"

"Because that's just the kind of husband Esther does want! One who won't be always pestering her!"

"Well, then I needn't be sorry for her," Cynthia retorted with a pouting shrug. "If she doesn't care any more about you than that, I can't see I have any obligation to her."

"Since when have you and I been bothered with obligations?"

Her eyes faltered as they met his. "Is that your way of telling me that you feel none to me?"

It was amazing, he reflected, that a woman of such passionate appetites should place so little reliance on the bonds of pleasure. The Coit family dwelt under a criss-cross of the arches of interfamily duties; in rebellion Cynthia only showed how true a Coit she was. If husbands were variables, marriage had nonetheless to be a constant.

"No obligation, no," he said flatly. "Obligation is a stale sort of thing. What I feel about you has more blood in it."

She seized his hand under the table gratefully. "Oh, darling, let's get out of New York! Let's go to the Fiji Islands!"

"On your money?"

"Who cares on whose money? I'm *sick* of Northfield!

I'm sick of women who talk about nothing but their children.
I want to be alive!"

"I thought you wanted to be a nice girl."

"All right. Can't I be a nice girl, too? Can't a nice girl be
divorced? Oh, God, how I want to be free!" She turned on
him with suddenly blazing eyes. "But you don't, do you?"
she demanded in a tone of whispered shrillness, her eyes
pleading with him to deny it. "You find Esther a great
convenience, don't you? A protection from me!"

"I wouldn't say that."

"Oh, *don't*, then!" She pinched him suddenly on the thigh.
She was greedy enough to read any commitment in his least
denial. But she had never looked more beautiful. It was odd
how discontent enhanced her looks. He shifted in his seat. At
that moment he would have married her if she had offered to
go to the apartment without waiting for lunch. He even
suggested it.

"What, *now?*" She looked startled. "But Marian Newcomb
over there just saw us order!"

He supposed this was the name of the girl to whom she had
nodded. Or did she know everyone in the restaurant? She
smiled again across the room, with a brightness that seemed
almost indiscreet. As he squeezed her hand again under the
table, enmeshing her fingers with his own, he realized with a
sudden shock that he knew the face of the man staring at him
across the room. It was Mr. Stillman! Reese had the presence
of mind to smile, even to wave his free hand. Stillman nodded
back curtly, but Reese already had ceased to care. The smile
had been only to make up to himself for a momentary reaction that had been shamefully like fear. Could he never
grow up?

"And I've been criticizing *you* for worrying!" he exclaimed laughing suddenly, but when she asked him to explain
he simply laughed again and ordered her a drink.

3

ESTHER did not hear that her husband had taken Cynthia out for lunch until a picnic on the following Sunday night at the end of the point at Parmelee Cove. These Sunday night picnics were a summer institution in the family. All of Mrs. Parmelee's grandchildren, the oldest of their offspring and the neighboring friends with their children would gather to grill hamburgers and drink beer and occasionally sing. In the fashion of the suburbs that had penetrated even now to the Cove, the wives were inclined to sit together and discuss domestic affairs while the men talked business and sports, except when Finny Coit was there, and then people listened to Finny. Finny was present that evening, and Esther sat at the edge of the circle, her head leaning against a rock and watched the reflection of the moon on the quiet sound. Andy Fearing, who had enough of his brother-in-law in the office without listening to him on weekends, had curled up at her feet, his chin resting on his knees, and occasionally murmured a comment at which she would merely shrug. Like everyone else, she was fond of Andy. He was so boyish and shiny-eyed, with his tousled brown hair and freckles; it was as if the rest of them had left him chronologically behind and he was hurrying after, shouting for them to wait. Esther was glad enough to linger for him, but she always knew it was lingering.

"I guess you and I ought to be jealous," he murmured with an odd little smile, jerking his thumb to where Cynthia was sitting by Reese. "There's no telling where lunches at French restaurants may lead to."

"Lunches?"

"Well, lunch anyway. And at the Tasse d'Or! There's something defiant about lunch in the Tasse d'Or, don't you think?"

His tone had suddenly lost its usual joking note, and she turned in surprise to see a glitter in his eyes. It was the nearest thing she had ever seen to a temper in him. In the past his only reaction to any provocation had been a brooding silence, usually followed by a sudden spirited change of topic. Reese had always said that Andy lived under the domination of a subconscious fear that a single burst of temper might blow him to bits. But was this glitter and this strained, dry smile really temper? Andy was excited, but his excitement had the breathlessness of a child's.

"I have no reason to believe there's anything serious between Reese and Cynthia," she said coolly.

"Well, you're about to have," he retorted, giving back her stare. "You know Minnie, my old nurse? Who takes care of little Angela now? You'd believe your old nurse, wouldn't you? Well, I would! Minnie's been suspicious of Cynthia for *months*. And last week she listened in on the telephone extension and heard her making an appointment with Reese. Apparently they meet in somebody's apartment at lunch time. Twice a week!"

Esther turned her face quickly into the breeze that was blowing from across the sound. She found herself thinking that a profile with blowing hair was a pose becoming to her. But she was embarrassed by her thought, and her embarrassment was followed by a moment when she tried to recollect exactly what it was that Andy had said. Then came a pain hard to localize and a sudden picture of herself, very pale and dressed in black, with her mother beside her, uttering little incoherent messages of sympathy. Finally, she saw an obituary page. She always scanned the obituary page in the newspaper, and when it was bare of any name she knew, there was a funny little dry sensation akin to disappointment. When, on the contrary, she saw the shocking black print of a relative's name, there was the quick intake of breath indicative of surprise, satisfaction, shame and ultimately, grief. She tried to divorce the game of finding a name from the truer feeling of her sorrow.

"Are you sure?"

"Would I be telling you if I wasn't?"

"I suppose not."

"It was inevitable," he continued bitterly. "All my life I've taken second place to Reese. In all the things that counted. At games in school. At drinking in college. At killing in the war. And now with my own wife! How he must despise me!"

"You're wrong there, Andy. Let's keep the record straight. Reese has always been very fond of you."

Even in the darkness she thought she could make out a gleam of satisfaction in his sudden surprise. But he shook his head quickly and angrily scooped up a handful of sand. "Fond enough to do me the honor of sleeping with Cynthia!" he retorted. "The greatest compliment, I suppose, he *could* do me! 'Well picked, little man!'" He snorted in self-derision. "Maybe I deserve it at that! Maybe it's what I've been asking for all these years!"

Esther's nose wrinkled slightly in distaste. "What are you going to do about it?"

"Well, I'm not going to be a well-bred Long Island husband, I'll tell you that! I'm going to fight!"

Esther had an odd feeling of alliance with her husband as she surveyed, half contemptuously, this presumptuous little man. Whatever she decided to do about Reese, she doubted that she would need his help. "Don't worry too much," she murmured. "Reese would never marry Cynthia. She's not his type."

Finny Coit's raised voice broke into her reflections. Finny had none of his sister Cynthia's good looks. He was rather softly fat with a pale, egg-shaped face, thick, red, curly hair and solemn, biting black eyes. But Finny did not seem to suffer from his inferiority in looks and muscle to the young people who gathered around him. Indeed, he gave the impression of consciously disdaining such things, as though, like college blazers and varsity sweaters, they pertained to the fantasy of youth and must now yield to the long reality of middle age and business things. Finny himself had taken over the family furniture business when still under thirty and had subsequently expanded and improved it to a point beyond the dreams of his late father and grandfather. The young Parmelees, Talcotts, Coits, Meanses and Fearings of Northfield, who were apt, with a friendly contempt, to expect very little of one another in the way of business success, as though the beneficiaries of an economic system were by their very birth disqualified from becoming its leaders, exploded with plaudits when Finny proved them wrong. Many of them, indeed, like Andy, were actually employed in the Coit business, which gave to Finny, although a bachelor in a suburban area of almost compulsory matrimony, a position of feudal preeminence, like a cardinal in a medieval court.

Except, Esther reflected, for Reese. Reese could not abide Finny Coit and took no pains to conceal it. She had never been able to fathom her husband's mysterious compulsion to communicate his hostile feelings. It would not have occurred to her, for example, that there was anything like a duty to be impolite to so important a client of Clark, Day & Parmelee. But then Reese, of course, could never be like other people; he couldn't be like his cousin, Fred Talcott, the secretary of Finny's company, who was even now shouting with laughter at one of his boss's dry little jokes. Reese would call such laughter the grossest hypocrisy. So would all the satirists of literature. And where would literature be, Esther thought irritably, without hypocrisy to laugh at?

"But that's just the point, isn't it?" Finny was saying now, his fluty voice rising authoritatively to command the general attention. "They haven't got the bomb yet. They *will* have it, of course. In time. Make no mistake about that. They don't have the luxury of the democratic process to hold *them* back."

"A luxury, I take it, that you would dispose of?" This, of course, was from Reese.

"A luxury I would cherish as long as I could afford it, Reese," Finny corrected him. "I sometimes wonder if that time will last forever."

Esther prepared herself for one of *those* evenings.

"And how would you take advantage of the time we have left?" Reese demanded. "Before they develop their own bomb?"

"Perfectly simple," Finny answered, addressing himself now entirely to Reese, who was indeed his sole adversary. "I'd lay down my demands right now. Evacuation of the satellite nations. Inspection behind the iron curtain to guard against further nuclear development. Free elections in China, and ultimately in Russia herself, supervised by the United Nations. This would be in the form of an ultimatum broadcast over the world for a period of weeks."

"And then?"

"And then I'd bomb them till they gave in."

There was a silence in the group, broken only by Fred Talcott's admiring whistle.

"And what sort of peace would you get out of that?" Reese demanded, very hot and red now. "How long would it last?"

Finny shrugged as he glanced around the group. "Maybe a hundred years. As long, anyway, as peace has ever lasted. Of course, Reese's humanitarianism is just what Moscow's counting on. They want us to stew in the juice of our own good will."

"Are you implying that I'm a communist, Coit?"

Oh dear, thought Esther. It was really rather worse than other nights. She could see that Reese was furious; his words were coming slowly, and he was breathing hard.

"Of course, I'm not implying any such thing," Finny responded with a small, conciliatory smile. "But I do suggest that you have been influenced by communist propaganda. Quite unconsciously, of course. Our press, our literature, our universities are saturated with it. It's hard to avoid being a dupe."

"I suppose I learned to be a dupe at Tarawa and Iwo Jima!" Reese exclaimed hotly. "I suppose I didn't have the advantage of all that clear thinking in Washington!"

Of course, now he had done it, Esther realized. Now Finny had won. There would even have to be apologies.

"The bad lung that kept me in Washington during the war, Reese," Finny retorted calmly, "also gave me a lot of time to think. I hope some of it was clear thinking."

"I'm sorry, Finny," Reese muttered sullenly. "I shouldn't have said that." And jumping up, he said gruffly to Cynthia, "Come on, how about a stroll down the beach?"

Esther watched his back disappear into the darkness, with

his rapid, short strides, his hands, as always, in his pockets. Cynthia, embarrassed, sat for a moment and then, perhaps feeling that it was more pointed to stay than to go, struggled to her feet and walked, slowly, almost casually, after him. Esther was glad that, sitting on the outer circumference of the circle, it was too dark for the others to learn anything from their covert glances at her. Did they think of what might happen down the beach? Did she herself? Or did she think only of what was happening in their minds? Did it matter so much *what* happened down the beach if she didn't think about it? Andy leaned over, smiling.

"You know at school Finny was only two forms ahead of Reese and myself," he whispered. "Tycoon though he may be now. Did Reese ever tell you what the boys used to call him?"

"What?"

"Tiny. Just plain Tiny."

"And was he?"

"No, he was a big boy. Or rather most of him was. Just one little part was tiny." Andy's brown, limpid eyes seemed full of a naïve affection for his brother-in-law. "I don't actually know if it still is. Finny is very modest at the beach club and always closes the bathhouse door. But hundreds of employees at Coit Stores have to sell hundreds more chairs and tables every year to make up for our calling him 'Tiny.'"

Esther got up in disgust to walk home. She had always admired Finny and despised Andy for imagining that his own puerile good looks justified him in sneering at his brother-in-law's success. Finny, after all, was the only member of their group who had really accomplished anything. She doubted very much if *his* wife, had he had one, would have strolled down the beach at night with another man under her husband's very eyes.

At home she went to bed and waited for Reese. His disappearance with Cynthia had been so pointed that she was afraid he might feel that he had to explain it, and any such discussion would be fatally premature. As soon as she heard him come in, she switched on the light and sat up.

"I don't see why you had to apologize to Finny Coit!" she exclaimed abruptly. "He deliberately goaded you into that crack about Washington so he could have the last word!"

Reese turned from his bureau in surprise. "No, that was bastardly of me," he muttered. "After all, he couldn't help his lung."

"Maybe not. But neither can I help being a woman. And that doesn't keep *me* from being a bit humble when I think of all that happened to you in the war and how little happened to me!"

"Oh hell, nothing happened to me," he said, turning away in embarrassment. "I wasn't a marine, for Christ sake."

"A lot more happened to you than ever happened to Finny Coit. And he might have the decency to recognize that when he accuses you of being a tool of Moscow!"

That was it, she felt with satisfaction, that was the note. By boldly placing her wreath, as it were, between them, she drove Cynthia into the background of shabby irrelevancies. He barely muttered good night now, before switching off the light, and long after she could hear his regular, static snoring, she lay awake, staring out at the moonlight.

She had always romanticized Reese, ever since the summer of her fourteenth year when her mother had rented that gingerbread house in Northfield, and she had attached herself to the group of children at Parmelee Cove of which he and his sister Joan had been the natural leaders. As they had grown older and life had become a more formal affair, Reese had tended to hang back, and it had been her decision to hang back also, waiting for him, as unobtrusively as possible. His silence and his aloofness had made up the bare canvas in which she had chosen to perceive the honesty and loyalty of a passionate and confused nature. Oh, she had reminded herself, time and again, that the finished picture was more the product of her fancy than of her powers of observation, but there were still undeniable signs that her induction of his character had not been wholly inaccurate. There was, for example, the innate decency of his instincts which everyone recognized: his way of promptly helping rather than making excuses in any accident or trouble, the way he always took the side, amid other children, of the weakest child, the way his eyes narrowed whenever conversation turned into gossip. And when she came to the drinking of his college days, it served only to prove that inner confusion which she had already divined and to offer her the opportunity, without competition, to take over, or to persuade herself that she was taking over, the happy task of his rehabilitation. Oh, that time of life, that wonderful time! The tears came to her eyes, tired of the moonlight, as she thought how happy she had been at their marriage and afterwards, even during the war. There would never be anything to equal the excitement of those leaves, as intense as they were brief, and going to night clubs with Reese, after making him put on his ribbons with the battle stars — for she *wanted* people to know, wasn't it natural? — and smiling at friends with that "No, please — don't join us — we have only two days" smile and feeling the radiation of their sympathy. She had even loved packing up and following him, with little Alfred, to San Francisco, to San Diego, to Portland, for brief visits before each embarkation, managing to find champagne and caviar and to make up some sort of gaiety in even the dreariest hotels. And in the long dark winters of waiting and worrying, there had still been something like exaltation in a shared concern with others, in war work, in the sympathy of his family. With the final year had come her second pregnancy, ending in the birth of little Eunice on V-J Day itself, which however dramatic, even "corny," as Reese had put it, was to her still an affecting coincidence. Always her vision of him as strong and stern, with a temper faintly rumbling like spring thunder, had filled the sky of his absences with gold dust. It was the old difference, of course, between the kiss and the imagined kiss, the act of love and its fancied counterpart — she knew something of the dangers of dreaming — but if it helped to drain the potential hell out of those days, could she really be blamed? She had paid for it, after all, when Reese had come home, and life had resumed its slow trickle down the long plateau of anticipated anticlimax. She had been prepared for it, and she could honestly tell herself that she had not betrayed her dissatisfaction by so much as a single sigh. He was what he was, as direct and prosaic as ever, but he was her bargain, and she knew how many of her friends, lamenting the lethargy of their own husbands, would have waxed rhapsodical over Reese's way of making love. Yet she had faced the fact that it left her curiously dissatisfied. She was careful to be always ready for him, and careful, too — at least she hoped — not to seem a pale Iphigenia sacrificed on the altar of his lust, but how she wished he were not so relentlessly physical! It was as if he were actually embarrassed by the least hint of sentiment, while she, on the other hand, felt naked and ashamed without it. It was part, she supposed, of the basic difference in their philosophies: for her the poor old face of the world was always in need of a touch of powder, a dash of lipstick, here and there even a beauty patch, while for him the primary duty seemed to be to stand by with a wet rag ready to scrub it off. There was only one sin for Reese in the universe, the sin of self-deception. His sullen refusal to be impressed with anything that suggested in the least bit any tinsel or lining or even color made her feel under a constant indictment for false values. Small wonder that their love-making had fallen off, had recently almost ceased. Yet that, too, she had been nice about. Was there no pleasing him, *ever?*

4

THE NEXT MORNING Esther walked across the big lawn to consult with Reese's grandmother. It was in accordance with her dynastic way of looking at things that she should go there first. She found the old lady sitting in the great, dark screened porch overlooking the sound where she spent all her summer days. Mrs. Parmelee was very little and very pretty, with lovely big blue eyes and a neat grey pompadour. She had a benevolent, queenly smile that seemed a perennial acknowledgment of the enthusiasm of younger generations as expressed in the cry: "Ah, *she* now, she's the real thing! There aren't many like *her* left!" To her descendants, who had long since ceased to see any but their own image of her, she was indeed the epitome of the gracious Edwardian lady. Only Esther, who had tried to establish a closer bond, had become aware of a difference. Always so neat in her appearance, Mrs. Parmelee sometimes appeared now with wisps of hair out of place or even with lipstick on her chin. And usually so patient and gentle with servants, she could now on occasion be shrill and petulant. But the deepest change was in the new note of her reminiscences, in her tendency to make what struck Esther as rather invidious comparisons between the careers of her late father and of her late husband. It had always been maintained by Mr. Parmelee and taken for granted by his descendants that the Hubbell family had been a rather vulgar lot whose highest boast was their alliance with himself. But in speaking of her father the old lady was now increasingly filial. "At least *he* did things," she would mutter; "at least, *he* accomplished something." The paternal collection of Meissoniers, the gaudy old steam yacht, the long trips in the private railway car to inspect new lines, aspects of a life that all Parmelees never referred to without a laugh of pitying derision, not dreaming that their condescension could be construed as envy, now formed the principal items of Mrs. Parmelee's nostalgic tales. Esther suspected that the value of her own companionship to the old lady was precisely that she had not been brought up, like the others, to laugh at such things.

That morning, however, it was Esther's turn to talk, and she talked, briefly and without mincing words, about her problem. Mrs. Parmelee listened to her intently, both hands clasping the handle of her cane, occasionally nodding.

"Ah, yes," she said, as Esther finished. "Cynthia Fearing. A lady — or what passes for a lady these days. That makes it worse."

"Why?"

"Because he'll think he has to get a divorce and marry her. Isn't that the code now? Isn't that the only thing there *are* any rules left about?"

Esther knew that she would have to act quickly if she was to deflect one of the old lady's excursions into the decline of manners. Mrs. Parmelee had a quick enough mind, but it was like the neat center of a garden approached by many narrow hedged paths. Once out of the center, one had to wait till she had come to the end of her particular path, and turned back. "But we're not even *talking* of divorce!" Esther exclaimed.

"I don't know what else wives can expect these days," Mrs. Parmelee continued, shrugging. "When you think what their husbands find when they come home. A set of screaming children dressed up as cowboys and the smell of burnt potatoes in the living room. It's no one's fault, I suppose. It's just the way you all live. When I tell my granddaughters how differently *I* was brought up, they throw up their hands and cry 'What a *dull* life it must have been, Granny!' Dull? They're whistling in the dark, poor creatures!"

Esther felt suddenly weary and defeated. She wanted more than this from the old lady, and she felt within her rights to expect it. For she had given her more; she had paid her the compliment of treating her as an individual, of daring to love her. Perhaps she was expecting too much. Perhaps, she reflected wryly, it was more sensible to be like Reese's father and aunts and to have kept one's image of the old lady firmly set in a valentine, one's ears deaf to the increased shrillness of her tone.

"But *there* isn't any smell of potatoes in *my* living room, Granny!" she protested sharply. "And my children *don't* dress up like cowboys! And when Reese comes home I've always changed my dress and have a drink ready for him." She felt a sudden twist of pain as she realized that what she was saying was true. She *was* different! "And it's not fair to confuse me with Reese's sister or his cousins!" she cried indignantly. "I've tried too hard!"

Even Mrs. Parmelee was affected by her appeal. She turned around, halfway down her cozy, hedged path of evasion, and gazed back at her grandson's unhappy wife with suddenly troubled eyes. "Oh, my poor child, I didn't mean *you*."

"Help me, Granny! Help me!" Esther leaned forward impulsively to clasp the old lady's thin hand and felt the hard bulge of her great yellow diamond.

"But, my dear, what can I do? What on earth can I do? An old woman who's survived her era?"

"You can talk to Reese. He loves you and respects you as he does no one else. He'd listen to *you*. You could find out what he wants."

"Ah, Reese. Who has ever understood Reese?" For just a moment it seemed as if she were going to focus on Esther's problem. For just a moment it seemed that there might be that much human sympathy left. But then the effort failed. Mrs. Parmelee was like someone awakened in the middle of the night; she turned away from the sudden light, burrowing into her pillow, warding off with a frantically waving hand anyone who approached. "There's no stopping these things once they've started," she went on in a shriller tone. "I've seen too many of them. If a man has a chance to be free, he's going to take it the moment he wants. Why not? How can you stop him?"

"By making him see he's needed."

"Doesn't do a bit of good." Mrs. Parmelee shook her head repeatedly with what looked almost like satisfaction. She seemed unaware now of the problem as one personal to Esther. "Divorce is like a dope. People may talk and talk against dope, but when the pain gets too bad, they'll always take it. In my day divorce wasn't available. For the respectable, anyway. We had to grit our teeth and bear it."

Esther, staring at her, slowly took in the shift in argument. "*Bear* it?"

"Certainly," the old lady snapped. "It wasn't all beer and skittles, you know, being married in my day."

"You mean to Grandpa Parmelee?"

"I don't mean anyone else."

"He wasn't unfaithful!"

"I don't know what you mean by unfaithful," Mrs. Parmelee answered with an impatient snort. "There are more kinds than physical. Reese, of course, would go in for the physical.

But at least you know then where you stand. His grandfather was always hanging around the ladies with little speeches and compliments and handpattings. And winking at the help. Ugh!" She gave a shudder of distaste. "It disgusted me!"

"But you'd never have divorced him?"

"It sometimes seems to me, my dear," Mrs. Parmelee retorted dryly, "that I'm so taken for granted now I might as well be dead."

Esther gave up. She had no wish to sit there any longer and hear the old lady destroy the past, turning the dignity of Parmelee Cove, with its decades of respectable family life, into the yelp of a pinched housemaid. On her way home across the lawn she felt her heart filling with something like panic. Was it really too late? Was she beaten before she had even started to fight? She saw the story of her humiliation leap now from tongue to tongue; she saw herself, like a sleeping Brunhilde, encircled with the crackling fires of a fatal sympathy. She visualized the antagonizing and ultimate alienation of Reese, the trial separation and at last the legal documents, stamping out, with their brutal and obfuscating definitions, any lingering hope of reconciliation. For modern society, she well knew, was like a dimly lit tank of undersea creatures. One could watch the slowly moving crustaceans, the jewel-like fish with their gently waving fins, and all seemed peaceful enough. But let one drop of blood appear in that green and blue darkness and see what teeth would come out of the corners and with what scuttling and rushing speed!

At home, in her own little garden, she contemplated her tulips and felt a bit calmer. She loved her tulips; they were always so straight and proud, hardly stirring in the gentle breeze from the sound. She drew courage from their example. If one bowed to the storm, one was lost. She had seen too many wives lose their husbands by looking the other way.

But if one lashed the troubled waters, if one whipped the storm into a hurricane? If one rallied all of Parmelee Cove and Northfield behind one? Had she not always thought of herself as something of an actress, a noble actress, a Katharine Cornell in *Antigone?* It was all very well to be pitied, but pity had to be followed by triumph. She was glad now of her call on Reese's grandmother. It had warned her that even the predestined victor had to fight. She would appeal to every wife in Northfield.

5

It was not long after Reese's lunch with Cynthia at the Tasse d'Or that he began to feel the small pricks of society's retaliation. He counted with a dry amusement the tiny red scars which they left. It started one morning in the office of Mr. Stillman who seized the occasion of a client's divorce to give Reese a thinly disguised lecture.

"It's amazing what hash even intelligent people can make of their private lives. Amazing. With taxes what they are today, even a rich man can hardly afford to split up his home. And what's the use, I ask you? In order to get tied up with another gal who'll bore him just as fast, if not faster!"

Like most of the lawyers in Clark, Day & Parmelee, Mr. Stillman showed the world all the outward aspects of domestic happiness. Yet it was at least suspicious that, for all his specialization in corporate work and professed horror of "matrimonial matters," he handled personally, and with an energy that smacked of zest, a number of divorces that could have been as easily delegated to juniors. He would open negotiations with a pious appeal for reconciliation, as perfunctory as a grace before dinner, and then spring into the fray with a violence that soon turned the mildest estrangement to bitter and permanent hostility.

"But there's always the hope the next gal may be better, isn't there?" Reese asked, straight-faced. "Isn't that what makes the world go round? Hope?"

In Northfield, among his contemporaries, he felt the inarticulate resentment of the wives. They were usually pregnant, and all had small children; obsessed in their minds and in their conversations with the problems of infants, they had little time or energy to devote to their husbands and depended heavily on convention to keep them in line. They had a dim awareness, in consequence, of their own vulnerability to the kind of thing that Reese represented, and they viewed him at dinner parties, huddled together as was their wont in discussions of formulas and kindergartens, as a herd of cows might turn suspicious eyes and horns on a dog that is frisking on the outskirts of their pasture. Yet none of them dared speak openly. It was Freddy Talcott, Reese's cousin, who was delegated to do this. Freddy was a homely, fatuously smiling, jocose, rather giggling young man whose conversation abounded in clichés about the battle of the sexes. It was always Freddy who could be counted on for the joke about women's hats or the number of items which they carried in their handbags or the damage they could do to an automobile fender, but these marked the outer limits of his independence. Basically, like most such jokesters, he was the slave and alter ego of his wife. Sitting by Reese one morning on the train, he opened the conversation with a man-to-man admission that he himself was no saint. It was as far as he got.

"What do you mean, not a saint?" Reese demanded.

"Well, we all have our little peccadilloes, don't we?"

"Do we?"

"Well, maybe *you* don't," Freddy retorted, flustered.

"Now it's funny you should concede that. I had an idea that my peccadilloes were just what you wanted to discuss."

Freddy scratched his brow. "Well, to tell the truth, Reese, it's rather difficult. I didn't want you to start out thinking I was being superior or a model husband or anything like that. I guess I've made as many slips as the rest of us."

"What kind of slips?"

"Must I dot every *i* and cross every *t?*"

"As many as you can."

"Well, damn it all," Freddy exclaimed, getting angry. "I'm only human, and even a happily married man isn't exactly blind to a shapely pair of legs —"

"Legs? Whose legs? Have you been looking at somebody's legs?"

"Oh, come off it, Reese. You know what I mean."

"Are you trying to tell me you've been committing adultery? Is that it?"

"Now, damn it all — !" Freddy began, flushing.

"Have you or haven't you?"

"None of your blasted business!"

"Good." Reese nodded abruptly. "That's the tone I like. Just remember, please, that mine is none of yours."

"But, Reese," protested his cousin, exasperated. "I have a duty in this. Won't you listen?"

"A duty? To whom?"

"To the family."

"Whose family?"

"Ours."

"Ours? I believe your name's Talcott, isn't it? Well, mine's Parmelee. And I don't for a moment concede that you're under any obligation to pry into my private life because your mother happens to be my father's sister. Shall we change the subject?"

Freddy gave it up, discomforted, but Reese began to wonder if the only people who were not talking about his affair were the two persons most injured by it. Esther's silence on the subject was nothing short of magnificent. She had always had a prodigious talent for turning her back on any fact whose existence she did not care to recognize. And once her back was turned, she showed none of the weakness common to her sex in yielding to the impulse to cast little covert glances over her shoulder. In fact, so strong was the impression that she managed to create of everything being all right between them that despite a delicacy on his part that would have normally impeded it, she had recently maneuvered him into a brief resumption of marital relations. Truly she was incredible! She had built a solid castle of evasion on the bedrock of her own failure to challenge him.

It turned out, however, that of Esther and Andy only the former could be counted on for silence. Andy called him at the office one morning and asked him to come uptown for lunch. "I'll be your host at the Midday," the slightly too cheerful voice went on. "And don't say you never get uptown. If you do it for Cynthia, you can do it for me!"

He jumped up when Reese entered the lobby of the Midday Club, and asked him, in his usual jovial tone, even adding the customary grip of the elbow, if he wanted a drink. Reese looked at him inquiringly.

"I don't usually before lunch."

"Neither do I. But today, I think, may be different."

They stood at the bar, in a group of men, and drank their drinks in silence while Reese tried to harden his heart. He could no longer afford the luxury of shame; he could not let himself pity Andy. There would be no end to it. His friend, however, seemed cool and coordinated; only two faint red spots on his cheekbones bespoke his tension.

"Shall we settle our facts before we start? Shall we 'stipulate,' as I believe you lawyers put it?"

"What shall we stipulate?"

"Well, let's start with your and Cynthia's affair."

Their eyes met abruptly over the word, and there was a sharp pause. Then Reese shrugged, half impatiently, and nodded. His mind dipped suddenly back to school, and he saw Andy at his desk, meticulously and beautifully drawing the intestinal tract of a frog. He heard his voice raised in the soprano solo of an anthem in chapel and saw the white cassock and the red skirt. Andy's innocence had always been a reproach to him, had made him feel like a smudge on that glistening cassock. "Did *she* tell you?"

"I was told by a good and loyal friend."

"One of *those*. Oh, all right, what the heck? I'll stipulate that Cynthia and I are having an affair."

"Thank you!" Andy exclaimed in a high, suddenly squeaky tone. "I decided it was up to me to speak first because I am the one who must take an attitude. You and Cynthia, being the 'wrongdoers' in the social sense, can simply pretend that you're innocent. Esther, as a 'wronged wife,' can simply look aside. But not the 'wronged husband.' He's expected to *do* something. Don't you agree?"

"They're just words, Andy. Don't mouth them so."

"Have you left me anything but words?" Andy's bright eyes were a bit too bright now. "That was always the contrast between us, wasn't it? You the doer and I the talker?"

"What's the use of all this? *Now?*"

"I'll tell you!" A small corner of Andy's surface calm had torn loose and was flapping noisily, spoiling the effect of his parlor comedy poise. "Because it's the most important thing that's ever happened to me, that's what's the use! If words let me down now, what good are they?" When Reese simply shrugged again, he went on excitedly: "I won't concede that! I believe that if you and I and Esther and Cynthia see this thing clearly — absolutely clearly — we can come out on top of it!"

"You mean we can *talk* our way out of it?"

"I mean we can try." Andy ordered himself another drink and leaned back, elbows on the bar, to explain himself. "You see, you have no conception of what you meant to me as a boy. I looked up to you extravagantly. Oh, I know I'm I'm going to embarrass you, but I don't care. You can jolly well stand there and be embarrassed for a bit. At school you were the athlete and at home all the little girls were mad for you. Even though you didn't know it. And at Harvard, when you went to cat houses, it wasn't to show off, like the rest of us, it was because you *had* to go. Oh, I admired you for that! You've no idea!" Andy paused as if to inhale the bouquet of his reminiscence. "I copied you in everything and almost became a drunk for my pains. I volunteered for amphibious warfare and almost got myself killed. I had you as best man at my wedding and mortally hurt my brother's feelings. Maybe now you get an inkling of what I went through when I found out about you and Cynthia? Because you have always been the one to do things. And now you were doing them with my wife!"

The discomfort that Reese suffered during this speech was tinged in the end with resentment. Was Andy trying to darken the picture of his friend's disloyalty by exaggerating his own affection for him? He had never asked for Andy's affection; he had never, indeed, asked for anyone's. Why did the world's heart always go out to the loving? Why did it admire their slow clumsy dance around the victim of their affections, the self-pitying display of their unwanted wares? The very thing that he had always most liked in Andy had been his consistency in not embarrassing him with any demands for intimacy. On canoe trips or sitting together at a Sunday night organ recital, or at college on long drinking nights or even in the war where they had served in the same flotilla, Andy had always been dressed in the sky-blue serenity of his oddly impersonal nature, never quite serious but never altogether joking, amused, tolerant, pleasantly mocking, compliant, undemonstrative, uninvolved. Had Reese told him that he was going to the moon and would never come back, Andy would have simply smiled and shrugged. At least so Reese had always pictured it. But now it appeared how little communication all those years of companionship had contained. If one never spoke of the heart, one never learned about the heart. Perhaps it was as simple as that.

"It's not a question of 'doing' or 'talking,'" he said brusquely. "Cynthia and I wanted to have an affair, and we had it. That's all there is to it."

"Well, not quite, I think," Andy corrected him. "Not quite. You say 'we *had* it.' Aren't you still having it?"

Reese was beginning to be angry now, but it was a relief. He met Andy's smugly inquiring look with defiance. "Yes!"

"Good," Andy responded with a faint, sad smile. "That's more the old Reese. You've got Cynthia, and you're going to keep her as long as you damn well please. And if I still want her back when you're through with her, that's my affair. Good." He nodded repeatedly, to express a satisfaction that he clearly did not feel, but that he wanted to feel and that perhaps he ultimately might feel, if he tried hard enough. "You see, I know you, Reese. I know you as nobody else knows you. You resent the world for trying to romanticize you. You're a heel, and you want the world to know you're a heel."

Reese looked down and breathed hard for a moment. "I hope that makes you feel better," he muttered.

"You think I'm getting back at you," Andy continued coolly. "I'm not so childish as to think you'd mind. I'm simply trying to be clear. You see, I know that Cynthia only married me to spite her family. It was inevitable when she discovered this that she should resent me. What she is obviously trying to do now is to humiliate me by leaving me for someone I admire. Or used to admire. If you and she can be made to see this, you'll understand that the whole basis of your affair is false!"

Reese felt little quivers of distaste throughout his frame. There was nothing he could do about the revulsion that he felt for Andy's detachment. Perhaps it was admirable to dissect oneself to this point, but wasn't there a fatuous pride in the very ability to do so that gleamed now in Andy's triumphant eyes and distorted the ego even more violently than a perfunctory jealousy, or even a perfunctory rage?

"I can't take any more of this!" he exclaimed. "You say I can't imagine what you went through when you found out about me and Cynthia. Maybe I can't. But I *can* imagine what you're going through right now! You're having the time of your life!" He turned away abruptly and walked to the door. Just as he left the room, however, he paused reluctantly and made himself look back and wave. Andy was standing immobile at the bar with a small, fixed smile. He barely raised his hand to acknowledge the gesture, and Reese hurried out, afraid of the impulse to run back and beg his pardon. It would have meant giving up Cynthia, and he was not ready to give up Cynthia. He had a funny empty feeling in the back of his head that when this happened, the last straining thread would break and he would tumble through the net into the bright blue void below.

But might it not be better for everyone if he did? The thought obsessed him on his subway ride downtown that the world he resented might be of his own invention. He conceded that the surface of life at Northfield presented a smooth, agreeable look, full of orderly busy people doing orderly busy things, justifying, to some degree at least, their constant application to each other of the adjective "nice." It was as if, like a petulant child, he had struck that surface with a stick and now could see in the ripples the faces of those about him grotesquely undulating: Andy grinning slyly, Cynthia restless and furtive, Esther smug and lofty, the friends avidly watching. If he went away, the ripples might subside and people might be themselves again. Esther could preside benignly over her little household from the throne of her abandonment, and Cynthia could make up with Andy or marry someone else just like him. And his own children — bitter as it was to contemplate — might flourish in an atmosphere where fundamentals were not always questioned. When little Alfred asked him, with deeply serious eyes, why he had to go to St. Lawrence's if Daddy had been unhappy there, what could he say? He had no alternative to offer; that was the desperate thing. And Esther knew it. Yet in spite of this and in spite even of the desolate prospect of losing Alfred and Eunice, there was still a fierce little hope flickering at the bottom of his darkest thoughts that if he could only get away and start again, he might yet find his place in the universe. He could even picture himself coming back to answer Alfred's questions and in front of Esther, too. Perhaps it was simply the final vanity of insisting that he, too, was a "nice" person. Or perhaps — and to this idea he clung — it was the birth long delayed, and coming at the most unlikely time, of a small, tough belief in his own powers against the world.

6

Esther's plan of campaign was directed primarily against Cynthia. She knew Reese's stubbornness too well to expect anything from the intervention of friends and relations. But it was a more feasible prospect to shake Cynthia's satisfaction in her affair by shaking her confidence in her own popularity, and to this end Esther made a series of long, searching calls on the various younger matrons of Northfield. "I'm not bitter, you know. I'm not even blaming anyone. I'm simply wondering what to *do* about it." She could count on each and every one of them to speak to Cynthia and to do it as awkwardly as possible. She expected to make the sun room at the Bath Club and the hairdresser's at Northfield places where the latter would not be able even to appear without being pulled aside for a bit of unsolicited and unwelcome "friendly advice." Her grounds once laid, the final step was easy. It was simply to destroy the financial basis of a possible elopement.

Happily, she knew how to handle Reese's parents. Alfred and Agnes Parmelee were members of the last generation on Long Island which could, with anything like equanimity, devote a lifetime to the pursuit of sport. They hunted and beagled and skated and skied with a grim pertinacity and much chattering of their day-to-day improvement, taking for granted that athletic progress, at any age and for either sex, was a subject in which even the palest city dweller

would feel obliged to pretend an interest. That their competence was small, that Alfred had no net game at tennis while
Agnes, because of a chronic elbow, had to serve underhand,
only made their efforts, in their own opinion, the worthier.
Reese's father had none of his grandfather's interest in civic
affairs, nor any, for that matter, of the old man's brains. He
was a small, dry, bustling, balding, paunchy man with eyes
whose very lack of expression betrayed an aggressive boredom with any human being whose interests were not identical
with his own. Agnes, on the other hand, very thin, with
bobbed grey hair in the style of the twenties, had at least the
remnants of looks and charm, but her roving eyes and long
delicate sniffing nose seemed to express her concern that she
might not have wholly succeeded in suppressing her childhood interest in non-Parmelee things.

Esther laid her proposition baldly before them. If Reese
should leave her, she wanted Mr. Parmelee to arrange that
Reese's share of his grandmother's estate would be willed instead to her and her children. Was it not only fair? She
marshaled her arguments impressively: Old Mrs. Parmelee's
fortune had dwindled; Reese's share would be barely enough
to support his family; in his present mood he might even
quit his job. The time had come for drastic measures.

It was the peculiar arrangement of the Parmelees that
Agnes always did the talking while her husband sat impatiently by, waiting for his chance to put an end to family discussion. It was she who had had to tell the children the
embarrassing things, stumbling over the facts of life as she
now stumbled over the facts of adultery.

"But it would involve telling Granny the whole story!"
she protested. "It would kill her!"

"I've already told her," Esther said shortly. "I thought she
took it remarkably well."

"You *told* her! Esther, how could you?"

"Because I'm fighting for my life, Mrs. Parmelee! I can't afford the luxury of fatuity!" She turned swiftly on her father-in-law. "I'm not asking for anything that's unreasonable, Mr. Parmelee. I simply don't see why the burden of supporting Reese's family should fall entirely on *you!*"

The only decisions that her father-in-law was capable of making were sudden ones, based on insufficient facts. He had long given up trying to understand a son so perverse as to prefer hiking and woodcutting to hunting or golf, and it made Reese's perversity only the more irritating that he should possess the natural athletic aptitude denied his father.

"She's right, Agnes!" he exclaimed sharply, jumping to his feet. "It'll be Reese's own fault. He's never taken my advice in anything! I'll call Mother's lawyer today. After all, she can always change her will back if he behaves himself!"

Esther's second and final interview in the accomplishment of her purpose was even briefer. Nothing in Northfield was more subject to popular discussion than the source and amount of people's incomes, and it had been an easy matter for her to ascertain that Cynthia depended for her and Andy's support on a certain "sprinkling trust" set up by her late father. Mr. Coit had provided in his will that the income of this trust should be "sprinkled" among his descendants as his trustees saw fit, and the trustees were his widow and his son, Finny. It was accordingly on Finny that Esther called next, in his office, full of large bronze masculine objects and photographs of factories and deceased directors, and put her proposition to him as succinctly as she had put it to the Parmelees.

"You want Reese for a brother-in-law about as much as I want Cynthia for a successor," she told him. "Why not tell her that during any period when she happens to be Mrs. Reese Parmelee her share of trust income will go instead to little Angela?"

"Starve her out, eh?"

"No. Simply threaten to."

"You seem to forget that my mother's a co-trustee."

"*You* seem to forget that the Coits are the one family in Northfield where the male still runs things! How many times have you told me that?"

Finny looked up with approval. How easy it was to handle him! She saw perfectly why none of the girls of Northfield had succeeded in marrying him. They had sought to allay his suspicions of their sex by persuading him that it was not Finny the tycoon whom they admired, but Finny the man. Yet it was precisely because he believed that Finny the man was a person whom no one could love that Finny the tycoon had constructed around his mortal counterpart so magnificent a series of towers and walls and moats. To admire the fortifications themselves was the way to the interior. It was a simple enough game if one knew the rules. Heaven help Finny if Esther ever decided to go to work on him!

"You're quite a gambler, aren't you?"

"What have I to lose?"

He nodded admiringly. "I'm damned if I know why you want to hang on to Reese. You're worth ten of him. But if that's your decision, you can count on me!"

"I knew it!" She stood up and gave him a serene smile. "And one more thing," she added, turning back from the door. "Granny Parmelee is giving Reese a birthday party on Saturday night. I think I wouldn't speak to Cynthia till the morning before. That might be just the perfect timing!"

Granny Parmelee loved to entertain the younger members of her family. Had Reese not had a birthday that August, another occasion for a party would have been as readily found. None of the intermediate generation ever appeared at these gatherings; Mrs. Parmelee liked to preside alone, in all her diamonds, over an assemblage of youth, holding her tiny court in the midst of a preoccupied world, talking volubly about greater days to the politely listening guest chosen by Esther to be her audience at the moment. The guest was always polite because he was always sure of being relieved. Esther was renowned in Northfield for her social proficiency.

Renowned, she reflected bitterly as she contemplated her seating list in the train going home, but hardly admired. Northfield distrusted social proficiency, and the Parmelees thought her officious in organizing the old lady's parties. Yet didn't somebody have to? They would never face the fact that Mrs. Parmelee was becoming senile. It was part of the family pattern of taking her for granted. It never occurred to any of the granddaughters, for example, to try to establish a personal relationship with her or to pay more than a perfunctory attention to her stories. They loved her, or assumed that they did, as people ought to love their grandmothers, always appearing glad to see her, always calling to thank her for presents, always describing her to others as someone who was infinitely kind and shrewd, two qualities usually summed up in the word "wonderful."

Yes, Granny was "wonderful," but to be always running into the house to chat with her, or actually to ask her advice, as Esther did, well, surely that was overdoing it, wasn't it? And the worst of it was that the old lady seemed to share this attitude herself. Like the others, she seemed perfectly content with the appearance of devotion, even with the appearance of love. No one, indeed, in Parmelee Cove seemed to need the kind of intimacy that Esther had to offer in such generous quantities. Very well, she would give up trying, she decided grimly. In the future she would let the others run the old lady's parties. They could sink or swim, so far as she was concerned. But this last party she had to manage. This last party was part of her plan.

7

REESE was beginning to feel as if he and Cynthia were conducting their affair in public, performing, as in a Paris brothel, to a snickering audience at the peepholes. It made him furious, and fury was a kind of solace. Surely, the audience was more obscene than the actors. The word "nice" had always been a favorite word on Northfield lips, but there were few limitations, apparently, on the activities of "nice" people. "Nice" people could divorce and remarry at will. "Nice" people could even indulge in drunken fornication on Saturday nights after the Bath Club Dance, provided other "nice" people didn't catch them. But no "nice" person could ever *think* of expressing the serious side of his nature in a serious love affair. Well, he was glad he was not a "nice" person!

He had to admit, however, that Cynthia still clung to "nice" standards. It was true that with the advent of general knowledge of their affair, she had become careless of concealment, but it was a rather hysterical carelessness. She telephoned him openly now at the office and no longer bothered to look up the street when she came out of the house where they met. If she was bored, she did not hesitate to show it, and if he started to tell a story that she had heard before, she cut him off abruptly. She made no further secret of her opinion that he carried his disapproval of Parmelee Cove and Northfield too far and even hinted that his bitterness towards her brother Finny sprang from jealousy about his own lesser success. Reese was as displeased at the discovery of her temper as she of his stubbornness. Indeed, their affair might have foundered but for the violence of their physical attraction, which seemed to be intensified by the very friction between them or at least by the summer humidity. If their meetings were briefer, they were also more frequent. In the dripping heat of the shabby little apartment they tore at each other like two cats.

She had once been modest, but now she liked to bound about the apartment, naked. It was singular that the act of love seemed to make her energetic rather than sleepy; he would lie in bed, smoking a pipe, watching her as she raised or lowered a shade, pulled at a curtain, transferred a lamp from one table to another.

"I can't bear this waiting and watching!" she protested one day. "If only I could *do* something about it. Don't you want to *do* something?"

"Nothing that I haven't been doing."

"You just want to lie back and smoke your pipe and feel superior to everyone. *I* know."

"That's it." He watched the irritation illuminate her grey-green eyes and laughed. "You hate that, don't you?"

"Well, naturally," she retorted, sitting on the bed and sulking. "A girl likes to know where she stands."

"You mean you want some kind of hold over me. You don't dare trust to your beautiful body!" He ran his hand down her back and let it rest on her thigh. "But that's where you're wrong. Very wrong. Because your beautiful body is the only way you *can* hold a man."

"Reese, I'm worried."

"What about?"

"Everything! Andy, for example. He came running into my room this morning with a four-leaf clover to say it was an omen that I was coming back to him!"

"Well, you didn't expect him to be *pleased* about us?"

"No, of course not." She pouted the way little Alfred pouted when he refused to promise him that dogs would go to heaven. "But I've always been surrounded by an approving atmosphere. And now I don't know how to behave. How *does* one behave under these circumstances?"

"Poor Cynthia," he said, "*I* approve of you. Does that help any?"

"No." She turned over suddenly and looked tensely into his eyes, catching his chin so that he could not turn away. "I want more than that, Reese. I want you to marry me. *Will* you?"

Her worried eyes, yellow now as well as grey and green, were extraordinarily beautiful. He contemplated them for several moments. "But are you *sure* you want to marry me?"

"Of course I'm sure!"

"Remember that what we started was an affair. Not a marriage." He continued to look at her questioningly, but she turned impatiently away. "We knew at the time that Northfield wouldn't like it."

"Well, isn't Northfield right?" she retorted irritably. "Isn't that the whole thing? Shouldn't we fish or cut bait?"

"I want you to know what you're doing," he warned her sharply. "I want you to know whether it's you or Northfield who's planning this marriage!"

"It's me!"

"Very well, then, I'll marry you." He lay back suddenly on the bed with his arms out and gazed speculatively at the ceiling. He was vaguely surprised to hear his own commitment. Yet he was perfectly sincere. If she cared so violently about being married, he had no belief in the sanctity of a sacrament strong enough to deny her this. Was he not finished with Esther, in any event? His and Cynthia's would hardly be a very happy marriage, but what did he know of happy marriages? Was he being a bastard? Not to Cynthia, anyway, for he was being truthful. To Esther? Ah well, it was too late to make up for all he had done to Esther, and she to him. He was glad, anyway, that he had not invented the whole fantastic scheme of the modern home. "If Andy will give you a divorce," he said soberly, "I'll ask Esther for one and marry you."

She looked at him fretfully. "You sound so cold about it. Don't you *want* to marry me?"

"No. I don't ever want to marry again. Marriage seems to me a very odd institution. The only thing that I know I want is what we have, here and now, in this room. I'm very sure of that." He reached over and gripped her knee until she winced. "And to hang on to that I'll even marry you. So there!"

She wrinkled her nose distastefully. "But that's so physical. So gross!"

"All right. I *am* physical. I *am* gross."

"But isn't there anything more?"

"What more do you want?" he demanded roughly. "A lace veil and bridesmaids? A sniveling mother in a big hat?"

"Oh, Reese!" she cried, sitting up abruptly. "Don't you believe in *anything*?"

He reached up to grab her shoulders and pull her down on top of him. "I believe in this skin I'm touching!"

"Nothing more?"

"Isn't that enough?" He released her shoulders with a sudden snort of laughter. "I suppose you want me to say I believe in marriage vows! Do *you*? What do you think you've been doing right here in this room?"

"I've been sinning, that's what!" She jumped up, very excited now, and started hastily to dress. "At least, *I* recognize it. There's some hope for *me*!"

Well, it was hard on her. He had to concede it was hard on her. She had tried so desperately to identify her boredom with his rebellion and to bind the two together with the brittle cord of sex. It was her bad luck that she should have picked as a lover the one husband in Northfield who wouldn't play the game by the rules. When he saw the bafflement on her face, he relented.

"Poor girl," he said more softly. "You want valentines and a ring and long, anguished love letters. But don't you see, that's all for a *first* marriage? People who do what we're doing have to be more realistic. Otherwise they become grotesque. Like the heiresses who tell reporters it's the 'real thing' when a Miami hairdresser becomes Number Six!"

But Cynthia did not smile. She did not even speak to him as she walked out. Nobody seemed to smile at him any more. They all looked as grim as his mother-in-law when he came home that night to find her sitting with his small, intense, preoccupied daughter in the living room, watching her as she opened the last of her birthday packages.

"Esther's taking Alfred to a picnic!" she exclaimed defensively. "I told her I'd just stay with Eunice till you got home!"

Mrs. Means, tall and pear-shaped, looked even older than her seventy years. She had been middle-aged when Esther, her adored only child, had been born. She was wearing a large, high, black shiny hat of no remembered style, a purple dress and black shoes. She would never admit that she had come to Parmelee Cove to see her grandchildren or even to see Esther. That would have been "getting in the way." She had always just "popped in" on her way to call on "dear Mrs. Talcott" or "dear Agnes Parmelee" or "Reese's darling grandmother." She had oval eyes with large dark pupils, a long, mottled face and thin, veined hands that were always in the air to illustrate by gesture the constantly repeated adventures of the immediate past: her brush with a streetcar conductor, her talk with an "angelic" taxidriver, her visits with the sick, her letter to her congressman.

"You've certainly made up for a bad Daddy, Mrs. Means," Reese said, reaching down to give her his customary kiss. "Eunie's birthday slipped my mind altogether. She knows it, too. Look at her, the minx. She won't even speak to me."

But there was no response in Mrs. Means, no return of pressure from her old soft cheek. As Reese straightened up and looked down at her he caught a glimpse of something like fright in her eyes, as if she had betrayed, by simple non-feasance, a hostility that she was under an obligation to conceal. He had always been fond of Esther's mother. He had found consolation in the warm bathtub of her sympathy and devotion. It was a shock now to realize that the tub had gone cold.

"I told Eunice the dolly was from me *and* Daddy," she hissed in his ear. "So it's all right, really."

"That was kind of you. But I don't want to horn in on Grandma's credit."

"You're very welcome to it. And now I must be off. Esther said not to wait after you came."

Evidently, she could not bear to be under the same roof with him. As he followed her out the door and down the flagstones to her car, he reflected sadly that she and he represented the ultimate extremes. It made him feel a curious alliance with her.

"I'm sorry about Eunice's birthday," he apologized again, for he hated to let her go without apologizing for something. "Too much on my mind, I guess. What with the office and everything."

She stopped at this, and standing behind her, he could see the tremor of her shoulders. "I'm not surprised," she said flatly. "Particularly with 'everything.'"

"Everything?" he echoed, for her attack had taken him by surprise.

She turned now, and her cavernous brown eyes took him in. "Surely I needn't be more explicit!"

Reese was permeated with a sense of regret. There were so few things he was sure of, but one was that he hated to hurt this old woman. The others — no, he did not care about the others. Esther had her self-pity and Andy the titillation of his theories; the Parmelees, even his own mother, were cushioned with preoccupations, and, as for the friends in Northfield, he could only despise the affectation of their pretended concern. But to this one old woman Esther's happiness was a matter of life or death. He could not submit to be ruled by her values, but he could at least admit that in this war she was an innocent casualty. He respected her hatred; he wanted to cry out: "Dear Mrs. Means, hate me to death, if you will, but I promise that if I could have listened to anyone, I would have listened to *you!*" But such a cry would have been an insult to her. He could only bow before her anger, with the respect that it deserved and murmur: "Oh?"

The sound of a car made them both turn around. "You needn't tell *her*, anyway, what I said," Mrs. Means hissed at him quickly as she hurried off to her car. "You can spare her *that* much, I hope!"

When Esther got out of her car, she gazed down the drive after her mother's and then asked him: "Why on earth was Ma in such a hurry? Did you shoo her away?"

"She didn't like being alone with me."

She met his gaze without the least change of expression. Then she merely shrugged and started back down the flagstone path.

"Esther!"

She paused. "Well?"

"Wouldn't you find it easier to come out with it?"

"What?"

"With what you've been telling your mother. And what you've been telling Andy. With what you've been telling God knows *how* many people!"

She walked on.

"Don't you think you and I should have it out?" he called after her.

"Never!"

"Esther!" She stumbled against a raised flagstone and staggered as if she were going to fall. He hurried up to catch her by the shoulders.

"Don't touch me!" she exclaimed with a sudden, shocking passion, and their eyes met in close surprise. "It's simply that I don't believe in discussing such things," she said, recovering herself. "I don't see anything to be gained. And there may be everything to be lost." She shook herself free of him.

"Yet you discuss it with others. You won't deny that, will you?"

"That's my affair!" she cried. "I must insist that's my affair! What you do is *your* business. What I do about it is mine. You want to strip me of my last defense, Reese! Well, you may defeat me. But you'll never talk me into surrendering my weapons. Never!"

"Esther," he pleaded. "I don't want to defeat you. Believe me. I don't want to hurt you."

"You're not hurting me!" she retorted. "Will you please get that through your big, fat head? You're not hurting me at all! There! Now, do you think we might go in and try to make Eunie feel we care *something* about her birthday?"

"I'll never understand you."

She tossed her head as she turned to the house. "Well, at least I still have *that* advantage!"

He lingered to watch her firm stride down the path. She could still, after all their years together, put him in the wrong as effectively as when they had gone to children's swimming parties on Parmelee Cove. How could any woman be so perennially and dramatically in the right? If he stood under the vaulting cupola of society's wrath, if he bellowed up his defiance into the dank air until he could sense the crumbling of masonry around him, until he could anticipate the angry avalanche of falling marble that would annihilate him, was it not the worst moment of all, as the inundation still mysteriously delayed, to discern, peering up through the threatening darkness, that the avenging structure was being held up by the strong white arms and shoulders of his passionately straining wife and to have for his only answer her bright and patient smile?

8

As CYNTHIA DRESSED for Reese's birthday party at old Mrs. Parmelee's she decided that she was the most ill-used woman on the north shore of Long Island. It was not simply that she was obliged, until Andy "took hold," as Finny put it, in the family company, to live in a cheap little cottage that looked as if it had strayed from a housing development and lost its way, embarrassed, under the stately elms of her mother's place. It was not merely that she was obliged every morning to remind her buoyant and eternally forgiving husband of the insults she had thrown at him the night before. It was not even that her brother Finny had threatened her that very morning with destitution and that her mother, persistently if unobtrusively alcoholic and totally absorbed in cards, had refused even to listen to her appeal. But now she did not even have a proper dress to wear to the party.

"Damn, damn, damn!" she cried as she discovered a spot in the yellow taffeta that she had finally decided upon.

What had she done to be used so? She might as well have been living in the heart of the Victorian era. Why did she have the bad luck to have the one husband and Reese the one wife who would refuse to behave in a perfectly normal situation the way normal people behaved? Everyone knew how it was done. There were tears and more tears and moving, violent scenes; there was a great deal of sad, true talk of the tragedy of broken homes; there were resolutions and even attempted reconciliations. But it always ended the same way; it always ended in Reno. And eventually everything worked itself out. But Esther! Would Esther behave like a normal person? Fat chance! She had raised the countryside! It was all very well for Reese; he didn't mind that sort of thing. He even seemed to derive a perverse satisfaction in outraging the feelings of his world. But she had no desire to antagonize people; it was their world, after all, in which she had to live. If she had told him that she wanted to get away, to see other places, other worlds, it was only for a year or two. In the end one always came back. But that was the kind of truth a man could *never* see. And Reese, of course, was even more visionary than most. No wonder he needed her! No wonder he needed *some* kind of a pilot!

She felt a bit better now, thinking how much smarter she was than Reese, for all his philosophic talk. What did it amount to, practically? She decided to try the yellow taffeta, after all. The spot was really hardly noticeable. And Reese, of course, never noticed what she wore. She remembered, with a small wry smile, what Freddy Talcott's wife had said about him: "I'm not asking any questions, my dear, but I can feel there's something up between you and Reese. No, don't say it! Just *listen* to me. That man would make the best lover and the worst husband in the world!"

Cynthia debated this for the hundredth time as she sat down, clad in the yellow taffeta, and started to work on her hair. But her heart sank with the sound of a step behind her, and Andy's face appeared in the mirror. His fingers were carefully adjusting his bow tie.

"Well?"

"I thought we might have a word about the evening,"

he said with his now customary dry pleasantness. "Considering where we're going."

"It was *your* idea to go!"

"Certainly. It would have been so pointed to decline. But everyone will be watching you and Reese. Have you considered that?"

She flung her comb angrily down on the bureau. "Certainly, I've considered it! What do you plan to do about it?"

His face wore the look of half-smiling patience that she most detested. "Simply this. I shall cut in every time Reese dances with you tonight."

She raised her hands to her temples. "Andy, what do you want?" she cried desperately. "Why do you torture me so?"

"I don't mean to hurt you, my dear." He looked actually troubled. "I only want to keep you."

But she was past being moved. His love, or whatever it was that he still felt for her, had degenerated during a single summer into mere stubbornness and tenacity. "I sometimes wonder if you really want to keep me," she said bitterly. "Or whether you only want to keep me from Reese."

Esther seemed particularly triumphant that night as she received Mrs. Parmelee's guests in the dark, high-ceilinged Jacobean hall of the big house, dressed in scarlet and wearing pearls that she had borrowed from her mother-in-law. She almost gushed over Cynthia's taffeta as she led her and Andy over to greet Reese's grandmother who was sitting in a high Italian armchair by the fireplace. But Cynthia, in sudden defiance, crossed the hall to where Reese was standing alone by the library door.

"Look at the birthday boy," she said, "all by himself. Won't the other children play with you?"

"I'm philosophizing," he said without turning.

"You look as if you were seeing us all for the first time."

"Or the last."

"I suppose it's very much the same thing."

"It's like in Stendhal," he said without heeding her. "Like the world after Napoleon. All these people are young and well off. They have good secure jobs and small, healthy children. Yet they're obsessed with appearances. Appearing normal, appearing adjusted, appearing warm and friendly and pleasantly informal. They're mannikins who repeat their clichés: 'I want my children to have the best education' or 'Every man should have a hobby' or 'I can't bear stuffy people,' just like monks telling their beads. In the hope that faith will follow prayer. As Christians they have accepted atheism. As Republicans they have accepted socialism. As snobs they have accepted everybody. Yet they still live by forms. They can't afford to turn over any more stones."

Cynthia had never heard him make so long a speech before. She had a faint foreboding that it might mark the end of something. "But these things have always been true," she protested. "What I can never see is why you *mind*. It's like being able to classify flowers. Does it make walking in a garden any less agreeable?"

"To find they're all weeds?"

"What does it matter what they're *called?*"

He gave her a level look. "I suppose that would be a woman's point of view," he muttered as he moved away to refill his drink.

Cynthia found dinner particularly trying. Esther seemed to have turned a simple birthday party into a glittering banquet to celebrate the solidarity of the Parmelees. In the middle of it she rose to make a long toast to Reese's grandmother. She told, with unabashed sentimentality, the history of her friendship with the old lady and how it bridged the years between them and even (here Esther had smiled charm-

ingly down the table) their becoming "in-laws," how Mrs.
Parmelee had consoled her during the war years, how Mrs.
Parmelee had even helped her raise her children. And then
she moved on to more general fields, praising Mrs. Parmelee
as a mother, a grandmother and a great-grandmother and
ending up by asking the table to drink the health of "Granny
Parmelee, as all of us here, whether actually related or not,
will always think of her — Granny Parmelee of Parmelee
Cove."

The toast was a great success. Cynthia heard her brother
Finny, who was sitting on Esther's right, ask her loudly for
"a copy of that." Then Andy, to her dismay, got up and
made his own little toast to Mrs. Parmelee, prefacing it with
an apology "for presuming to say a word after all the beautiful things Esther has said." The long board fairly throbbed
with approval. But Esther's real triumph came amid a tap-
ping of knives on glasses and a renewed frenzy of applause,
when Granny Parmelee herself rose to acknowledge her
toasts.

"I make it a point never to play favorites with any of my
'descendants' or their 'spouses,'" she began in a high, quaver-
ing tone and paused to cast her sweetest smile down the
table. "You will see by my words that I have been talking to
my lawyer again. And I believe I can truly say that I *have*
no favorites. But I'm sure that none of my dearly beloved
children or grandchildren would have any objection to my
telling all of you tonight that if I had to start life over again
and if I had to choose someone else to be, I should without
hesitation choose to be Esther Parmelee."

There was a vociferous round of applause, and it was
several seconds before Mrs. Parmelee could go on with her
toast. When she did, it was to tell in warm and simple terms
what Esther and Reese had meant to her since they had

taken up their abode in the nearby gatehouse. The mood that Esther had evoked had caught the old lady completely. A queen at a jubilee, she bowed from her carriage, becoming once more the legend that everyone wanted her to be.

After dinner, when the ladies had withdrawn upstairs, Cynthia faced an even harder test. She had an uneasy sense that the curiosity of the ladies had suddenly become hostility. No one, of course, was going to make unpleasant hints to her, but no one, on the other hand, in view of the renewed blaze of public recognition of Reese's and Esther's domestic bliss, cared to be seen in any intimate tête-à-tête with a presumably defeated home breaker. Cynthia had been drawn willy-nilly into the admiring court that surrounded Mrs. Parmelee and by like token the Parmelee status quo. With however poor a grace she could do nothing now but go through the form of dropping her own sour little curtsey. It was Esther herself who sought her out and found her sitting alone on a wicker chaise longue on the porch looking at the dark sea and drinking brandy.

"It'll just take me a moment to say what I want to say, Cynthia," she began in a soft, low, benignant voice, sitting down on the end of the chaise longue. "When are you going to give up?"

Cynthia, watching her sullenly, made no answer.

"Reese was never the person for you," Esther continued in the same smooth tone. "Because you were tired of Andy, you had to look for his opposite. I don't blame you for being tired of Andy. But I shall blame you very much indeed if you mess up your life a second time. *And* mine."

Cynthia felt herself hypnotized by those all-assuming eyes. "What would you advise?"

"Never to try to be something you're not!" Esther turned away abruptly and stared out over the water. Her voice was suddenly bitter. "You should know now that you belong in your brother's world. You're a Coit through and through. I don't know why your family ever encouraged you to think you were different, just because you were young. It made you grow up to believe there was something for you beyond their way of life. You couldn't tell that your little flare-up was only a passing phase. But it was hard on Andy. Because he *was* that passing phase!"

Cynthia did not like this at all. She was still enough of a little girl to believe that no one should be disagreeable to her at a birthday party. But before she could answer, Esther had gone, as quickly as she had come, and Cynthia watched her from the porch, assembling the ladies to go down to the dance floor.

Reese himself came up to Cynthia as she reached the foot of the Jacobean stairway and asked her to dance. She shrugged and nodded, but before they had moved more than a few steps, Andy appeared suddenly at Reese's elbow and tried to cut in.

"What's the idea, Andy? We just started."

"I saw that."

"Aren't you going to let us dance?"

"No. It's *one* thing I can stop."

Reese stared at him, his head tilted slightly back, his body still, his eyes expressionless. Cynthia knew it was the prelude to one of his violent fits of temper and clutched her hands together in a misery of suspense.

"I'm going to dance with Cynthia," Reese said in a slow, menacing tone. "And if you cut in before ten minutes' time I'm going to knock your block off!"

"That's always the privilege of a bully."

Cynthia looked desperately from one to the other. Andy was smiling serenely; Reese's fists were clenched. In another

moment it would be the end of everything; there would be a
scuffle, Andy would have a black eye and in the uproar she
would be humiliated forever. She wondered in her sudden
anger if she did not hate them both.

"Andy," she hissed, "for the love of God, give us five
minutes, will you!"

It was another shock when her appeal succeeded. Maybe
the real anguish in her tone persuaded him; maybe it startled
even him into seeing how terrible such a scene would be. At
any rate, his smile disappeared; he looked puzzled for a moment, and then, with a silly little bow to save his dignity, he
walked smartly away. How odd, she thought, that her last
remnant of respect should disappear with his granting the
favor which she had so earnestly begged.

"Come on outside," Reese said brusquely, and she followed
him to the terrace. It was windy now, with a half-moon, and
she could make out whitecaps on the sound. Everyone else
had stayed inside, and they were alone. "I'm through," he
said curtly. "Tonight has done it. I can't take any more of
this. Esther has gone too far."

She put her hands on the stone parapet and gazed up at the
moon. She was having the most curious sensation. She felt
all of a sudden that she was very glad that she had had her
affair with Reese. Perhaps it had made a woman of her, after
all. But at the same time she was not sure, as long as she had
her memories of him, that it was absolutely essential to her
happiness to continue their meetings.

"Where will you go?" she asked, detached, formal.

"Anywhere you want."

"Where *I* want? Am I going?"

"Aren't you?"

She was distracted by a small carbuncle, inflamed and
very red, on the side of his nose. Such things had always

repelled her. "You want me to go with you?" she asked coolly. "Without further formalities? Leaving my child, I suppose?"

"Oh, we'd take Angela."

"Andy might have something to say to that!"

"Andy'll come around," he said with a snort. "Andy always comes around. That's his role. Everyone will come around when we really go off. You watch. There'll be a hysterical drive to cover it up and make us respectable."

"What about your job?"

"I'll get another."

"What would we live on?"

"I've got a little saved. Esther can have the rest."

In later months Cynthia was to wonder exactly what effect that carbuncle had on her decision. She had been watching it ever since she had turned her gaze from the moon. She was positively angry with him for having it and spoiling her picture of him. And yet it seemed very lucky that he should have had it that night. By concentrating on it, she was able to remind herself of a dozen things that were true and fixed. For she was quite clear now that she was facing the ultimate crisis of her life. Here was a man of remarkable quality — oh, she faced that! — asking her to change her very scheme of existence. He offered a new, perhaps a more exciting life. He was no Andy. In fact he was like no other man among her friends. But she remembered what Freddy's wife had said about him. Did she really *want* a new and exciting life? And suddenly, as she stared at that carbuncle, she knew that she didn't want to leave the world of all her friends, the cozy, gossiping, accepting, even the hypocritical world. It crackled before her, as warm and easy and welcoming as Reese's world seemed dark and chill and austere. He, of course, did not mind such qualities. But then he did not mind his carbuncle. He was probably not even aware that he had it. His immorality was too stern for such trivia.

"No, Reese," she said at last. "I can't."

He seemed to take in the finality of her decision, even through her hesitation, for he nodded. "I haven't the 'right' to ask you, I suppose," he said with a hint of a sneer.

"Couldn't we go on in the old way? For just a bit more?"

"You don't understand. I shan't be here."

"You've really made up your mind?"

"It's a decision long overdue."

As she stared into his now almost surly blue eyes, a feeling of anger rushed over her. "You're *glad* I'm not coming!"

"I wouldn't want you if you didn't want to come!"

She turned abruptly and went back into the house. She had to get back to the party and truth before that blue stare should knife its way into a decision which, despite her rapidly beating heart, every other conscious part of her being told her was the right one. She hurried to the table in the library where drinks were being served, but just as the waiter handed her a whiskey, Andy came up.

"You see!" he exclaimed, like a boastful child, "I did what you wanted!"

"You did indeed!" She threw back her head and laughed a bit wildly. "You're much too good for me! I've decided to get that divorce, after all!"

He turned white. "What about Finny?"

"Oh, Finny won't mind. He never could bear you. All he wants is that I shan't marry Reese. Well, I'm not going to marry Reese!"

Andy turned immediately to go to the dance floor to find her brother. As she raised her glass to her own reflection in the mirror behind the bar table, she felt that at long last she was drinking to a real freedom and a real future.

9

ESTHER was dancing with Freddy Talcott when she suddenly sensed that Reese was no longer on the floor, and she had an immediate conviction that he had left the party. She dismissed Freddy with the quick smile that was the hostess's prerogative and crossed the floor to say good night to a couple who were leaving. When they asked her where they could find Reese, she simply replied that he had gone home. She then escorted Mrs. Parmelee, who was very tired, to her bedroom and kissing her good night, made no excuses for Reese. She was through with making excuses for him. Downstairs she looked about for him again, but her search was perfunctory. She knew he was not there. She stayed at the party until the last guest had gone, talking with animation to Finny Coit about the menace of communism in our schools and government. Then she supervised the turning off of all the lights, and, refusing a lift from Reese's sister, walked home alone over the dark lawn. She had little hope now for the interview that lay before her. Reese, in his usual fashion, had made her feel like a child surprised in a foolish game. But the foolishness, if it was that, had consisted only of her fantasy in assuming that there was anything in the world that could overcome his surliness and induce him to play. She was weary, and it angered her that he should take it for granted that he was the only one who could be wearied by the life they were leading, by life on Parmelee Cove, by life itself. Did he think that like one of his grandmother's cows, she was incapable of boredom?

As she had anticipated, she found him in the living room, smoking his pipe and reading Stendhal. He closed his book as she came in and looked up defiantly.

"Well?" she asked flatly. "Are you through with her now?"

"I am."

She stared at the challenge in those wary blue eyes and knew there was no triumph for her in them. His head was reared up like the head of a suspicious stallion. "Very well, then," she continued. "I'm willing to talk about it."

"You've been to a great deal of trouble to save me from Cynthia. It's almost inconceivable how much. If effort could make a happy marriage, ours would be the happiest on record."

"Is that a compliment?"

"It's a statement of fact."

"Go on," she said, nodding. "Go on."

"We live in different worlds, Esther. With different premises. To you, if a marriage is threatened, another woman must be outwitted. To this you direct all the resources of your fertile imagination. You outwit the woman, of course. She goes down like a ninepin. Who could resist you? And then, of course, the weakling husband must see the error of his ways and the sterling worth of his spouse. And the curtain, as in a Lonsdale parlor comedy, will descend upon the connubial embrace of Lord and Lady Lavering."

Esther sat down slowly on the sofa. She felt suddenly an overwhelming weariness. It came over her with a rush that in all the years of her efforts, since the first picnics with the blond schoolboy hero of Parmelee Cove, she had never once really succeeded in altering by so much as a jot or a tittle his stubbornly consistent philosophy of negation. There was not even any gain in making a temporary impression on him; it was only a question of time before he snapped back to his original point. She felt sickened by the waste of a lifetime of effort. And then as she closed her eyes she became aware of a dull red along the dark horizons of her consciousness. Was she going to hate him? Had she always hated him?

"I see," she said in a dead tone. "It seems that all this time I've misconceived my rival. She was never Cynthia. She was myself."

"And a far more formidable rival than Cynthia ever could have been."

"Are you through now? Is that what you're trying to tell me, Reese?"

"I'm through with everything, that's what I'm trying to tell you." He had got up and turned to the window now, his hands in his pockets. "With Parmelee Cove. With Clark, Day & Parmelee. With my old self. With Cynthia."

"And with me! Say it!"

"All right, Esther," he said quietly. "With you, too."

She clenched her fists in a sudden spasm of rage. "My God, when I think how I've worked to hold you!" she cried. "I've fought and fought! It's so damned unfair!"

"You've played by all the rules," he conceded. "Your rules, anyway. What good do they do when the other side doesn't recognize them?"

"Poor Cynthia," she said bitterly. "She played by my rules, too. She's just as licked. I guess one is always licked when one plays with a — with a —"

"Heel," he said, turning around defiantly. "That's the word, isn't it?"

"How proud you are of it," she said disgustedly. "And

yet how true that's what you are! After St. Lawrence's and
Harvard and the Navy and a large, loving family to back you
up, what have you finally succeeded in becoming? A heel!
And pleased as punch, too! Why not? It was no mean task
to accomplish, with all those obstacles!"

"But it's not the end of the story," he retorted with a sudden heat that showed that this shot at least had grazed him.
"It's not the end of the story yet. All right, everything I've
done so far has been undoing. But there was a lot to undo.
And now I'm starting again from scratch. Now we'll see!"

"Life doesn't give second chances."

"You beg the question, Esther!"

Once more they stared at each other, and it struck her now
that she could discern behind the blue blankness of his stare
the struggle between his principles, if principles they could be
called, and his pity, maybe even the remnants of his affection
for her. When he turned away suddenly, she was sure that
she had guessed it correctly, but her sureness only turned
her heart into a desert. That he should actually fight against
the innate decency of his nature was too great a perversity
for her any longer to forgive. If life *did* give second chances,
it was time for her, too, to let go. She closed her eyes and
felt dizzy with the sense of all she was having to let go; she
wondered if the operation would not be too grave for the
patient; she could not seem for the moment to imagine what
life would be like without Reese to worry about. When she
looked up and saw his head still turned to the window, she
forgot everything but the sudden eruption of her anger.

"Very well, then," she said in a cold, low tone with a
slight tremor, "there's one thing I'll do to help you. I'll
take as big a load off your conscience as I possibly can. By
behaving as badly as the worst wife in Northfield."

He turned around. "How do you mean?"

"I'll keep the children, and I'll keep this house and every bit of money I can get out of you!" Her shoulders were trembling now, and she realized with a shock that she was shouting. "And I'll get your father to see that Granny's money goes straight to me and not you! He will, too, you know! He's told me so!"

"Of course he will. In fact, it's done already. I told him I hadn't the slightest objection."

"If you're going to walk out on your wife and children, you're going to have to pay for it!" she continued passionately, jumping to her feet. "If I've got to be Daddy as well as Mummy, you've got to leave me in a position to do it!"

"But I will, Esther, I will." He sat down at the desk and started jotting figures on a pad. "I want you to have everything, of course. It won't be too much, but when I get a new job I'll be able to add to it. I want you to take my place at Parmelee Cove. In my family and in every way. It's always been a way of life for you and not for me. You're welcome to it! And I mean that nicely, too. With you it makes sense; with me it makes none. Look, I figure that if I give you my securities and the income from my little trust and this house —"

As she watched him making marks on the paper, energetically putting into execution a plan that he must have been considering for years, she wondered bleakly how it was possible — how it was even conceivable — that she could have molded so little the one man she had ever loved.

PART II

Exile

I

NOBODY watching Rosina Street step swiftly down Fifth Avenue in the midtown area would have taken her for the feature editor of *A Woman's World*. One would have imagined for such a post a woman over rather than under thirty and at least as well tailored as one of that magazine's models: brooding, chin in hand, white, slim, a kind of western odalisque. Rosina, hatless, with blowing curly, short brown hair, a high brow and smooth, heart-shaped face, with slanting eyes that wore an almost contradictory expression of cheerful preoccupation, her briefcase swinging purposefully from a shoulder strap as she strode along, seemed to belong rather to the world of the art periodical or the liberal quarterly. Yet in fact she was no exception to the staff of her magazine who, partly in reaction to the elegance from which they made their living and partly to shun competition with Mrs. Doremus, their senior editor, who liked even on the business scene, to play the bird of paradise, affected a simplicity, even a casualness in their daytime dress. In the evenings, of course, each and every one of them was a Gilda Doremus in miniature.

Rosina's air of preoccupation that morning, however, was not any mask of daydreams. She was on her way to the office of Amos Levine, counsel to *A Woman's World*, to discuss a law suit, or at least the threat of one, that might well mean

the end of her career with Gilda Doremus. She had brought
it on herself; Rosina always brought things on herself. How
else could one get ahead? It had been a calculated risk, but
now it seemed that she might have miscalculated. On only
her second issue as feature editor she had published a piece on
Charles Paturo, the owner of the entertainment agency. Mr.
Paturo, avid for free publicity, had opened his files to her,
and she had extracted a great deal of fascinating material to
support her thesis that the charity ball had become an indispensable tool in the old but ever changing craft of social
climbing. But the most fascinating material of all she had
found in Mr. Paturo's desk, an area into which she had not
had permission, specifically, to delve. It had all appeared, well
stocked with names, in an article which had enjoyed a grati-
fying vogue. Rosina had calculated that with success everyone on the magazine would forgive her. In this she had been
quite correct. But she had also figured that Paturo would
prefer any publicity to no publicity. In this, it seemed, she
had been quite wrong. He had fairly howled with pain and
sent his lawyer to Amos Levine with demands for apology,
for retraction, for damages, for anything, in short, that a
lawyer could get.

Amos Levine's office was in Rockefeller Center, and the
door carried the legend of his name alone. Yet Rosina de-
duced from the size of the waiting room, a smooth, grey, boring modern, and the huge circular desk of the receptionist,
that other people besides Mr. Levine worked there. They
must have been, however, incidental figures, mere concealed
ducts and arteries in the corporate mind of Amos Levine,
the man who was always on the "other" side. The "other"
side, she surmised as she glanced around, must have been the
lucrative one.

"Mr. Levine will see you now, Miss Street. You can go
right in."

Rosina stepped into the next room, finding it, as she had anticipated, a larger, greyer version of the reception hall. She took in the Utrillo over the sofa — it reassured her that she should have predicted it — and then glanced about for the — yes, the small Dufy of the race track, directly over Mr. Levine's chair. Maybe it was all going to be easier than she had thought. She smiled into the dark, brooding, rather melancholy eyes that were fixed on her.

"Do you like painting, Miss Street?"

"Enormously."

Because of his eyes and because of the thick, smooth, dark hair through which he now ran his fingers he seemed at first almost young, conceivably romantic, the kind of man whom many women might have loved to console. But as she took in the wrinkles under his eyes, the long oval face, the rather blunt, coarse nose and chin, the cashmere suit, too soft, too good, the huge gold cufflinks and the ruby pin in the Burmese tie, she recognized the litigator in late middle age. It struck her, however, that where she had expected him to be sharp, maybe a touch "greasy," he seemed relaxed, indifferent, in fact almost sleepy. He laughed, and it was a soft pleasant laugh.

"I bet Dufy is to your generation what Bouguereau was to mine: Grandma's front parlor."

Rosina, sitting down, was thinking already of a feature article: "Antimacassar in the nineteen-fifties." "Oh, no," she said politely. "Dufy has his place."

"In a lawyer's office? Is that it?" But when she made no answer he went straight to business. "I've read the famous piece on Charlie Paturo, and I loved it. Don't do one on me, Miss Street. Will you promise me that?"

"I promise you nothing." She glanced around the room. "In fact, I've already started it."

"Maybe we'd better see what we can do about Charlie first.

Then you'll know how far you can go with me." He placed a silver paper cutter neatly in the middle of the bare black blotter on his desk and regarded it quizzically for a bit. "Charlie Paturo happens to be a very good friend of mine. Of course, that doesn't make the slightest difference. You know my reputation?" He raised his eyebrows mockingly. "Something, I believe, about pennies and a dead grandmother's eyes. If we get into court, I will, of course, conduct the trial. But any preliminary negotiations had better be handled by one of my associates. Someone who doesn't know Charlie Paturo. That is why, if you don't mind, I'm going to take you in and introduce you to Mr. Parmelee. He has already been thoroughly briefed."

Rosina didn't mind in the least. A subordinate in charge might mean a smaller bill. A few minutes later she was sitting in a much smaller office with only one picture, a Picasso, this time a reproduction, facing a large blond man with a disconcerting blue stare. He was smoking a pipe, but he had asked her first if she minded. He had seemed to sense instinctively, as his employer had not, that what she really needed was reassurance.

"There's nothing to any of this, you know," he said brusquely, slapping some papers on his desk. "Old Charlie Paturo is simply howling because he's hurt. But he hasn't thought the thing through. He hasn't faced up to the simple little fact that he can't afford to go to court."

"He can't?" Rosina realized from the sudden rough jolt of her relief how deep her anxiety must have been. "Are you sure?" she continued, taking a quick breath. "Mr. Levine seemed to think he might."

"Just a lawyer's trick. We all do it. Build up the case, and you build up the fee."

She wondered, astonished, if Mr. Levine had any suspicion

of how casually his associate dealt with his little tricks. "Why can't Mr. Paturo afford to go to court?"

"Because the truth is always a complete defense. He'd just bury himself six feet deeper."

"But could we *prove* all those things in my article?"

"Maybe not. But we could do worse. We could *try* to prove them. We could put his biggest clients on the stand and ask them embarrassing questions. I think we could make a nice little dent in his business. And he knows it, too. Don't worry."

Mr. Parmelee's set jaw carried an extraordinary conviction. Rosina, who only a few minutes before had seen herself discharged from her magazine, now saw Mr. Paturo in bankruptcy. "But why do you tell me this?" she demanded. "Why do you minimize your own work?"

"Because I saw you were worried. And worried sick. The moment you walked in here."

"And I thought I hid it so well!"

"Oh, you did. It's just that I've had some experience with women of character. I know how they do it."

She stared, intrigued, at those unrevealing blue eyes. For a moment she almost forgot Mr. Paturo. "You're very perceptive," she observed. "What else do you see in me?"

"Well, for one thing, I imagine that peeking into Mr. Paturo's desk was mostly your idea."

"That's right."

"And I seem to imagine that you never cleared the article with Mrs. Doremus. Or at least that you never cleared the final version."

"That's right again."

"And if it costs the magazine anything, it's your neck?"

"Even if it costs them nothing, I'm stuck with Mr. Levine's fee. That's why I'm so grateful to you for keeping it down."

"If you let them put that fee business over on you, you're a dead duck!" he warned her with sudden brusqueness. "That woman Doremus will walk all over you from then on. This is a tough world, Miss Street!"

Rosina did not like his tone. In fact, she was suddenly very much put out with him. It was her particular pride that she knew a great deal about the toughness of this world. Who was he to talk to her as if she were some society girl, killing time with a silly job before marriage? Her gratitude vanished. "I think I know my world, Mr. Parmelee," she said with dignity. "I think I know it quite as well as you."

"All right," he retorted with a smile that only made her angrier, "let's get on with it, shall we?" He pushed the papers aside and sat back in his swivel chair, puffing hard at his pipe. "Do you have any other material on Paturo? I don't care what kind."

"A little."

"Put it all together and make it as bad as you can. Then give it to me, and I'll show it to his lawyer. I'll tell him it's the sequel. Due out next month. That'll give us a bargaining point. There'll be a certain amount of inconclusive chatter, a few recriminations and then *A Woman's World* will do the handsome thing. We'll offer to quash the sequel, and everyone will end up in everyone else's arms!"

When the interview was over, and Rosina walked back up Fifth Avenue, she was still irritated with his method of reassurance. She had had her worries, it was true, but they were the worries of a capable woman who had taken a long chance for a clearly conceived goal. It was galling to have Mr. Parmelee console her for thinking she was in a jam when she wasn't. How had *she* been supposed to guess that Paturo had no case? Was *she* a lawyer? And who was Mr. Parmelee to be so sure that he knew her world? For all his dour determination and despite his obviously subsidiary position in the office of a man who seemed in every way his opposite, she thought she had detected in his accent and in the easy confidence of his manner a certain upper class note. It seemed impossible to her that anyone who had really emerged from what Mrs. Doremus referred to as the "top drawer" should work for a man like Amos Levine, but on the other hand she could hardly picture Mr. Parmelee as having ever belonged to any world like the one in Roanoke, Virginia, that had been the scene of her own childhood. Now *there*, she thought with a snort, had been a school for toughness. And had Mr. Parmelee ever had the ineffable experience of being married to anyone quite as rotten as Cyrus? Had he ever had to work for anyone, even Amos Levine, who was as exacting and crafty as Mrs. Doremus? It was intolerable, after the tussles of *her* life, to be thought naïve!

Her mood had not changed when she met Grace Chess for lunch. Grace was Mrs. Doremus's executive officer and had been so for fifteen years. It was notorious to everyone in the business but Grace herself that Mrs. Doremus had appropriated not only her ideas but her very brain. Grace was that not wholly rare phenomenon of the journalist world, an old maid in her middle forties with a sophisticated mind and a totally unsophisticated soul. She was even considered a bit of a saint, untouched by the meanness in those around her. She was a gentle, shy, ladylike creature, of prodigious energy and conscientiousness, with black hair, already dyed, parted in the middle and pulled straight back to a large bun and skin as smooth as pebbles washed by years of clear water. She was supposed to have had an unhappy love affair with a famous poet when she had been very young, and she was inclined to drink rather a lot, but without adverse effects, at literary parties. She and Rosina had become good friends, although Rosina suspected that Grace found her methods at the office too bold and aggressive. She prickled now at the inconsistency of the charges that she suddenly felt were being leveled against her that day. Could she be at once crafty and naïve? Could Mr. Parmelee and Grace both be right? Almost brusquely she told the latter about Paturo and Mr. Parmelee's plan.

"Oh, I'm *so* glad, my dear," Grace said with that note of vibrant sincerity that made her so valuable a listener. "Now it'll all be over. Do you think maybe we should have a little cocktail? Just to celebrate?"

"Not for me." Rosina cared very little about drinking. "You go ahead."

"Oh — no."

"Tell me something, Grace," she pursued, "something that's been on my mind. You thought it was terrible of me to put those things in the Paturo article, didn't you?"

"I? Oh, no. Not at all, dear."

"Yes, you did. *You'd* never have done it, would you?"

"Well, I don't know." Grace's puckered brow showed the burden of her honesty. "Perhaps not. But what does that prove?"

It seemed to prove a lot. Rosina gave in altogether now to her sense of being misused. She suddenly wanted to reach behind the soft veil of Grace's benignity and grab hold of that small head-shaking critic who never emerged. "You think I'm hard, don't you?" she demanded in a sharper tone. "You've always thought I was hard. Or is tough the right word?" But then she pulled herself up abruptly. What was she doing to poor Grace? How could she so wantonly ripple those big pools of eyes with pain? Was it because Mr. Parmelee had so easily seen through her, spotting her right off as the guilty party? The memory aggravated her anew. "You think only a tough person would have sacrificed Paturo for her future on the magazine?" she went on in the same tone. "Isn't that so?"

"My dear, I don't judge people."

"Of course you do! You just don't tell them."

"Rosy, what do you want me to say?"

"Oh, anything but to the point!" Rosina cried in exasperation. "I suppose everyone thinks I'm hard and designing. Except those who think I'm silly and small-town. I don't know which is worse!"

"But nobody thinks of you either way!"

"It's all very well for you," Rosina went on bitterly, shrugging away her friend's denials, ashamed of herself for hurting her. "You always had loving parents. You still have that sweet old mother whom you live with. But my father was a drunk. And not the kind of drunk a daughter can love or hate and then write Thomas Wolfe novels about, but a plain, dull, common or garden drunk. He bored me to death as far back as I can remember. And Mummy, who had to run a gift shop in Roanoke, you can picture her, can't you? With dirty grey hair and square glasses and lots of useless energy and a cliché for every occasion? The kind of woman with whom it's impossible to have the smallest communication. The very smallest!"

"Poor Rosy!" Grace shook her head with concern and surprise. And why not? Rosina had never told her a word before about her background. "Was there no one you could talk to?"

"No one!" Grace's sympathy, now that she had it, was repellent to her. "And I didn't want anyone! Even Grandpa, though he was the best of the lot. A minister. Methodist. He was the one who sent me to college. But there was no real communication with him, either. I played a part for

him, the devout little girl. I rehearsed ahead of time everything I said to him. But I *had* to, Grace, don't you see?
People like that can't handle sincerity. You've got to give
them what they want. Till you can get away!"

"Do you ever see any of them any more?"

"Oh, I write Mother two or three times a year." Rosina
shrugged impatiently. "I even send her money if I can. But
that's that. I never go down, and they never expect it. I've
even shed my Southern accent!"

"Well — almost."

Rosina had to smile at this, and her mood softened. What
was she doing, anyway, telling Grace her life story? But
she had started, and she wanted now to go on. "Anyway,
that was my first mistake. My family."

"But surely they weren't *your* fault!"

"I have no use for the word 'fault,' " Rosina said scornfully.
"What difference does 'fault,' make? A mistake's a mistake."

"Very well, then. You say it was your first. Have you
made a second?"

"Yes. My husband. Or rather, my ex-husband."

"Rosy, I never knew you'd been married!"

"I don't advertise it," Rosina said with a brief shrug. "Cyrus was one of those advertising boys with a magazine cover
face who never grow up. I thought I could help him. I was
only twenty-two. But I learned. There was no baby, no alimony, no nothing. I even got an annulment. That's why I
took back my own name and the 'Miss.' "

Grace permitted herself a faint smile. "You wiped him out
pretty thoroughly," she observed. "If the police ever came
looking, they couldn't tell he'd been here."

"I won't even tell you his last name. That's how anxious
I am to forget it. So there you are, Grace. I've had two
strikes. One more and I may be out."

"But out of what?"

"Why, out of the game of making anything of myself!" Rosina exclaimed, as if it were the most obvious thing in the world. "Anything real, that is. And I'm not just talking about our particular rat race, either. Gilda Doremus isn't my entire ideal, whatever you may think. I'm no Emma Bovary. I want perfectly good things: I want to make good in my job. I want to marry a man who *is* a man, not an advertiser's model of one, like Cyrus. And I want to have children and treat them as people, not just dummies of myself. I don't want to spend my whole life walking in my sleep!" It struck her suddenly that poor Grace herself was just such a somnambulist, and she leaned over quickly to pat her hand. "I think *you're* a live person, Grace. I don't know anyone to whom more people have poured out their hearts. It's the penalty, I suppose, of being a saint. And now your hospitable basin is overflowing with mine. I, who never tell a thing to a soul!"

"Maybe it's time you did."

"Maybe I'm just on a talking jag." Rosina smiled ruefully. "Maybe it's the relief about Paturo. You see, before I went to Levine's office today I thought I might have made my third mistake!"

Back at *A Woman's World* she went to Mrs. Doremus's office and told her what had happened. The latter seemed a well decorated rather than a well dressed woman; the lavender and orange that blended to drape her figure might have been chosen for curtains. Mrs. Doremus was handsome in a heavy, forward way; her big nose, her big black eyebrows, her large white teeth and raised jaw made people first introduced to her glance nervously about for a means of egress. The impression was not softened, as it was meant to be, by the fixed smile on her lips, or by her brief schoolmistress nods or by the purple pencil that she twiddled between her fingers except when she paused to jot a note on a clean pad, a miracle, one felt sure, of synthesis. She gave a final nod when Rosina's tale was over.

"Good," she said. "Then there's nothing left but to wait and see?"

"That's it." And then, because Rosina felt pricked by the memory of Mr. Parmelee's warning, she went on: "I hope Mr. Levine's fee won't be excessive. I noted that he collects Utrillo."

"Well, I've done things for Amos in the past," Mrs. Doremus informed her. "I guess he'll do a little something for me. Only you know," she added, and her tone hummed with a faint warning, "I hate to waste my credit."

Rosina composed the memorandum that Mr. Parmelee had wanted, and he called her several times in the ensuing weeks, always reassuringly. Mr. Paturo, it seemed, was already weakening in his demands. As Rosina's article receded into the past, and his wounds began to heal, he dreaded the prospect of opening them afresh. He had been horrified at the suggestion of the second article. Finally, one morning Mr. Parmelee walked into Rosina's office and handed her a form of general release to be signed by Mrs. Doremus. Rosina glanced vaguely over the small printed clauses.

"But why should *we* release Paturo?" she asked.

"Because he's releasing us. It's customary at the end of these things. An exchange of releases of all claims from 'the beginning of the world to the execution of these presents.' We lawyers are nothing if not comprehensive."

She reflected a moment and put the paper down on her desk. "Then it's all over?"

"All over."

"I don't know how to thank you. And will — are you planning to send us a bill soon?"

"There won't be any charge. I talked old Amos into that. Don't worry about it. Your boss has sent plenty of big flies into his web."

Gratitude had always been difficult for Rosina. She found it an exhausting emotion. But Mr. Parmelee did not seem like the kind of man who expected gratitude. "Do you always speak so disrespectfully about Mr. Levine?" she inquired.

"Does it shock you?"

"No, but it surprises me." She almost felt that she had to turn away from that blue stare. "I had always heard that younger lawyers were subservient to their superiors."

"Most of them are."

"Why are you different?"

"If you're free for dinner tonight, I'll tell you all about it."

Rosina was taken aback. It was not that she was unaccustomed to sudden invitations, even propositions, but it seemed peculiar from a lawyer on a professional visit. She had always supposed there was something sexless about the law. Was *this* why there was to be no fee? "You move rather fast, don't you?" she said, dryly.

"On the contrary, I move rather slowly. I didn't ask you the first time we met. But our little case is over. If I let you go now, I may never see you again."

"Are you married, Mr. Parmelee?"

"Did I ask *you* that?"

"No. But you know I'm *Miss* Street."

"How do I know that isn't a professional name?"

"As it happens, it's not."

"I'm glad to hear it," he said, smiling. "Well, then, I'm not married either. Any other questions? About previous marriages? Children? Legitimate or otherwise? How about a loyalty oath?"

She got up and picked up the release to take it to Mrs.

Doremus. "That won't be necessary," she said with the briefest responding smile. "But it *will* be necessary for you to take me to a cocktail party first. If I go out with you. Is that agreed?"

He agreed readily enough, and she took him that evening to a party at Anstiss Stranahan's.

Anstiss was one of the new friends whom she had met through Grace Chess. "Friend" was perhaps not quite the word: Anstiss was really more a way of life. She liked to think of herself as the leader of a liberal, artistic coterie, and if most of its members came, like herself (born a DeLancey) from old Manhattan families, it was because only those similarly situated could assess the full accomplishment of her liberation. Anstiss was a lean, tall, red-haired, black-eyed, dryly loquacious woman in her early forties, obsessed with the dialectics of her own political position. She had given away her money — that was the big thing — or rather she had given away a part of it. She had given away a million dollars inherited from a maternal grandfather in Pittsburgh whose name in labor relations had been particularly odoriferous. On the other hand, she had kept the smaller but still respectably sized fortune of her father's mother which had been derived originally from Yankee clipper ships. Every dollar from every branch of her family tree had thus to defend itself at the bar of her justice. Nor was the decision ever final. The question of whether or not the clipper ships had been used in the opium trade was always open to further debate amid the little group that gathered in the 1810 house on Ninth Street with its red plush curtains, its empire furniture and shelves of books to the ceiling. In the midst of these discussions the high, jarring voice of bald, tall Jack Stranahan could be heard declaiming about the publishing firm that he and Anstiss could have started had she not given away quite

so much. Yet he was not protesting. It was the "thing" about
Jack that he had a dull job as an insurance adjuster. This,
in addition to a naturally bad temper, kept him from being
altogether overlooked. Everyone in the group had a "thing,"
and everyone's "thing" was freely discussed before the others:
whether Grace Chess should go on living with her mother,
whether Duer Lispenard should give up his job to finish "that
play," whether Cliffie Suter's analysis was hurting his painting. Very few in the group were married; and more than
half were in the Social Register. They talked a lot about
moral problems and temptations with which they were rarely
faced, and all agreed that their upbringing had been deplor-
able. A great many drinks were absorbed at their meetings,
and they called themselves, after an amusing mistranslation
of Grace's from Molière, the "precious ridiculers."

Rosina was not only the youngest and genealogically the
least distinguished, but she had no "thing," or at least no
thing that she was willing to talk about. She made up for it,
however, by her ability to listen, which, as Anstiss used to
say, was no mean asset in a group of babblers. Rosina would
sit quietly, looking pretty, while the others drank and talked,
and in a few months she found herself not only the most popular member of the group, being the only person with whom
nobody had quarreled, but certainly the best informed. Yet
seeing the little group as clearly as she did in no way lessened
her desire to remain a member of it. If one wanted to make
friends, one had to start somewhere, and even the precious
ridiculers might in time open doors to other and more interesting groups in the city. Their roots, whatever had become of their branches, were still deep. Rosina had learned
that in New York one could move only by passing from
group to group. Oh, it was easy enough to make an *appearance* almost anywhere, as she had done, once or twice, at

Mrs. Doremus's Saturday nights. But appearances were nothing; it was belonging alone that counted. And Anstiss Stranahan's little group was the only one to which she could then
belong which might at the same time provide an opening to
others. The world of Greenwich Village in which she had
spent her first years after college she would have nothing to
do with. She abominated it, as she abominated everything
that reminded her of the mistake of her marriage. To her
the Village was nothing but dirty lofts and cheap whiskey
and self-pity, no hours, no rules, no gradations. As a man
who has starved in a prison camp may never feel quite secure
of his food again, so Rosina wondered if she would ever now
get over her craving for neatness and order and meals at
proper times and conversation without rude personal remarks
and sex relegated to its proper place. One might be bored
at Anstiss's, but one was rarely angered. The single men, a
rather neutral lot, never bothered her. When she thought
what Cyrus's friends had been, it was, on the whole, a relief.

"Reese," as she now had to call him, behaved very well at
Anstiss's. Although he knew nobody there, he did not cling
to her, as so many men might have done, but moved about
the room on his own. She noticed that he introduced himself to Grace Chess, and she saw the latter flush with pleasure.
But Anstiss almost immediately cut this short. Obviously, it
was her duty as leader to examine personally any candidate
for the little group. Rosina, watching them over Duer Lispenard's shoulder, wondered if her new friend would ever be
able to sit quietly through an evening of Cliffie Suter reading
aloud from *Typee*. She doubted it. Obviously, he was not
in the least awed by Anstiss. The jerky way in which he
moved his arms when he had a point to make, taking his elbow off the mantel on which he had been leaning, seemed to
spring more from a need to emphasize than from any feeling

of constraint. He appeared to be very emphatic. Too much so, perhaps. She hoped he was not going to get angry with Anstiss; at the moment his fist was going up and down as he talked. It was curious how awkward his gestures were; one might have expected more coordination from so muscular a frame. It was as if the very act of articulation were painful. But the most distinctive feature about him was the way in which he appeared to be different persons from different distances. Across the long room his blond hair, wide shoulders, and clear, boyish features made him seem like a Nazi storm trooper, a mere handsome receptacle of maleness. But closer up one took in the circles under his intent blue eyes and the stubborn intelligence of his short straight nose and square chin. Also, the hairs of his close-shaven beard were distinctly darker than those on his head. Oh, he was a man, all right, she decided with an almost irritated shrug. But what on earth was she going to do with him?

"What does Mr. Parmelee *do?*" "Duey" Lispenard asked her suspiciously. He was younger than everyone, except Rosina, and everyone's darling, except Rosina's. The small, heart-shaped face under the blond crew cut was contracted into a scowl. Duey represented the flame of youth at Anstiss's and took for granted the tribute of his elders.

"He's the lawyer for *Woman's World.*"

"Since when have we taken up lawyers?"

"Oh, since we got tired of unproduced playwrights."

Duey stared at her for a moment with remote, wide-open eyes. He never resented things. It was as if he had no time, in the constant polishing of his ego, for resentment. "Is he a *good* lawyer?" he demanded.

"Well, I wouldn't get in a tussle with him if I were you."

"Why do you say that?" he asked, immediately suspicious. "Is he something special to you, this Mr. Parmelee?"

"What on earth gives you that idea?"

"Your tone! As if you'd like nothing better than to see him chew up everyone in this room!"

"Not at all," she retorted in a lighter voice. "Reese is strictly business to me."

"I wonder." Duey continued to stare at her, now with a mocking look. "I think I've even ruffled you a bit. I declare I have! The unrufflable Miss Street! You who sit so quietly, like a cat, taking us all in. Tell me, Rosy, are you planning a novel about the little group?"

"No. And I'll bet I'm the only one here who isn't!"

With Duey so curious she dared not look at Reese again for several minutes. When she did, she saw that he had finished with Anstiss and had crossed over to the bar table where he was standing by himself, his eyes taking in the room carefully as he occasionally sipped his drink. Rosina thought how uncomfortable it always made her to be left alone at a party. Obviously it did not bother him in the least. She went over to him.

"I think you've done your duty now. And very nicely, too. Shall we go to dinner?"

He took her to a small, cheap Greek restaurant where he seemed to know all the waiters. In accord with what she had now decided was his predominant characteristic, he made no apologies for the place, told her what to order and asked their waiter to bring him what was evidently a favorite wine. After this there was a slightly awkward pause. Fortunately, however, Anstiss's party gave them something to talk about. What, she wanted to know, had he thought of Anstiss? Had he liked her?

"As a specimen, yes," he replied.

"As a specimen? I would have thought she was unique. How many women can you point to who've given away a million dollars?"

"Probably none. But I can point to dozens who like to torture their husbands."

"You think Anstiss does? Why?"

"I only have to look at her husband. Think what fun it must have been, giving the fortune away, piece by piece! Holding up each tempting morsel before his slobbering jaws and saying: 'Now tell me: are you *quite* sure you didn't marry me for my money?' And then, when the poor guy says no, tossing it out the window!"

"But he approved!"

"He *had* to!"

She was beginning to be irritated again at his presumption. Who was he to assume that he knew all about the Stranahans after a single meeting? "I think you're taking a great deal for granted."

"What do you see in those people?" he asked in a more aggressive tone. "What can they offer a girl like *you?* They're frozen stiff in their little mental routines!"

"Anstiss happens to have a very beautiful house," she replied after a moment's reflection. "Don't you think it's beautiful?"

He shrugged. "I suppose."

"That doesn't mean anything to you?"

"Very little."

"Well, that's where we're different." Her tone was flat. If he was going to be one of those people who made a fetish of fundamentals, he could *have* his fundamentals. "If I had a house like that I wouldn't care who I had in it. Or whether I had anyone at all. I'd just stay home and love it in peace and quiet."

"I don't believe it."

"That's because you don't know me!"

He changed the subject by asking her about her job on the magazine. He showed a polite enough interest, but she found herself hesitating before each answer. He had an air about him that made her feel that it was important to tell the truth. The exact truth. Or else be silent. He wouldn't have minded silence, she was sure. They ate several small courses, and she even began to find that she did not object, every so often, to having a sip of the sweet, strong wine.

"But I'm sure you don't care about magazines like mine," she protested finally. "Aren't they the epitome of everything you dislike?"

"Now that you mention it, I guess they are."

"You're very sure of yourself," she retorted, nettled. "Is there all that difference between your world and mine?"

"How do you mean?"

"Well, why is working for a man like Amos Levine so much better than working for Mrs. Doremus?"

"A 'man like' Amos Levine? Do you imply he's some kind of shyster?"

"Well —" She hesitated before that stare. "You know the kind of thing people say about him."

"I don't know what he may be *supposed* to be," Reese retorted coldly. "I only care what he is. And for my money he isn't any shadier than half the partners in half the big Wall Street law firms. He calls a spade a spade, that's all."

It was a subject that was obviously important to him, and for the rest of their dinner they discussed ethics in the law. He seemed obsessed with his theory that the only distinction between the reputable lawyer and the ambulance chaser was one of outward appearance. Rosina was not particularly interested in the problem, but she was interested in him and in the quantity of anger that he seemed to have stored up. It appeared to be directed entirely against hypocrisy, which she had learned to regard as a harmless, even a rather necessary vice. But to him it was always a grinning mask, never a veil behind which the features might be safely relaxed. She was startled when she looked at her watch and saw the time.

"I must go," she said, jumping up. "It's a weekday night."

"Won't you come up to my flat for a nightcap? It's only a block away."

"No, thank you."

"You're a very decided young lady," he said, taking her arm as they walked out of the restaurant. "I have a feeling 'no thank you' means just what it says."

"You're right. It does."

"I won't be coy," he continued in a perfectly matter-of-fact tone, when they were seated in a cab. "I was hoping that if you came up, I might induce you to spend the night."

When she turned to him indignantly, however, she saw that there was nothing matter-of-fact in his look. It was a direct, almost a defiant stare. "You don't hold much with preliminaries, do you?" she asked, and it irked her that her voice sounded just a bit breathless.

"You're right. I don't."

"Well, I suppose there's no law against trying," she said, nonplussed, and turned away with a shrug to look out the window.

"Is it because I'm premature?" he continued aggressively. "Or because I'm unattractive to you?" When she said nothing to this, for she could think of nothing to say, he went on: "What about next week? Would you go out with me again?"

It was imperative for her to reassert some kind of control. "Look here, Reese," she said firmly, turning back to him, "let's get one thing straight. I'm not the kind of girl you can take out once to dinner and then spend the night with."

But his stare was unblinking. "How many times do I have to take you out?"

"If you're going to insult me," she cried angrily, "you can stop the cab right now!"

"I'm not insulting you!" he retorted. "You're insulting yourself! *I* never suggested there was any connection between my buying you dinner and your spending the night. I made a perfectly natural suggestion. Why not? You're grown up. You've been married. You know what it's all about."

"How do you know I've been married?"

"Mrs. Stranahan told me."

Rosina felt a tremor in the dais of her dignity. "Trust *her*," she murmured. But she had to admit to herself that Anstiss had extracted the same information about his own marital status and whispered it to her in the bedroom while she was putting on her coat. "I suppose any divorcée is considered fair game," she continued bitterly. "In any case, let me assure you that you're wasting your time. I don't believe in love outside of marriage."

"Is that what marriage taught you?"

"No, I learned it before," she replied, breathless again at the rudeness of his persistence. "I know what I can handle and what I can't, that's all!"

"Then it's not for moral reasons?"

"My reasons can hardly matter to you. My conclusion is all that counts."

"What a funny girl you are!" he exclaimed, suddenly laughing. "I like you. Will you go out with me again?"

They stopped before her house, and she leaned forward to open the door. "Keep the cab. I have my key."

"What about it? *Will* you?"

She hesitated. "Call me tomorrow. I don't know what I think tonight any more. Except one thing. You'll have to promise me one thing." She got out and closed the door

firmly, turning back to look in at him. "No more propositions!"

"Done." He moved quickly forward to the open window.
"But you'll have to promise *me* something."

"What?"

"No more proposals!"

She stood for a moment, shocked, her mouth open in a
conflict of surprise and indignation. Then she suddenly burst
out laughing. "Done!" she exclaimed, and the cab drove off
as he waved after her. Upstairs in her room she found that
she was in a state of tense excitement and had to take a
sleeping pill. It would never do to lie awake through the
night and consider how much she would have rather been
with Reese in his flat.

2

WHEN Reese and Esther had been finally divorced, he bought a secondhand car and motored to California. He went out by the northern route and returned by the southern, talking only to hitchhikers and strangers in bars. Yet the long hours of solitary driving and the great flat spaces acted like a massage to his disposition, smoothing out the kinks of his resentment and making him feel a less discordant part of the universe. When he returned to New York he rented a room in Greenwich Village and started to look for a job. He had no wish to go back to Wall Street where he knew that his sudden demission from Clark, Day & Parmelee, with hardly a week's notice, would have given him a bad name to live down. He refused his family's offers of assistance or advice; he had made over what he had to Esther, and that would have to forestall their further criticism for the present. His father proposed to give him a small allowance and, when this was declined, to pay his club dues, but Reese answered that he had resigned from his clubs, and Alfred Parmelee then gave him up. Obviously, the boy had gone off the deep end, and the family's hopes were transferred to the curly head of sober little Alfred who could now be sent to St. Lawrence's without further opposition.

As it turned out, Reese did not have to look long for a job. He applied to Amos Levine because of a will contest, much publicized at the time, between a rich manufacturer's mistress and his widow and children. Levine represented the mistress who had been left half the estate in a will drawn shortly before the manufacturer's death. What had fascinated Reese who, with time on his hands, had attended the trial, was the bland way in which the family and friends affirmed the testator's insanity. It seemed quite clear to Reese that the man had been sane, but none of the plaintiffs' witnesses appeared even to consider the consequences, legal or moral, of perjury in the light of what they evidently considered a holy battle. The issue was clear: it was the home against vice. Levine was slow, courteous and soft-spoken; he never antagonized the judge or jury by molesting or disparaging the widow or her family. His sad, tired eyes seemed to be haunted with the larger tragedy of domestic discord, with the innate frailty of man of which this lawsuit was only a minor manifestation. He was remarkably undramatic for so famous a court lawyer, and his questions were simply phrased and sometimes haltingly articulated. How the trial would have ended Reese was never to learn, for like so many of Levine's cases it was settled out of court, but the newspapers carried the rumor that the cause of vice had received a substantial portion of its bequest. The next day Reese found himself facing those same tired eyes across Amos Levine's desk in Rockefeller Center.

"The Parmelee of Clark, Day & Parmelee," Levine was asking. "Was he a relative?"

"My grandfather."

"I see." Several slow nods followed this. "May I ask why you left them?"

"I wanted a different kind of practice. A court practice. The kind you have."

Again the slow nods seemed to indicate that the applicant's

desire was the most natural thing in the world. The eyes were now moving down the form which Reese had filled out. "I see you have very little experience in my line."

"I can learn."

"I think you can, Mr. Parmelee," the soft voice agreed. "And if you will accept an opening salary in proportion to your inexperience, you may start with me on Monday."

He offered Reese exactly half what he had been earning at Clark, Day & Parmelee. It was outrageous, but Reese took it, and before a month was out, he knew he had done the right thing. The office staff consisted of an accountant, four stenographers and a bookkeeper. There were only two other lawyers, a Mr. Isaacs and a Mr. John, both middle-aged hacks who had been with Levine for more than a decade. They looked up the law, wrote briefs, drew legal instruments and had obviously gone as far as they were going. What Reese had wanted he was soon able to achieve; he became Levine's trial assistant. He went to court with him; he prepared cases with him; in time, he argued the motions that Levine did not care to argue and tried the smaller suits. It was a perfect education in court work, and Reese never begrudged Levine the night work that he had so begrudged his former employers. For he felt that he was a real lawyer at last, and he was almost ashamed of how much he enjoyed it.

The world in which he spent his working day was hardly one that his mother would have considered, to use her term of ultimate moral sanction, "attractive." It was a world of child custody fights, of bitterly fought divorces, of plagiarisms and libels, of contracts wriggled out of or too tightly enforced. Often the client was personally objectionable, frequently his position morally dubious, but there was always something to be said for his case — the issues were never entirely black and white. And Reese could partly assuage his sometimes uneasy conscience by reminding himself that the opposing side invariably had both money and good counsel. It would have been going too far to have pictured Amos Levine as a latter-day Robin Hood, robbing the unworthy rich for the deserving poor, but it would have been quite fair to have labeled most of the fights in which he participated as cases of dog eat dog. To Reese who loved a fight it was a more satisfying existence than any he had known. He was living at last in the very heart of New York's fetid jungle of competition.

Amos Levine, however, viewed his own world through different eyes. He had become intimate with Reese in the course of their first year together and was evidently satisfied with his work, though he never praised or dispraised it. But he loved to wax philosophical with his assistant at lunch after a morning in court.

"My specialty isn't really law," he would tell Reese as he lit his cigar. "It's people. I think I have some inkling of what makes them tick. It's my only stock in trade, really. Working out a human problem. And that's the big satisfaction, too. Don't forget it, boy. Not the power or the glory. Or the money which all goes in taxes, anyway. But the sense of having solved a human riddle and helped a human being. I like to think of myself as a bit of an artist, Reese. That's why I buy paintings. I want to see how other artists do it. Because basically we're in the same racket."

Reese would merely grunt to such effusions. It gave him a dry amusement to find that his new world was no freer of hypocrisy than his old. Levine might profess an indifference to money, but he would never grant the smallest raise in salary, however deductible on his own tax return, unless faced with a sincerely intended threat of resignation. In fact, his feeling for money was probably one of the prime reasons for his success in the law. He had an uncanny sense of what cases, whether won, lost or settled, would mean good fees, and he never touched one where there was a serious risk of missing his compensation. He kept his office completely cleared of the small, non-paying matters that clogged most lawyers' desks: income tax returns, servants' accidents, traffic violations. He would do no little favors to hold that vague intangible: a client's good will. And yet it seemed to work. Reese knew from the girl who typed Levine's tax return the astonishing size of his income. Surely, so large a figure was not earned by mere competence in the law. Besides, Amos was not all that competent. He was lazy and frequently ill-prepared; he never checked the papers drawn by Isaacs or John; his judgment out of court was erratic, and Reese had discovered amazing holes in his knowledge of elementary legal principles. His two great assets were his nose for a fee and the lazy, easygoing charm of his court manner which continued to disarm juries who had come into the courtroom expecting just the reverse.

Outside the office Reese's life was uneventful. He lived more cut off from his old world than if he had moved to another city; there were no bridges between Greenwich Village and Parmelee Cove. He read a good deal of evenings when he was not working and sometimes went to off-Broadway theatres or sat in bars. He met girls in the latter or at an occasional cocktail party given by a client; he had several short affairs, easily terminated. Cynthia Fearing, now divorced from Andy, had wanted to take up with him again, but he had made too clean a break with his old life to admit of the retention of even this slender strand. She had moved to Park Avenue and a life of parties; he read with amusement in the social columns of the evening papers of Mrs. Coit Fearing and her dinners for the international set. He imagined how exasperating she must have found the success of her ex-husband who, according to the same columns, was a favorite in the same circles. For Andy was delighted with his restored bachelorhood and the renewal of his popularity, free of the domination of the Coits. All the former sunniness of his disposition had returned, and he had proposed to an unobjecting Reese a renewal of their old friendship. Now they dined together, perfectly pleasantly, once a month. Cynthia, no longer tied to either, had in the end become a bond.

"You know something, Reese?" Andy said one night. "I think you're happy. I think you're happy for the first time in your life."

Well, there was some truth in it. Reese had certainly lost his nagging, daily sense of the disapproval of the world. He was less jumpy, less sullen, less quick to take offense. He felt a new peace, alone at night in his bare apartment. But there were prices to be paid which still hurt. There was first of all the question of his children, whose custody he had had to surrender to Esther. She allowed him to see them on weekends, but when he took them for a walk around Parmelee Cove on a Sunday afternoon, he always had the feeling that he was interfering with other plans which they had made. Young Alfred and Eunice were nice to him, but it was their very niceness that hurt. They had to explain all their references now, and he knew that this bored children. Basically, he had ceased to play any real part in their lives.

The balance of the price was his concern about one aspect of Levine's practice. However little he worried about the rough-and-tumble of his employer's litigating habits, he could not regard with equal complacency his rather unctuous solicitude towards certain rich female clients. Especially objectionable was his attitude towards old Miss Emma Howland, a resident of the Stuyvesant Hotel. Reese had overheard several of their telephone conversations while working in Amos's office, and he had disliked the note of flattery in the latter's tone. But he had disliked even more being asked by Amos to go to the Stuyvesant to confer with her on the preparation of a new will.

"I think it's better if you go instead of me, Reese," Amos had explained a bit self-consciously. "In case the old girl decides to make me an executor or trustee or something like that."

"What difference does sending *me* make?" Reese had demanded. "I'm only your clerk, aren't I? If you think she needs an independent lawyer, let's get her an independent lawyer!"

"No, no, that would only be necessary if she was going to leave me a lot of money. It's perfectly all right for a lawyer to draw a will making himself an executor. At the client's request, of course."

"Then why send me?" Reese insisted. "Why not go yourself?"

"Because it *looks* better," Amos retorted impatiently. "From every point of view. Now go ahead and do what you're told!"

By Reese's third visit to the Stuyvesant, he had become very fond of Miss Howland. She was about his grandmother's age, and as she had told him on their first meeting, a distant cousin of the Parmelees. She had met Amos Levine when he had represented the tenants of the Stuyvesant, a great dark brownstone late Victorian hotel, in a successful suit to enjoin the landlord from evicting them and converting their apartments into smaller units. Miss Howland, like many of her co-plaintiffs, would not have known where to go had she had to leave the Stuyvesant. It was the living tomb of some two hundred old people, mostly spinsters and widows.

With her companion and constantly changing nurses she occupied three high-ceilinged rooms filled with her own black
mahogany furniture and large faded photographs in plain
brown frames of Greek and Roman ruins. Here and there a
Howland ancestor in oil surveyed his changed surroundings
with a look of placid early New England contempt. In a
corner of the farthest room stood a fully equipped dentist's
chair. For Miss Howland never went out. The last time she
had penetrated the great out-of-doors had been to visit her
sister, similarly incarcerated in the Plaza, ten years before.
The sister survived, and they talked daily and at length on
the telephone, but they had not seen each other since that
final outing.

It had been Miss Howland's idea to hire Amos Levine to
represent the tenants. Like Reese, she had read about him in
the newspaper, and she had decided that he was just the kind
of "hard, two-fisted, fighting lawyer" that they needed. The
lawsuit had been the most exciting event in her long but uneventful life, and she had been ecstatic over the victory for
which she regarded herself as at least half responsible. Afterwards, she had happily confided all her affairs to "dear Mr.
Levine's" hands, and he called on her at regular intervals during the year. On each anniversary of the famous victory they
opened a bottle of champagne.

On the afternoon that Reese brought her the new draft of
her will, he had to listen again to her account of the famous
struggle against the landlord. Like George IV and the battlefield of Waterloo she had almost persuaded herself that she
had been in the courtroom itself.

"You can imagine that I've had the best of service ever
since," she concluded with a firm shake of her head. "Oh, my
yes. Not that I like to threaten people or anything like that.
But in a building like this one, Mr. Parmelee, it pays to keep

an eye on the landlord. So if my newspaper is late two days
running, or if my coffee is watery, or if I begin to find things
swept under the rug — those little signs that the hotel is beginning to take you for granted — I get the manager on the
telephone, and I tell him — oh, right straight out, yes, I do —
'Now, Mr. Prime, you don't want me to have to get Mr.
Levine in here again, do you?' That *fixes* him, I can tell you!"

There was no point telling Miss Howland that the hotel
had changed owners twice over since the famous suit and that
the present owner was a friend of Levine's. The landlord
for her would always be the would-be-evictor. Reese
thought she even looked a bit like a judge, sitting up straight
in her high armchair, her wide figure covered in black silk,
with her crown of snowy white hair, her round, red, cheerful
face aglow and her small eyes snapping. But Miss Howland's
judicial pose, the "old tartar," was only a pose, like all her
others. Fundamentally, she abounded in sentiment. The principal role that she loved to play was the intrepid, impulsive,
out-of-doors girl, a Jo March, the child who had been
a sporting father's favorite, but whom a beautiful, wistful
mother had sometimes found a bit too much of a tomboy,
the hater of lace and frills, the scoffer at doctors, at illness
of any kind, impatient of the least inquiry as to a bodily ail-
ment. It took a little while for Reese to grasp this pose, faced
as he was with the inconsistency of her nurses, her dentist's
chair, the contrast of her long confinement and evident good
health, and her many references to her "poor old arm" or
her "poor old knee" as if they were faithful but worn-out
servitors who had to be forgiven for their inability to keep
up with the unflagging spirits of their mistress. Yet this
very inconsistency, he soon learned, was a characteristic of
the valetudinarian, as was the contrast between the attitude
of casual superiority that she displayed towards her business

affairs and the detailed notes on them which she kept. To hear her talk of her will, for example, one might have thought it the hen-scrawl of a soldier, thinking at the last moment of his loved ones on the eve of a bombardment, and never of a highly technical thirty-page document with dozens of constantly changed legacies of small, worthless objets d'art.

"I would suggest it's not necessary to bequeath *every* item to a particular person," Reese suggested cautiously as he looked with discouragement over her new list which was even longer than the preceding one. "You might leave something to the discretion of your executors."

"Ah, yes. But who *are* my executors?"

He looked up in some surprise, for she was usually very clear about such things. "Why, the People's National and your nephew, Sam."

"Oh, that reminds me. Last time he was here, I think I told dear Mr. Levine that I wanted *him* to be an executor, too. Would you add him, please, Mr. Parmelee?"

Reese hesitated. It really was a bit thick. Levine would be counsel for the estate in any case and get his minimum four per cent while the bank and the nephew did all the work. A third executor was totally unnecessary.

"You've got two already," he pointed out, "and one of them is a bank. Don't forget that each executor gets two per cent of your estate. Putting Mr. Levine in would simply amount to giving him a present."

"But I should *like* to give Mr. Levine a present!" Miss Howland exclaimed, clasping her round, plump little hands. "Mr. Levine has been so lovely to me! Can't I be lovely to him? Why not?"

"Well, then I suggest you leave him a small legacy."

"Very good. Let's leave him a legacy. What would you suggest?"

Reese glanced appraisingly about the room. "How about one of those photographs?" he suggested, pointing to the Roman Forum. "I heard him say the other day that he loved your pictures of Greece and Rome."

"Well, of course, I was going to leave the whole set to my cousin, Caroline," the old lady said dubiously. "But if you think Mr. Levine really wants it —" She hesitated. "Oh, well, Caroline will never miss one. Yes, let's leave the Forum to Mr. Levine." But Reese was discouraged to hear her continue: "That's just a token, of course. I want to give him a real present, too."

"I'm afraid that's a rather delicate matter," he said, looking up at her firmly. "I don't mind putting in a legacy of a picture. Or even a small cash bequest. But if it gets to be anything much bigger, I think you ought to have someone else write the will. It looks very bad when a lawyer puts in a bequest to himself."

Miss Howland seemed faintly embarrassed. "But it's not a bequest to *you*, Mr. Parmelee. Much as I like you and much as I appreciate your giving me the time you have. It's a bequest to Mr. Levine."

Reese could not help smiling. "But, you see, in the eyes of the bar," he explained, "as I work for Mr. Levine, it's the same thing as if he were drafting the will himself."

"How very odd. And you mean I have to go to another lawyer and do a whole new will?"

"Oh, no. You'd only have to go to him for a codicil. Just one page containing the new bequest."

"But that seems such a bother," Miss Howland said with a sigh.

"It *is* a bother."

By the time Reese left, he was hoping that she had forgotten the codicil. Levine would get his picture and his counsel

fees, and that was that. The next day, when the will had
been typed, he took a copy into Levine's office and laid it on
his desk.

"What's this?"

"Miss Howland's will. Do you want to check it?"

Levine gave it back to him with a shrug and a small enigmatic smile. "I trust you, Reese. Don't you know that yet?
If you say the will's okay, then it's okay."

Reese looked at him hard for a moment. "I say it's
okay."

"Then, fine!"

But for a period after this episode Reese was uncomfortable
in his mind, not only about Amos's relations with Miss Howland, but about his own relations with Amos. Even con-
ceding that the cultivation of an old and wealthy recluse was
objectionable on its face, had he not still been rather shabbily
disloyal to his employer to have adopted such a ruse to
thwart him? The whole thing left a bad taste in his mouth
and cut down materially on the pleasure that he had come
to count on in his work. It was fortunate that at just this
time, when he was most in need of distraction, Rosina should
have walked into his office with the troubles of *A Woman's
World*. There was an intensity about her that he found immediately appealing. He doubted very much if he would care
for any of the things that she cared about, but he liked her
for caring so much. Esther, of course, cared; she was even
ruthless in the tenacity of her caring, but then Esther always
dramatized herself, which was just what he felt this girl did
not do. Esther saw herself as a brooding, eternal mother
figure. Like a woodcut illustration in a novel of the soil she
seemed to be always on her knees in the good earth, her arms
outstretched to a lowering sky. He had often suspected that
the role of Ceres was a substitute for that of Venus, that

Esther compensated for her concealed distaste for the fundamentals of procreation by her emphasis on the fundamentals of motherhood, as if she meant to wall out of sight the offending male with the bricks and mortar of her domesticity. Rosina was not like this. Rosina wanted less fundamental things, but she wanted them desperately, and she knew very clearly and precisely what they were: to get ahead on her magazine and to be respectable and respected. In the assiduous pursuit of these small specific goals, sex was not a missing factor for which compensation was being sought; sex, on the contrary, was a dangerous, vibrant force which might any moment topple over the small, gay pagoda of her preconceived scheme of life. All her defenses, indeed, were primed to keep just this force at bay. Very well. He would accept her challenge and the rules of her game. They would see who would be the first to crack.

Soon they were dining together once a week. They argued about almost everything, sometimes bitterly, but both enjoyed it. One of their most sharply contested issues was whether or not he should accompany her to Anstiss Stranahan's evening gatherings, and this was finally resolved in a compromise. She would go to one of his off-Broadway plays for every party at Anstiss's he attended. Reese tried to stave off boredom at the Stranahans' by analyzing the little group. He found it significant that it should revolve around its youngest male member. For Duey Lispenard struck him as perfectly humorless and perfectly self-centered, serenely satisfied with a small imagination and a second class mind. This self-assured young man had decided to be a playwright for the sole reason that success might be attained more quickly in that field than in any other. His sour little boyish face was the reflection of a vanity so grotesque that Anstiss and her friends found it charmingly novel. How delightful that Duey should *really* want a Cadillac or that he should *really* pine to see his name in headlines! How refreshing to find someone who really believed in mink coats and diamond tiaras! His play, parts of which had been read aloud to the little group, was a moody version of a mood drama by Williams or Inge; it was unlikely but not impossible that he would get it produced. Anstiss, after all, might finance it.

"But what do they see in him?" Reese would ask Rosina. "He's like a smug, bad-tempered little cat. One that would scratch its mistress, too."

"Some people like cats."

Which it seemed they did. Anstiss was obviously intent on being Duey's guide and mentor; she must have foreseen a long line of dedications to herself. She was heard frequently now to refer to him as the one "truly creative" member of the group. This offended, as it was meant to offend, her principal rival for Duey's affections, the big, cheerful, temperish, rather screaming Cliffie Suter, a children's portrait painter who was the only self-supporting artist ever to be ensnared by the Stranahans. On several occasions he and Anstiss came perilously close to open battle. Yet it was to Reese himself, the one member of the group who despised him, that Duey most docilely turned. The would-be playwright simply could not believe that anyone existed whom it was out of his power to charm. He would sit by Reese at the readings and whisper to him all his choicest comments. Sometimes he would leave Anstiss's with Reese and Rosina; he would dog their steps until they had to stop in a bar or café to get rid of him. And there he would at last succeed in making Reese laugh by holding up the members of Anstiss's little group, one by one, to a ridicule that was more amusing for its exaggeration than its wit.

"You shouldn't encourage him so," Rosina warned Reese

one night after they had left Duey. "He's a born trouble-
maker. He'll go and repeat it all to Anstiss and say he got
it from you."

"Let him."

"But Anstiss will be livid!"

"So what?" Reese shrugged. "She won't throw *you* out.
She'll limit her revenge to my poor head."

"But I like taking you there. Don't you like going there?"
Her face suddenly drooped. "Oh, of course, you don't. You
hate it, don't you?"

But he didn't hate it, that was the point. He would have,
of course, except for her. But now the dreariest evening at
Anstiss's was filled with the happier prospect of discussing it
afterwards with Rosina, of watching her grey eyes flicker
with anger across the table in a coffee house, of hearing himself called a puritan red. And then, of course, they did not
always go to Anstiss's. Sometimes they went to the large
old-fashioned apartment that Grace Chess occupied with her
mother. Grace was a determined romantic and matchmaker;
she tried hard, but unsuccessfully to elicit some confession
of feeling from either of them. Sometimes they went for late
evening parties at Cliffie Suter's studio, amid the uncompleted
portraits of expensive children with poodles, and heard dissident members of the little group being catty about the Stranahans. And once Rosina even took him to a cocktail party
given by Gilda Doremus in a great room high over the East
River with love seats and papier-mâché tables and huge
looped curtains of red and gold. Mrs. Doremus explained to
Reese in that unyielding monotone that she used alike to
prince and pauper the role of her magazine in the redecoration
of embassies and the role of embassies in the preservation of
peace.

"Help!" he whispered to Rosina when he finally escaped

to her corner. "I've got to get out of here before that woman catches me again!"

"But we just came!"

"I don't care. It's not safe."

"It's *quite* safe," she said cuttingly. "Gilda only spoke to you once because I brought you. You're far too obscure to be spoken to twice."

"But I don't even like to be in the same room with her!"

"Really, Reese! You don't like Anstiss. You don't like Gilda. I'm beginning to wonder if you'll ever like any of my friends!"

"Anstiss is pathetic. This woman is dangerous. There's a difference. I'll meet you at the Greek's."

"You'll do no such thing! If you leave now, I'll never speak to you again!" She was suddenly excited and forgot, as she always did when in a temper, to lower her voice. He loved this forgetfulness in her, for Esther had never forgotten, and he even smiled broadly as she went indignantly on: "Who are you, anyway, to look down on Gilda Doremus? She runs a magazine that gives pleasure to thousands of women! Thousands! But of course you care nothing for that kind of thing, do you? It's too superficial, isn't it? All you care about are your old fundamentals of sex and greed! Like the way you interpreted that story you told me about your boss and the old lady. Of course, you took it for granted that he was after her money!" Mrs. Doremus, surveying her party like a general on horseback, had stepped back a few paces and was almost within earshot. He tried to warn Rosina, but it was too late. "Of course!" she continued heatedly. "That's the way you see everything! He couldn't be interested in the old lady for herself, could he? She's too old. Therefore, it must be her money. If it's not rape, it's larceny! What else?"

Mrs. Doremus turned around. "Dear me, is somebody going to be raped?" she asked mildly. "Come, Rosina, I want you to help me with Mr. Pforzheimer. You can't just stand here talking to the man you brought. Cocktail parties are work, darling!"

Reese almost burst out laughing at Rosina's expression of dismay as Mrs. Doremus hurried her off. But he had no idea of leaving the party, even though, as it turned out, he had to wait a full hour before her return.

3

Rosina had to admit that Reese was good to his word. When he took her home after they had been out, he would wait until she had fitted her key in the lock of the downstairs door and then say good night with that funny little jerky bow from the waist which was a habit of his, a courtly hangover, perhaps, from early days at dancing school. For she was beginning to learn from occasional references, little though he discussed his childhood, that it had been full of just such things. She had even discovered, on better acquaintance, that his rough and blunt way was actually the cover of the most sensitive kind of good manners. He could perceive immediately, for example, if a movie bored her or if a topic of conversation pained her. Indeed, she thought he was carrying things too far one night when he declined to come up to her apartment for a drink on the grounds that it was "inadvisable." She began to feel uneasily that she was slipping under the dominance of a stronger personality. Why else should she wake up in the early morning angrily remembering the perfect rebuttal to one of his arguments that she had not been able to think of the night before?

It was impossible not to be honest with him. He was too keenly aware of any kind of sham. This was irritating to her, as so much of life was made up of small pretenses, but it was less irritating to her than his adamant refusal ever to be in the least impressed with anyone else's success in the world. She could never catch him in an open statement of admiration; his moral sense seemed to find expression only in his likes and dislikes. As a philosophy it was certainly a grudging one, but there was a certain bleak logic in it. And it was catching, too. At least she liked to think it was catching and not that she was falling in love with him. She would find herself using his arguments to other people, even arguments with which she had passionately disagreed to his face. She carried this so far one day as to hurt Grace Chess's feelings in talking about Anstiss's little group.

"You never talked that way before you met Reese," Grace reproached her. "It's always easy to laugh at people who are trying to cultivate their minds. But the thing I object to is that the scoffers are usually intellectuals themselves. Like Molière and the *Femmes Savantes*. Or Mary McCarthy and *The Groves of Academe*. Those of us who care about art and literature are few enough. We ought to stand together and not tear each other apart to make a Philistine holiday!"

Rosina dropped the argument promptly. She did not like Grace's immediate assumption that her point of view was adapted from Reese's. What good did tact and discretion avail a girl? If she was seen out twice running with the same man, it was generally assumed that she was infatuated. And wasn't she? Hadn't she been absurdly disappointed when he had refused to come up to her room for that drink? And what had she hoped he would do when he was there but break his promise? Sometimes in the middle of the afternoon at her desk she would find that she had been sitting motionless, without working, for as much as ten minutes at a time, her mind a riot of the most graphically indecent fantasies. She would shake her head and go to the water cooler, but when she returned to work she would feel as if she had been almost physically weakened by the violence of her imagination.

If Reese was critical about the Stranahans' little group, the little group was no less critical of him. It was not only that he made no secret of his boredom during the readings aloud, getting up and noisily cracking ice for his drink; it was not merely that he openly objected to the word games that Anstiss loved to play, but worse, far worse, he had, albeit innocently, made greater strides in the affection of Duey Lispenard than either Cliffie Suter or Anstiss herself. These two, usually so critical of each other, became almost allies in their recognition of a common enemy. When Cliffie first broached the subject of Reese to Rosina, one night at the Stranahans' when Reese was not there, she suspected that it might have been prearranged with Anstiss.

"Sweetie, do you mind if I'm frank with you?" he began in his loud, deliberate, gravelly tone. Cliffie always smiled, but his smile, his heavy jowls, his big forehead and messy, thick, greasy black hair trembled with incipient anger. Like many large men of his type, he combined to a surprising degree the qualities of a flabby softness and a dangerous eruptability.

"That always means you're going to be, anyway."

"How right you are. Then tell me: are you planning to marry the boy?"

"Do you mean Reese?"

"Now come, little sister, don't be coy with me."

"I have no reason to believe that Mr. Parmelee has any such plans," she said coolly.

"Who cares about *his* plans? I asked about yours."

"You may not know this, but he was only divorced a year ago." She fixed her eyes on Cliffie's and spoke very distinctly. "I have every reason to believe that he was badly burned. I should doubt if he goes near that fire again for a bit."

"Pooh," he retorted, "the American male always remarries. No matter how much he rants and raves. There must be something hymeneal about the air on this side of the Atlantic."

"You seem to have resisted it."

"If you're going to be catty, I shall have to slap your little wrist."

"What about the American female?" she asked, pulling away her hand. "Is she a marrier, too?"

"Worse!" He threw his arms up. "This country must be her paradise. She can marry to her heart's content!"

"Then why ask my plans?" she said with a shrug. "Obviously, Mr. Parmelee and I must be destined for the altar."

"Well, I don't altogether deny some *small* residuum of free will," he conceded. "It's just possible that you could turn him down."

"Why should I want to?"

"Why indeed? A husband's a husband, isn't he? But, my dear, I'll tell you." Cliffie's broad, heavy face became almost serious now. "You couldn't bear another divorce. You couldn't bear to fail twice. You see, I've studied you!" He smiled, triumphant, as he saw the surprise in her eye. "You'd put up with anything to save this marriage. And you'd succeed, too. Mr. Parmelee would be for keeps. That is why Mr. Parmelee's qualifications must be so carefully assessed."

"I have a feeling they already have been," she retorted. "What are your conclusions, Cliffie? Maybe you can save me the trouble."

He cleared his throat in noisy introduction to what was evidently a prepared lecture. "There are two worlds in this city, Rosy, and the first is ninety-nine per cent of the whole.

I call it the world of maintenance. It's made up of the people who keep the wheels turning: doctors, lawyers, mothers, streetcleaners, politicians, prostitutes and so forth. These people are always dealing with things they call facts. The other world, the one per cent, I call the world of fantasy. It's made up of artists and editors and interior decorators and poets. People whose job is to make beautiful, useless things. People who live to have fun. It is usually fatal for a woman from the world of fantasy to marry at all. But it is absolutely fatal for her to marry a man from the world of maintenance."

"Why?"

"At worst she will be bored to death. At best she will come to regard her husband as a kind of useful handyman whose function is to rearrange the furniture in the living room. In either case, if he is any part a man, he will end up resenting her."

"And why do you assume *I* belong to this world of fantasy? How do you know I'm not up to my neck in maintenance?"

"Because I can always tell a fantasist," he said solemnly. "And what is more, I can always tell a fantasist who is going to succeed. Make no mistake, my dear. You're going further than old Gilda Doremus ever dreamed of!"

The sudden, unexpected compliment almost unnerved her. She knew that Cliffie was discriminating and that he hated to praise; a compliment from him was a kind of diploma in itself. But at the same time she felt something like panic that he should be thus trying to take Reese from her, and her protest had a note of shrillness. "But Reese doesn't bore me in the least, Cliffie!" she exclaimed. "That's where you're wrong!"

"Give him time. At the moment you're dazzled by his masculinity. But even that can become a bore. Believe me, dearie, I *know*. Wait till he starts drinking too much and is rude to your friends."

"You think he's a Philistine," she retorted angrily. "But he's not! He hates sham and pose, that's all. But if something's real enough —"

"I know all about that attitude," he interrupted brusquely. "You'll be telling me he likes Walt Whitman next. But don't you see that hating sham and pose is the very essence of Philistinism? What he really hates is beauty! Because what is beauty made of but sham and pose! And strut and swagger! And blood and sweat and genius! That's why the world of maintenance is pledged to destroy it!" Cliffie was becoming strident in defense of his fancied minority. "Don't try to sell me these down-to-earthers, Rosy! What would they leave us but mud?"

Well, he was silly, and he exaggerated, of course, but his point of view stuck in her mind. It was quite true that Reese was apt to check her in flights of the imagination that he considered too high above ground. He had little interest in the splendid or the dramatic. Yet there were things that nonetheless made a deep imprint on his imagination, things for which he used the word "terrific." He could stand for minutes on end, totally rapt, before a derrick in an excavation, or a man welding, or pigeons in the park or a Picasso. And she never ceased to be amazed by his geographical knowledge of the city in which they lived. He loved to go on Sundays to remote areas, to Staten Island and Hell Gate Bridge and the upper limits of the Bronx. He knew, it seemed, every animal in the three zoos and had a photographer's eye for the best views of the harbor and East River. Yet he could dismiss all French art before Cézanne as "gook," all religion as a fear of spooks and the poetry of T. S. Eliot as "pompous twittering." And even this paled before his real crime, which was that he took out other girls and made no secret of it. If Rosina would not satisfy certain needs, his careless attitude seemed to imply, did such needs not still have to be taken care of? She would have given much if he had at least pretended that he could wait until she had gone back on her word.

When Anstiss Stranahan followed Cliffie in taking up her cudgels against Reese, Rosina decided that there was less of a conspiracy between the two than she had imagined. For the leader of the little group took just the opposite tack from that of the portrait painter; she warned Rosina that the danger of Reese was not that he would marry her, but precisely that he wouldn't.

"Of course, it's your own affair," she told Rosina, one evening when the latter had arrived ahead of the others, "but I hate to see a good friend wasting her time. That man is out for one thing and one thing only. Oh, you can rely on me, dearie, I know the type. He has that hungry look. If ever I saw a man who's allergic to the altar, it's that one. You're a very attractive girl, Rosy, and a real catch, but Helen of Troy couldn't get the price of a marriage certificate out of him."

"I think he knows where I stand on that."

"Don't be too sure." Anstiss snorted down at her from the rocky peak of her superior knowledge of men. "He's the kind who thinks we all give in in the end. Just the way I'm sure he thinks people only read poetry if they're frustrated. Do you remember what he said about why Joan of Arc joined the French army? Why, it was perfectly disgusting! I'm sorry, dear, if I'm saying too much. But you can't expect a real friend to stand by and do nothing while you're taken in by a half-baked Freudian!"

Anstiss always went further than she intended. She generated her own anger as she talked, and if she was not interrupted it was bound to carry her on to untenable positions.

She could work herself into a terrible tantrum without the least apparent provocation. But once taken, her positions could never be abandoned, and her conversation was like a thinly spread army trying desperately to man a long chain of remote and useless fortifications.

"I think that's going a bit far," Rosina remonstrated. "Whatever else Reese may be, you'll have to admit he's a gentleman."

"It depends what you mean by *that* antiquated term. If you mean that he's a graduate of St. Lawrence's, as he was boasting the other night —"

"Oh, Anstiss, he wasn't! If there's one thing you can't accuse Reese of, it's boasting about his background!"

"You might let me finish." Anstiss paused, eyeing her friend severely, until she had regained the conversational initiative. "It's not nearly as difficult to get into those schools as you may think. What do you conceive this 'background' of his to have been?"

"Well, aren't the Parmelees old New York or whatever you call it?"

Anstiss sniffed. If she had turned a broad and decisive back on her own antecedents, it had not been before a thorough analysis and evaluation of all that she had been leaving. She had become an expert on the social world, though she always claimed that her interest was sociological rather than snobbish. It was sometimes difficult, Rosina reflected, watching that flared nostril, for an underprivileged girl from Roanoke to appreciate the distinction.

"If you mean, is he a member of the Hoyt Parmelee family," Anstiss said disdainfully, "I should say, obviously not."

"Who are they?"

Anstiss was always happy to show how detailed her study of the enemy had been. "Old Mrs. Hoyt Parmelee was a

Hubbell. She's still alive, I believe, probably the last of that generation. Of course, the Hubbells were 'common as dirt,' as my mother used to say, but they had money, and that kept the Parmelees from slipping off the social map. The old man was a rather colorful figure in his day. But, you know, an ass. The son, Alfred, is supposed to be God's own bore. Not that I give a damn about people like that, but it's a question of using your terms accurately. If you know what those families are like, you know that your friend Reese simply isn't out of the same drawer."

"But I think Reese's father's name *is* Alfred."

Anstiss got out a copy of the Social Register which she always claimed made "amusing reading." It apparently amused her to see her own name in it, for she had maintained her listing. She turned now to the P's, glanced at the proper page and then handed the book to Rosina with a silent gesture of triumph. The latter read: "Parmelee, Mrs. Hoyt (Eunice Hubbell)" and "Parmelee, Mr. and Mrs. Alfred Hoyt (Agnes Forest)" and "Parmelee, Mrs. E. Means (Esther Means)." All of them lived in a place called "Parmelee Cove" in Northfield.

"Perhaps your friend Reese had his name removed," Anstiss said sarcastically, "in a burst of democratic fervor."

"Which is more than some other people I know have done!"

"I'll tell you something else about your darling Reese," Anstiss exclaimed, thoroughly angered now. "He doesn't believe in limiting himself to one girl. Duey saw him in a bar the other night with the most obvious kind of tart. He said they were practically — well, as close as one can in a booth!"

"Reese is not accountable to me for his actions."

"No? Well, I'm glad to hear it. I think it's perfectly disgusting, behaving that way in a public place."

Rosina had had enough. Her heart was aching, and she

was afraid that at any moment she might burst into tears. "I'm sorry you dislike him so," she said bitterly. "I'll certainly not make the mistake of imposing him on you again."

Anstiss's expression promptly changed. "Oh, Rosy, come now," she said placatingly. "Don't be that way about it. I never meant that I didn't want him at our little gatherings. Of course I do. He's quite entertaining, really. It's just that I don't see him as a husband for you."

Rosina nodded grimly. Anstiss would never be willing to let Reese go while he was still capable of taking anyone with him. She was always haunted by the possibility of a Pied Piper in her little group. But the brief satisfaction of making Anstiss back down hardly compensated for the painful picture of Reese at the bar, and Rosina cried that night when she had gone to bed, a rare thing for her to do. She was determined that somehow she would have it out with him, somehow she would manage to give him the hell which the peculiar terms of their friendship gave her no right to inflict.

The next time he telephoned, however, it was to give her an invitation that took her quite by surprise. It was on a Sunday, and he asked her to drive down to Long Island to lunch with his parents. She was so pleased and excited that she decided to postpone for the moment any discussion of his conduct in bars. It was a beautiful early spring day, and Reese seemed in unusually high spirits. He had rented a car and drove with the zest of a person long deprived of such activity. He even hummed, off key, a Mozart aria. She had never seen him in just this mood before.

"Do your parents really want me?" she asked. "What did you tell them?"

"That I was bringing a girl."

"Just that?"

"Oh, I said she was a nice girl."

She speculated during the rest of the drive as to what his parents would be like. She decided that they would be quiet, respectable professional people living in simple and dignified retirement. She pictured them as having a more distinguished past than a present, which could explain the discrepancy between Reese's expensive education and his current lack of means. She was certainly not prepared at the end of an hour, when he turned suddenly into a long macadam drive and they sped through clusters of white and pink dogwood with glimpses of old shingle turreted buildings, all of a similar style.

"Your parents live *here?*" she murmured.

"Well, they live on the place. It's Granny's, actually. But we're like a Chinese family. None ever moves."

"Except you?"

"Oh, I escaped. More or less. But I had to leave part of my tail in the door." They turned a corner, and Rosina caught her breath at the sight of the long, rambling façade of the big house. "That's Granny's house there. Isn't it a beaut?" He laughed. "What the well dressed girl *would* wear in the eighteen-nineties. Let's go to the garden first. I'll show you that before lunch."

He stopped the car by a long, closely clipped hedge, and they got out to walk through enormous clumps of azalea, white and pink and magenta. When they came to a round clear wading pool with a small Roman temple rising in the middle, she stopped with a gasp.

"You *are* an odd one," she said with an embarrassed laugh. "I had no idea your family was rich."

"It looks a hell of a lot more impressive than it is," he said with a shrug. "This place eats up capital a mile a minute. My sister, Joan, and I call it 'The Cherry Orchard.' "

"But there must have been a fortune once!" she exclaimed,

looking down the vista at old Mrs. Parmelee's house. "What did it come from? Oil?"

"No, railroads." He smiled. "Granny regards oil as rather 'nouveau.'" He reached down under a tile by the side of the pool and turned a crank that made two little fountains start up. "Her father was an old pirate called Abram Hubbell."

"Hubbell," she murmured. "So your grandmother *was* a Hubbell."

She thought of Anstiss and almost burst out laughing. It would have been a laugh of joy as well as triumph. For it was infinitely satisfying to be able at last to fill in Reese's background. Her mind was too orderly not to have found something faintly ominous in the preceding void. Just to watch now the simple gesture of his turning off the fountain was reassuring. He knew so exactly the location of the hidden handle that he grasped it as soon as he had reached under the tile. It was part of his profound knowledge of the place, a knowledge that obviously went back to his early childhood, and part also, despite the sarcasm of his descriptions, of his deep affection for it. Reese now had roots, so to speak, like the azaleas, and the discovery of this gave a singular buoyancy to her spirits. He seemed kinder and gentler, too, in his native habitat. She thought of *Pride and Prejudice* and how Elizabeth Bennett first realized her love for Darcy on seeing him at Pemberley. It was not the size of the park or the grandness of the house that impressed Elizabeth; it was the reassurance of seeing a man at home in a place he loved.

Her new sense of gentleness in Reese's disposition was intensified at lunch with his parents in the red brick house at the end of the garden. Mr. Parmelee, a small, busy man who mumbled into his soup, paid absolutely no attention to her, but she had a comforting feeling that this was the way he treated everybody. Reese talked to him at some length about improvements and repairs to the place, probably the only subject of conversation in which they shared an interest. Mrs. Parmelee, whose red tweeds and golf shoes sat oddly with her thin nervous appearance, troubled Rosina scarcely more. She could see by the way her hostess kept touching the tip of her long, bony nose with a handkerchief that she was even more apprehensive than her guest. Reese had evidently told her about *A Woman's World*, and she probably expected someone very smart and unsettling. She started by asking Rosina if she was related to the Street family in New York, but before she could answer, Reese, turning from his father, called down the table in his bantering tone:

"Rosina comes from a very old and distinguished Virginia family, Ma. They owned slaves while Mr. Hubbell was still a hired hand on that farm in Astoria. Now we all know each other, let's proceed to more interesting topics."

Mrs. Parmelee, however, did not seem to have many more interesting topics. She asked Rosina politely what she did on her magazine and sat unlistening while she was told. Obviously this was a different world, and different worlds did not exist for Mrs. Parmelee. Rosina thought it possible that she might have known Mrs. Doremus and asked her this, but any acquaintance with the senior editor was denied with some spirit. Then Mrs. Parmelee told Rosina about the problems of her golf game and how she wished that Reese would keep up his. After this conversation lapsed, and they both listened to Reese and his father discuss the question of repairing the garage roof. Yet Rosina had no feeling that Mrs. Parmelee was bored with her. She sensed, on the contrary, that Reese's mother was curious to find out more about her, but simply lacked the conversational means to go about it.

After lunch Reese said that he would walk over to see his

children. Rosina understood that she was not invited, as it would be awkward for her to meet his former wife. Afterwards he would call briefly on his grandmother who was too ill now to see any but the immediate family, and then they would return to town. Mr. Parmelee disappeared to his study, and his wife and Rosina were left alone on the terrace to look at the sound. Mrs. Parmelee was silent for a long time, and then without any introduction at all she started talking almost intimately about Reese.

"The thing that I can never get used to, Miss Street, is his not seeing more of his children. Of course, I know that Esther is entitled to have them, but it still seems to me the worst thing in the world for them to be so little with their father. And Reese is such a wonderful father, too. You might not think it because he sometimes has a brusque manner, but he has extraordinary warmth and understanding. Esther is an admirable girl — I have absolutely *no* criticism of her — but nothing can make up for a father. Nothing!"

Rosina was not quite sure how she was meant to react to this or even if she was meant to react at all. Mrs. Parmelee was looking fixedly at the water, and her little speech might have been in the nature of a monologue. She felt her way cautiously.

"I know he likes to talk about the children," she murmured. "He's terribly proud of them."

Mrs. Parmelee looked at her for a moment as if she were trying to recollect who she was. "He *adores* them," she said in a correcting tone.

"And, of course, I suppose he can only see them on weekends."

"It's the only thing in his new life that I can't reconcile myself to," Mrs. Parmelee continued in her monologue tone. "He thinks I mind his working for that Mr. Levine, and I do a bit, but not the way his father does. Things like that aren't terribly important to mothers, as I'm sure you will discover one day, Miss Street. If Reese could be with his children more, that's all I would ask."

"It certainly is the tragedy of divorce," Rosina agreed, a bit lamely.

"Of course, you mustn't think he hasn't done everything for those children that he could possibly do!" Mrs. Parmelee exclaimed. A new defensive note now entered her tone. "He's stripped himself for them. Literally stripped himself! He made over everything he had to his wife, and he pays her half his salary to boot. And he knows that his own grandmother has changed her will to leave his share to Esther!"

Rosina began to feel uncomfortable. Was Mrs. Parmelee trying to warn her off? Was she saying, in effect: "Look here, Miss Street, if it's a fortune you're after, you're wasting your time"?

"I'm sure he'll always be able to earn his living, Mrs. Parmelee. I've had firsthand knowledge of how good a lawyer he is."

Mrs. Parmelee looked blank. The idea that her son might ever make a respectable income out of Amos Levine's office had obviously not occurred to her. "Oh, I'm sure he will," she said perfunctorily. "I know he's very clever. But I had hoped that he might someday own this place. I had hoped that he might run it and keep the family together. But with what he has done for Esther and the children and at the rate my mother-in-law is encroaching on her capital — oh, Miss Street, it's hard to know what to look forward to any more. It really is!"

Rosina asked if she might walk in the garden again, and Mrs. Parmelee, looking just a bit surprised, said, "Of course."

She walked across the wide lawn and down the path again to the azaleas. It was an intoxication to be alone with her new impressions. She was no longer in the least suspicious of Reese's mother. The last speech had quite reassured her. Mrs. Parmelee was not concerned about her; she was concerned *for* her. She must have felt it her duty to warn any girl who came with Reese to Parmelee Cove how illusory was its opulent look. For how indeed was anyone to suspect such a discrepancy between fact and appearance or to divine that the heir of the Parmelees had already been plucked dry? Rosina fairly hugged herself with joy. She had found at last the husband that she wanted. Now that her mind was made up, she would only have to make up his.

Was she really so unworldly? she asked herself as she came again in sight of the Roman temple. Did it really mean so little to her that in a few years, or months even, this whole place, so suddenly and dazzlingly opened up to her, would be put on the auction block, and Reese would again be the Reese whom she had known up till that morning, a clerk of Amos Levine's with a rented room in the Village? But such things were of little importance compared to his ceasing to be an enigma. She had placed him, and that was basically all he had lacked. He fitted into a picture and it was a picture that she liked. What did it matter to her that his father was a stuffy, narrow man and his mother a nervous, frightened woman? They could be boring — formidably boring perhaps — but who in the world had ever been hurt by boredom? The point was that they belonged to a system, an honorable and respected system, and as long as it was honorable and respected, it made no difference to her that it was antiquated or even dead. So few people could ever understand the simple truth that she prided herself on having mastered: that direction and organization, however trivial and however outmoded, were never to be despised in a world whose greatest danger was chaos. She knew that as a daughter-in-law of the Parmelees she could talk nothings with them happily for the rest of her life. It was all she required of her husband's family.

When Reese came to get her in the garden, he looked pre-occupied and worried. She assumed that it had distressed him to see the children and to realize with each visit how far the paternal relationship had dwindled, and she asked no questions. As they drove back to the city in the thickening traffic, she felt the approaching week of unwelcome duties settle over him to smother the joy in the spring that he had manifested on the way to Parmelee Cove. But when he spoke it was evident that something besides the children was on his mind.

"What a terrible thing old age is!" he exclaimed.

"Why do you say that?"

"Because it exposes people. It strips them. It's like a last judgment."

"Are you thinking of your grandmother?"

"Yes." He moved his hands together on top of the wheel and accelerated their speed. "Shall I tell you why only the family are allowed to see her? And only certain of the family at that?"

"Do you want to?"

"Yes. You can see these things in their proper perspective. Granny's mind is beginning to go. Quite fast now. She suffers from mental delusions." He cleared his throat, and she knew that it was the new, the modern Reese, establishing his ascendancy over the sentimental child of Parmelee Cove. "One of her delusions," he continued almost harshly, "is that she's the victim of a white slaver, locked up in a bawdy house. She thinks her male visitors are — well, you can im-agine."

"Oh, Reese!" All the joy in her heart at the early spring

of the garden and at her picture of the Parmelees at home in their idyllic retreat fell suddenly to pieces. She might have known that he would destroy it, that nothing would be safe from the bleak, chill wind of his fear of self-deception. "You shouldn't have told me!" she cried resentfully. "Those things are irrelevant. They have nothing to do with your grandmother's long good life!"

"On the contrary. It shows the kind of thoughts that have been going on under Granny's white pompadour through decades and decades of ironclad respectability!"

"Oh, Reese, shut up!"

"Why should I shut up?" he demanded indignantly. "Do you think it means I don't love my grandmother? Well, you're wrong! I'm simply trying to understand what —"

"I mean it, Reese. Shut up!"

They finished the drive in silence. When he stopped before her house, however, he looked at her sideways and said in a milder tone: "I've spoiled it all, haven't I? The whole day?"

"You have, more or less."

"I'm sorry."

"Oh, it's all right," she said wearily. "It's not your fault, I suppose. I was just a bit carried away by the azaleas. Maybe I've been pent up in the city too long."

"Shall we go down again next week?"

"Next week may be a bit soon."

"But you'll do it again?"

"Oh, I think so, Reese. Please don't ask me now."

She climbed her stairs alone, very tired, and fell on the daybed to weep bitter tears. Where were all her plans, all her discipline, if a few flowers, a family lunch and an old lady's wandering mind could so undo her?

4

THE NEXT MORNING, when Reese arrived at his office at nine o'clock, he found a message that Mr. Levine wanted to see him immediately. It augured a crisis that Amos should get in before ten, but Reese sat at his desk for fifteen minutes while he finished the *Times* crossword puzzle. He still had the problem of his early morning temper, and that Monday it was worse than usual. When he finally went down the hall to Amos's office, he found the latter looking grave. He asked Reese to close the door.

"I'm sorry to tell you that our poor old friend, Miss Howland, passed away on Saturday morning. It happened very quickly and peacefully, in her sleep. A wonderful way to go."

It was the way death had always been announced at Parmelee Cove. As a benignant grey lady, swathed in clichés, who had the tact to make her visit as brief as possible and to depart with her victim amid a low murmuring of "What a mercy!" and "What a wonderful life!" Was she called a leveler because she elicited the same phrases from all lips, from Amos's as well as his grandmother's?

"I'm sorry. Shall I get her will out of the vault?"

"That's been taken care of." Amos frowned slightly. He was offended by such dispatch in turning to practical things. "I was very fond of Miss Howland, you know," he said reproachfully. "It's odd how close we were. I had almost the feelings of a son for her. At least of a nephew. And I believe she cared about me, too."

Reese said nothing. If Amos was looking for sympathy, he could get it from someone besides his hired hand. "She left you a bequest," he said casually, glancing up at the wall. "One of those prints. But I don't suppose it will go with the Utrillo."

"I shall always treasure it!"

Reese shrugged. "Shall I draw the probate papers?"

"Isaacs is taking care of that." Amos was forced to give up sentiment at last, and he turned with an air of reluctant dutifulness to the business in hand. "There's something more important that I want your help on. There's not only a will." He paused significantly. "There's a codicil."

Reese searched the expressionless lines of the other's face. "I didn't draw one," he said tersely. "Did *you?*"

"No. It was drawn by Pat Shea. You remember Pat?"

Reese certainly remembered him. Mr. Shea was currently counsel to the Stuyvesant Hotel and a good friend of Amos's. Together they had worked out a *modus vivendi* between the old tenants and the new management. "Did you send Miss Howland to him?"

"I never heard a thing about it." Amos raised his right hand. "So help me!"

"So help you?" Reese stared hard. "What's *in* that codicil?"

Silently Amos handed him a sheet of paper, and he sat down to read it. It consisted of a single paragraph: "To my devoted friend and faithful lawyer, Amos Levine, who has made it possible for me to finish my days in the home I love, I give and bequeath the sum of one hundred and fifty thousand dollars." Reese's breathing came in pants as sudden anger pricked through him. He glanced quickly to the bottom of the page and saw that the paper was correctly executed and witnessed. The date was only of the preceding week. "It looks as if she did 'care about you,'" he said sarcastically.

"So help me, Reese, my first inkling of this was when Pat called me Saturday morning!"

"Can the estate pay a legacy that size? After administration fees and taxes?"

"Oh, yes. She's left easily half a million."

"Congratulations, then!"

"Now, wait a second, Reese, wait a second." The weary dark eyes pleaded for sympathy. "Don't be like that. This thing has hit me like a ton of bricks. What the hell am I going to do about it?"

"Do about it? What is there to do about it but stretch out your hand to the executors and say: 'Thank you, gentlemen'?"

"It's not quite as simple as that. The executors won't pay. The nephew and niece have already retained your old firm, Clark, Day & Parmelee. I got a telephone call from a Mr. Stillman last night. Sunday night, mind you. Before the poor old lady's even been buried. The family, he tells me, will oppose probate of the codicil. If I fight, they'll throw the book at me. Fraud, undue influence, the works. Even a conspiracy between Pat Shea and myself to divide the legacy!"

Reese smiled bitterly at the idea of how intensely Stillman would enjoy such a role. Saint George and the dragon. "And if you don't fight?"

"I get fifty thousand by certified check this afternoon."

Reese pondered the significance of Stillman's speed. "They must think you have a pretty good case. You could get them up to seventy-five thousand, I guess." He shrugged. "I suppose you'll settle?"

"And admit what Stillman's charging?"

"It's no admission. Every lawyer knows that."

"But what about my duty to Miss Howland?" Amos cried in a high-pitched voice. He got up, agitated, and paced back and forth under the Utrillo. "Is it fair to her to let her relatives browbeat me out of my bequest? It's not just the money. You know what my taxes are, Reese. What's more money to me?"

But Reese was inexorable. "This would be income-tax free to you, Amos. You couldn't save that much the way you're living in ten years. Let's be frank about it. It's a fortune."

Amos found himself in the novel position of appealing to his subordinate, and he accepted without a murmur the change in their status that this brought about. "But she left it to me!" he protested. "It was what she wanted to do with her money. If she'd thought I was going to go chicken and turn over most of it to her nephew and niece, she wouldn't have left me anything but that photograph of the Forum!"

"Maybe."

"Well, what would *you* do in my shoes?"

Reese pulled out his pipe and slowly filled it while he thought. "If I'd had nothing to do with her going to Shea," he said finally, his eyes carefully following the pacing figure, "and if I were convinced that she was of sound mind when she wrote that codicil, I'd fight the Howlands. I'd fight them to the last ditch. I wouldn't settle for a penny less than the full legacy."

Amos ceased his pacing and paused to stare down at Reese as the latter lit his pipe. "But I tell you I didn't know a damn thing about her going to Shea! And, of course, she was of sound mind. Sound as a rock!"

Reese threw away his match as he stood up. "Very well, then," he said conclusively. "I'd fight."

"Now, wait a second, Reese," Amos said petulantly as his associate turned to the door. "Sit down, will you? I haven't finished. Why are you so impatient this morning?"

"I have work to do."

"It can wait." When Reese was seated again, he stated flatly: "I want you to represent me."

This time Reese was really taken aback. There had been too many surprises for one morning. But his astonishment began to abate when he remembered that Amos would naturally prefer to have his bequest undiminished by legal fees. And then, too, there was the public relations aspect. Might it not make Amos's case seem more respectable to the newspapers if he were represented by a man who was not only a relation of the testatrix but a former employee of the very law firm that was attacking him?

"Wouldn't you do better with a more experienced trial lawyer?"

"I know your work, Reese. It's better than that of a lot of 'experienced' trial lawyers. And I'll make it worth your while, too. Is that what's worrying you?"

"Not in the least."

"What is it, then?"

"I'll tell you." Reese leaned forward, slapping a hand firmly on Amos's desk. "I'm worried about why a man as smart as Pat Shea would stick in a legacy that size without more explanation. More preamble. People are apt to use codicils to add legacies to old friends and servants. A few hundred dollars here and there. Not a hundred and fifty thousand!"

Amos became suddenly very calm; he smiled almost affably. "Are you implying the figures were tampered with?"

"I'm implying nothing. Miss Howland might have mistaken the sum herself. She might have said a hundred and fifty thousand and meant fifteen hundred. My point is that it's all too quick, too big, too near the end. I don't like it. I don't like any part of it."

Amos had now quite recaptured the old, lazy charm of his habitual manner. "Well, I tell you what I'll do," he said, balancing his silver paper cutter between his fingers. "I'll let you be the judge of it. If you'll take the case, I'll fight. If you won't, I'll renounce the legacy. Even the fifty grand they're offering me now."

Reese sat open-mouthed. If it was a bluff, it was a magnificent one. "I never said you shouldn't take the settlement."

"But where's the logic in that?" Amos demanded. "Either Miss Howland meant me to have the legacy or she didn't. She certainly never intended me to have *part* of it. Would it help you to talk to Pat Shea?"

Reese got up for the second time. "Not yet," he answered curtly. "You've told me all you know?"

Amos smiled as he solemnly again raised his right hand. "So help me," he repeated.

Reese happened to be having lunch with Andy that day, and when they met, he told him the whole story. Andy, who knew Mrs. Anthon, Miss Howland's niece, in the world of night clubs and benefit parties in which he now complacently moved, was outraged at the idea that so "prehensile" a woman, as he described her, should be allowed to collect Levine's legacy without a struggle. It was more, he insisted, than flesh and blood could bear.

"You're supposed to be a lawyer!" he exclaimed vehemently. "You should be able to review the facts dispassionately. All right: what do we find? An old lady client tells you she wants to leave a legacy to your boss. You think it's improper for you, as his employee, to handle this. So you tell her to get another lawyer. And what does she do? She gets another lawyer. What the deuce are you crabbing about? Do you begrudge Levine his pound of flesh? Even when it's legally sliced?"

"But isn't it rather odd that she should happen to go to one of his cronies?" Reese demanded. "A man whom she'd never even met?"

"Not a bit. He was the lawyer for the hotel, wasn't he? She probably got his name at the desk."

"And not from Levine? On one of his 'friendly' visits? For you can be damn sure he went to the files and read the will *I* drew. And when he saw that measly legacy of the Roman Forum, what do you think he did? He beat it right around to the Stuyvesant to thank her! Oh, he's smart! And *then* she asked him for the name of a lawyer!"

"And he suggested Shea?" Andy's face brightened into a broad smile as the theory struck him. "And Shea slipped in the extra zeros, which the old girl never noticed? Having agreed with his pal, Levine, that they'd divvy up later? I'm to assume all that? My dear Reese, I suggest you're neurotically prejudiced against your boss!"

Andy at last carried the day. Reese could not seem to escape the logic of the facts that he had told Miss Howland to hire another lawyer and that she had done just that. How could he without some proof of fraud not stand behind the codicil?

"You've told me about a lot of your cases," Andy concluded. "I've never known you to show such moral nicety before."

"But this is different! This is *me!*"

"And 'me,' of course, is special," Andy retorted. "Pardon me, Mr. Parmelee of Parmelee Cove! I should have recognized you sooner!"

And so the case of "In re Howland's Estate" started in the old courtroom of the Hall of Records beneath dark paneled walls and between two huge fireplaces, modeled on the fireplaces in sixteenth century banqueting halls in châteaux along the Loire. In the center of the chamber, on a raised mahogany bench between two flaring orb lamps, the surrogate looked down with a dry attention on this as on other struggles that marked the passage of property from the dead to the living. Reporters were there in number, and even the *New York Times* carried a daily column on the case. It had all the elements of popular appeal: a rich recluse living in an ancient hotel, a niece already known in the social columns and for her cigarette endorsements, a famous trial lawyer in the witness box and the possibility of infinite dirt. It lacked only sex, and it seemed that the inexhaustible Mr. Stillman might even produce that. He introduced in evidence a series of letters from Amos Levine to the decedent, couched in a sentimental style that occasionally bordered on the "purple," which he read aloud to the jury in a high, sneering tone which left no doubt as to his own conviction that their purpose had been to turn the head of an addled and romantic old woman.

" 'It is two days now since my last visit, dear Miss Howland,' " he read, " 'and the memory of it is like a little patch of violets in the dull grey of my litigating life. What good is it to gain success in the eyes of an indifferent and easily impressed world, if one is never understood, if one can never communicate on the simple basis of one unencumbered human being to another? And such a relationship, I dare to say, is only possible between two people of different sexes.' "

How Stillman loved it! Reese could almost forget that they were antagonists in his fascination at studying his former employer. Stillman, who had been raised on a small farm in New Hampshire, could never have enough of his New York success. His tweeds could never be tweedy enough, his clubs solemn and cavernous enough, his senior partners pompous enough. Yet the world that his imagination had created or at least supplemented, unlike most such worlds, was evidently satisfying to him. Reese knew that Stillman reveled in the company of his shy, plain wife and of his plain, expensively schooled children and of the shy, plain wives of his contemporaries who enjoyed the same success and the same cozy beach club on the Connecticut shore. For Stillman was no social climber; he and his friends wished only to form an honorable and "nice" society to take over and continue what they deemed to have been the honorable and "nice" traditions of the people who would have been their parents had they been born to New York parents of established wealth. And how he swung his clean, glittering blade on behalf of the scions of the Howland family! What a joy to kill the infidel at the gates of the holy sepulcher! Such a crusade, anyway, had to dignify what might otherwise have seemed rather a mean investigation: the relentless examination of chambermaids about the vagaries of Miss Howland, the thunderous questioning of nurses as to her small complaints, the savage heckling of a stubborn old doctor who admitted her eccentricities but refused to deny her capacity to make a will. Reese marveled at Stillman's quick change to geniality after a session in court if they met in the elevator, the pound on the back, the grip on the shoulder, the hint of basic alliance between lawyers against a world of clients. "Well, Reese, old boy, quite a fight, quite a fight, isn't it?" But for Levine himself, there were no smiles, even in the elevator. Stillman's conviviality had its limits when it came to Beelzebub. And in court, with the monster on the witness stand, he would soar to a pitch of violence that ran the danger of driving the jury into sympathy for the very victim so blasted.

"What did you mean, exactly, Mr. Levine, when you wrote the testatrix that a relationship such as hers and yours was only possible between persons of different sex?"

"I meant there could be an understanding between a man and a woman not possible between a man and a man."

"Is such an understanding not commonly thought of as the understanding between two people in love?"

"Possibly. But there's such a thing as Platonic love, Mr. Stillman."

"Ah yes, of course. Platonic love!" Stillman's eyelids soared in the sneer of a man who meant to show that to one of *his* virility, such matters must be the rankest hypocrisy. "An unbodily love! And it was this incorporeal passion, unknown to cruder mortals, that you proposed to Miss Howland?"

"It was not a case of proposing, but of defining."

"I see. Did you 'define' it, then, to Miss Howland?"

"I think she understood without that."

"You do? I admire your confidence. I wish I could share it. But it strikes me that Miss Howland was less versed in her Socratic dialogues than you. For example, we have heard testimony this very week from Nurse Allen that the testatrix referred to you as her 'beau'? That is not a word that I find in my Plato. But I confess I know only the Jowett translation. Miss Allen testified also that Miss Howland described you on one occasion as her 'cavaliere servente.' Is that term in *your* Plato, Mr. Levine?"

"No. It was Miss Howland's little joke."

"Oh, I see. A joke. A *little* joke. Thank you, Mr. Levine. My sense of humor seems a bit defective today. Was it also a little joke when you wrote her that there was an 'immediacy of communication' between you and her that you had never felt with another person?"

"No. That was quite serious."

"I'm sorry to hear you say that, Mr. Levine." Stillman
turned away from the witness box with an elaborate shrug
and what was almost a wink to the jury. "I had hoped perhaps that Mrs. Levine might have enjoyed the privilege of being your closest communicant!"

But Amos was a perfect witness. He never lost his temper;
he simply turned to the jury and courtroom, in moments of
greatest provocation, a small, weary half smile, as though to
express his patience with the small probings of small men into
matters which they were not fated to understand. Reese had
discovered early in the proceedings that Amos was his own
best advocate and had put him on the stand for hours in his
own defense. Amos had always had the habit of dictating
long memoranda after interviews with clients, and these now
came in very conveniently to demonstrate the range and content of his discussions with Miss Howland. It made for a be-
lievable and innocent picture of their relationship to be able to
bring out her love of zoos, not visited in years, her collection
of photographs of the English royal family, her habit of pos-
ing as the incorrigible and lovable "tomboy," her strong opin-
ions against high buildings and city politicians and her suspicions that the frequent visitations of her nephew and niece
were not entirely disinterested. Amos's lazy drawl and neat,
conservative appearance went far to rebut any picture that
the jury might have conjured up of a sleek and oily shyster
preying on an addled old woman. Yet what, Reese kept asking himself more and more intently as the trial wore on, *had*
been the true nature of their relationship? Simply that of an
unctuously flattering Disraeli at the feet of a vain and peppery
old queen? Or had there perhaps really been a drawing together between two natures, basically in some way congenial,
from two widely disparate bases, a touching of fingertips
from two arms stretched across abysses of possible misunder-

standing? How could such a thing be credited in this dark room filled with men who grinningly acknowledged the existence of only the simplest drives of sex and acquisitiveness? Who would have despised even more than trickery the very thing that Amos was trying to prove?

Reese had never before so wanted to believe in anything as he now wanted to believe in Amos. It could have then been the battle of his life symbolized. There across the long counsel table sat Stillman, a grotesque but effective parody of the mores of his past. Behind him, next to her brother, sat Mrs. Schuyler Anthon, so tall and thin and chic and falsely blond, concentrating more on her look of intelligent attention than on the case itself, occasionally whispering and briefly pointing, looking as she looked in her last advertisement, stepping out of a green Mercedes-Benz with the Newport Casino in the background, holding up with her charming smile the cigarette that she was currently endorsing. Reese knew just how such a woman would have felt about her aunt; he could hear her little wails at lunch at the Colony on the days of her monthly afternoon visit to the Stuyvesant. Yet for all her wails she would have valued the presence in the family of such a font of funny stories. She would have adored astounding her dinner partners on the night after the visit with the cry: "Do you know, the poor dear even has a *dentist's* chair in her room?" She would have reveled in such eccentricity as something indigenous to old and aristocratic stock. And now this whole delightful trial—why it was worth more than the legacy itself! When she was on the stand she testified as if reluctantly about her "poor aunt's" little weaknesses, with small understanding smiles at the jury, as though to convey the idea that mental haziness in the Howland family was an ancient mark of distinction, an indication of vintage and that it was the sad duty of the survivors in each generation to go into court and wash the dirty linen rather than lose it altogether. When Reese cross-examined her, he let his irritation at all that she seemed to stand for betray him into Stillman's error. When he suggested that her motives in visiting Miss Howland might have had something to do with the latter's will, she cried in a clear, indignant tone:

"I loved my aunt, Mr. Parmelee!"

"Yet you have heard what Miss Howland herself suggested?"

"I've heard what Mr. Levine *said* she suggested," she retorted, "but I don't believe it for a moment. And even if it were true, what sort of a niece would I be if I couldn't forgive the poor old darling the suspicions of her senility!"

But as the trial drew to its close it was becoming increasingly evident that Mrs. Anthon and her brother, however justly indignant, simply did not have a case. For all Mr. Stillman's probing, he had not been able to show any convincing evidence of conspiracy between Levine and Shea, and he had failed utterly to prove that Miss Howland lacked testamentary capacity. Vagueness and eccentricity, yes — these he had proved in abundance — but it was still certain that she had known who her relatives were and what she had been doing when she had signed the codicil. The jury might well believe that Amos was a tricky lawyer who had played on an old woman's feelings in the hope of a legacy, but there was no law that prohibited a foolish and credulous old woman from leaving her money to such a man. Stillman himself was clearly aware that his case needed something more; he was putting witness after witness on the stand, chambermaids and bellboys of the Stuyvesant who had barely known Miss Howland, in the forlorn hope of rounding out his shadowy sketch of mental incompetence. The surrogate was bored, the jury was bored, even Mrs. Anthon seemed to have wilted, but Stillman kept doggedly on. Only Reese in all the courtroom listened attentively to each witness called, and Reese's attention was more riveted to them by his personal concern with the truth than by his duty as a lawyer. For to know the truth of what Amos and Shea had done had now become almost an obsession with him. It was as if the court and the lawsuit had faded away and he and Stillman were alone in a dark void shouting their questions up at the dim outline of a smiling sphinx. Sometimes it seemed to Reese that he was actually on Stillman's side, that they were working together, joined in the same quest. This feeling, despite the fact that he was doing his utmost for Amos, was particularly acute on the morning of what promised to be the last day of the trial.

Reese had briefly recalled an earlier witness, one Miss Knott, a large, smiling, talkative woman who had worked on the switchboard at the Stuyvesant, to establish again the fact that it was Miss Howland who had called Shea on the day the codicil was signed and not he her. Stillman had not cross-examined Miss Knott the first time Reese had called her. She had been employed by the hotel only in the week preceding Miss Howland's death, and it had already been established that she had never met the testatrix. Now, however, a more desperate Stillman proceeded to cross-examine her at some length. How had Miss Howland sounded? Had her voice not seemed frail? Had the witness detected any note of apprehension? No, the witness had not.

"Of course, if Miss Howland's tone had changed, you wouldn't have known, would you?" Stillman continued. "I mean, you hadn't heard her voice before, had you?"

"Oh, yes. Several times."

Stillman proceeded immediately to his next point, but Reese was struck by this last response. He himself had asked Miss Knott very few questions, in court or out; he had taken for

granted, as Stillman had, that an employee of two days' standing who had never even seen Miss Howland, could have little
to contribute to the trial. But how then had she heard Miss
Howland's voice "several times"? Had she and Miss Howland talked together on the telephone? By day? By night?
Had Miss Howland been one of those sleepless old ladies who
liked to chat with the switchboard girl in the early hours of
the morning? Reese's heart began to beat faster. He knew
he had to have that answer for his own satisfaction, even if it
cost him the case. For if he re-examined Miss Knott now,
God only knew what revelations might be forthcoming,
what new aspects of poor old Miss Howland's confused plans
for the distribution of that little heap of securities that had so
long supported her voluntary incarceration in the Stuyvesant.
But in sudden desperation he knew that he no longer cared.
He *had* to find out! As Stillman was about to dismiss the
witness, he rose.

"One question more, Miss Knott, if you please," he said,
coming forward. "You said just now that you had heard Miss
Howland's voice several times. Would you tell the court on
what other occasions you heard it?"

"Why certainly." Miss Knott, who loved being a witness,
settled back in the chair to prolong her testimony. "Miss
Howland was a very friendly lady and told me she always introduced herself to each new girl at the switchboard. The
first morning I was on, she called up and said: 'This is Miss
Howland. I'm the oldest lady in the world.'"

She paused, and Reese moistened his lips. "Was that all she
said?"

"Oh, dear me, no. That was just her little joky way of
starting out a conversation. Then she went on and asked me
all about myself, where I lived, what family I had and so
forth. She was a dear, she was."

"Was it only to chat that she called?"

"Well, that's what I thought at first," the witness continued, "but I was wrong. She wanted the name of a lawyer. She said she had to do something to her will and that for some reason — I don't know what — she couldn't use her regular one. So I gave her Mr. Shea's name."

The whole courtroom leaned forward in tense silence. Reese barely could hear his own lowered voice ask: "Why *his* name?"

"Well, it was on the number board in front of me. You see, he was the hotel's lawyer, and I didn't know of any others, so I asked if he'd do."

"And what did Miss Howland say?"

"She said that he would do fine — it was a simple matter — and would I get him on the phone for her?"

"Which you did?"

"Which I did."

When Reese took his seat again to watch an almost distracted Stillman try vainly to break down Miss Knott's testimony on cross-examination, he felt that he was in danger of hysterical laughter. The whole case seemed suddenly not only senseless but gloriously comic.

"It's in the bag now," Amos whispered to him. "Great work, my boy! But why didn't you bring that out before?"

"I didn't know it."

Amos's stare was blank. "You mean you asked those questions blind?"

"I had to."

"Gee!" Amos pursed his lips as if to whistle. "You don't mind taking chances, do you?"

"What chances were there?" Reese turned his head to look directly into Amos's eyes, a foot away. "Didn't you tell me everything was on the up and up?" He smiled grimly at Amos's quick nod and averted face.

5

THAT NIGHT Reese had to talk about the case, and he called up Rosina to ask her to cook supper for him. At first she protested that she had to work on an article, but when he insisted, she gave in. It was singular, he reflected, walking to her apartment, that they should be on such terms that he *could* insist, when nothing, not even a good-night kiss, had passed between them. He was more intimate with Rosina than he had been with Esther, even in the beginning. It was interesting, perhaps even significant, that of all the women he had known, he should be closest to the one who had yielded him the least. Yet it was not, he knew, that there was nothing between them. Far from it. They were a very long way from that Platonic goal that Amos had described in his correspondence with Miss Howland. Rosina's impatience, her sudden, violent flare-ups were more exciting to him than his most passionate moments with Cynthia. It was clear to him, and he was sure it was clear to her that they could not go on much longer as they were going. How they would eventually work it out he did not know and was certainly not going to plan. It was enough — for the time being — that he should have the upper hand.

Rosina's apartment consisted of one large room in a converted brownstone with a tiny kitchenette. It was characteristically neat and spotless. The daybed was covered with a gay Mexican blanket; there were three hammock chairs in red, yellow and green, and the two abstracts on the wall had been rented from the picture library of the Museum of Modern Art. It was all predictable, but it was all attractive. During supper he told her about the case and his doubts. She listened well, in her usual way, with a few intelligent interruptions. But was she seeing it, he wondered suddenly, as a feature for her magazine? With Rosina there was always that.

"Well," she said, when they had finished supper, and he was sipping brandy, "you should be feeling good. It's a big case, and it looks as if you'd won it."

"But don't you see that's not what's worrying me?"

"Of course I see it. But if you go to law, you go to win." She shrugged. "How many times have you told *me* that?"

"Yes, but this is different. If Amos swindled that old woman, if he even bamboozled her into doing what she did, this whole new life of mine has been wrong. It's even worse than my old one! That's why I took the chance and asked the switchboard girl that question. The chance I had no business to take."

"The chance that will win your case!"

"That's luck. Pure luck."

"You judge yourself too harshly, Reese. You're a gambler at heart. You wanted to cinch the case, and your instinct told you to go ahead. That instinct was sound."

"But it wasn't instinct. I was after the truth! Whether it made or broke Levine!"

Rosina rose and carried her coffee cup to the old white marble Victorian mantel. She peered down for a moment into the empty grate and then turned resolutely around. She seemed suddenly irritated.

"I sometimes feel there's no end to your relentless self-analysis," she said. "It's as if some demon inside you would

never let you take anything for granted. But as long as you're
at it, do you really probe deeply enough? Why don't you go
all the way? Are you *really* concerned with the truth? Are
you sure it isn't an atavistic prejudice coming out at last? An
old St. Lawrence School snobbishness about a lawyer who
writes sentimental letters to an old woman that no gentleman
would write?"

He laughed easily enough at this, for, like Andy, she was
wide of the mark. But it was evident that they were both
tired, and he stood up. "I've argued enough in the last three
weeks. I'm not going to start a fight now. Besides, it's bed-
time. But what about giving me a kiss good night? No breech
of agreement on either side, just a simple good-night kiss? I
need it, Rosy."

Her face crumpled, and she came quickly forward to throw
her arms around him. She clung to him desperately as he
kissed her lips. Then he gently removed her hands from his
shoulders.

"There," he said. "Now that's all."

She was still panting. "You can be very provoking."

"Do you mean you want me to break my word?" For as
soon as she had resisted his effort to loosen her hold, he had
felt rising within him the old brutal need to assert his inde
pendence, the old intransigence about making the least concession to female inconsistency. He looked at her now with
suddenly fixed eyes. "If you mean it, say it!"

"No, I don't mean any such thing, damn you!" she exploded suddenly, hitting him on the chest with her fists.
"Who do you think you are, anyway?"

"I think I'm someone the law calls a reasonable man," he
retorted, seizing both her fists and holding them tightly. "Get
hold of yourself, will you, Rosy? You've always put yourself in a special class. Now live up to it!"

He released her when she stopped struggling, but she glared up at him furiously. "I'm not asking any special privileges!" she cried sharply. "And I'm not being unreasonable! What makes me so angry is your parade of self-control when I know what it's based on!"

"Based on?"

"All your other girls! The one Duey saw you necking with in that restaurant! Of course, you can afford to be cool with me when you have one of them to go to!"

Reese flushed angrily as he remembered seeing Duey. "That's my affair."

"Your affair!" she exclaimed. "Your *affairs!* If that's not too dignified a term for them!"

"Good night, Rosina," he said curtly, trembling with anger. "You're too excited. Thank you for my supper. I'll call you tomorrow."

Out in the street he was still quivering with irritation. That she should expect him to stay away from other girls when she gave him so little was an absurdity that he could not even laugh at. Was she going to be another Esther, after all? Were there any women who *weren't* like Esther? He thought of Agnes Damon. She was a model who had given him a key to her apartment. Sometimes he went there in the evening and waited for her to come home. Behind the door of the bedroom he would hear her saying good night to the man who had taken her out. Sometimes she would even give the man a kiss before closing the front door and going into the bedroom to call: "Reese? Is that you in there with the light on?" Their understanding was admirable. He thought he would use his key that night.

6

EVERYONE at Parmelee Cove had been very nice to Esther. It was agreed among the family that there was no absolute rule that one had to take the side of the blood relative, particularly when the blood relative had behaved as badly as Reese. There was something rather splendid, they thought, not to say novel and exciting, in lining up so solidly behind an abandoned in-law and showing the family's united front in matters of morality. Esther had been much touched by the buoyant support which she had received from all of them when she had returned after six dreary weeks in Reno. Even her father-in-law, usually silent with the neutrality of his stubborn indifference, took upon himself to murmur to her:

"Nothing's going to be any different, my dear. You're just a daughter now, that's all. No longer a daughter-in-law."

And for many months, indeed, it had seemed that things were going to work themselves out this way. Reese's sisters and his cousins always included her on Saturday night parties; his aunts first visited, and later telephoned, and his grandmother, who had assimilated only vaguely the shocking fact of this divorce, treated Esther with the same combination of petulance and good manners as before. But it was clear to the latter, before the end of her first year without Reese, how universally he was missed. It was remarkable to her, in view of the fact that he had not even wanted to live at Parmelee

Cove, how indispensable a part of the place he had become. Nobody, for example, seemed to understand the electrical connections in the big house but Reese. Nobody else could get the motorboat to work properly. And Freddy Talcott was a miserable failure with the children's summer sports class which had always run so smoothly under Reese's direction. There were more and more remarks like: "One thing I'll say about Reese is that the children really jumped when he told them to do something" or "You have to hand it to Reese that he had the trick of keeping that old swimming pool at the right temperature." Whenever he came down of a Sunday to see the children and lunch with his parents, there were always a series of accumulated problems for him to solve. It was rumored about the place that he was living in a cold-water flat and working for a man who was no better than a crook. Esther, who had always slightly disturbed the Parmelees with her competence and good spirits, began to sense the slow but inevitable shift in the tide of sympathy. It was as if the simple facts of Reese's absence and her own presence at Parmelee Cove must mean that she had driven him out. It was still true, she reflected grimly, that blood was thicker than water.

When she went over to lunch one Saturday with Mr. and Mrs. Parmelee and Reese's sister, Joan Blackwell, she gathered from the sudden silence which greeted her entrance that they had been talking about Reese. She knew that he was coming down that Sunday.

"Why don't you bring Reese over to lunch with me tomorrow?" she asked boldly. "I think it's much more natural for the children to see us together. As a matter of fact, I told him he could spend the night at my house any time he wanted. There's always the guest room."

The suggestion caused a profound shock. Agnes Parmelee looked nervously to her husband and daughter and got no help from either. "Well, I've ordered everything here," she faltered. "So maybe we'd better go to you another time, my dear."

"But I could come here and bring the children," Esther pursued relentlessly. "How would that be?"

"I suppose I'd have to ask the cook. Three more, you know, and on such short notice."

"Oh, we could bring sandwiches!"

"Oh — yes. Well — I really don't know."

"What Mother's trying to say, Esther," Joan broke in bluntly, "is that Reese is bringing a girl down for lunch to-morrow." Joan had more than her share of the Parmelee in-tractability. She had gentler features than her brother, but her brown stare was even less compromising than his blue one.

"Oh, is he?" Esther's eyes shone brightly. "Well, I can quite see that it might cramp his style to have an ex-wife hang-ing around. Who is the lucky lady?"

"A Miss Street," Agnes Parmelee answered. "Miss Rosina Street. She comes from Roanoke," she added dubiously, as though not sure what value to attach to such a source.

"Hasn't she been down here once before?" Esther de-manded. "Yes, of course! Well, that seems to be becoming rather a thing!"

The others, however, made no comment, and the subject of Rosina was allowed to drop. Conversation was desultory until Joan, who had not seen the morning papers, asked what progress had been made in the Howland case. This was the one subject on which her father could be drawn. That Reese should be involved in such a case was evidently a far worse crime to Alfred Parmelee than any abandonment of a mere wife.

"The boys were talking about it this morning in the locker-room at Piping Rock!" he exploded. "Of course, they stopped when they saw me. But I promise you, Agnes, I could hardly hold my head up! That a son of mine should be mixed up with a shyster lawyer in defrauding an old woman is the limit. It really and truly is!"

Even Joan, who had more of Reese's independence of mind than others of the family, seemed to go along with her father. Parmelee Cove, after all, was united in its confusion of morality with the out-of-doors, and what was Amos Levine but the very symbol of closed windows and stuffy parlors? Alfred Parmelee evidently pictured him as the kind of man who would be capable of spending a beautiful Saturday afternoon in a country club bar, drinking whiskey and playing the coin machines. Esther was roused to his defense.

"It seems to me you're begging the question, Mr. Parmelee," she pointed out. "Whether or not Miss Howland was defrauded is just what the court has to decide."

"Oh, come, Esther, it stands to reason," he retorted impatiently. "You get a man like Levine oiling his way into the confidence of a senile old woman —"

"But *was* she senile?" Esther interrupted. "I've been reading the testimony rather carefully. It strikes me that she may have known very well what she was doing."

"How could she? And leave that much money to a man like that? When she had a nephew and niece of her own?"

"People do strange things with their money."

"Well, it shouldn't be allowed!" Alfred Parmelee expostulated. "It's perfectly obvious that if Levine gets a cent of that money, there's no justice in the State of New York!"

"You mean that it should be against the law for people to leave legacies to lawyers?"

"Now there you go, putting words in my mouth! You're as bad as Reese!"

The general feeling at the table seemed to be that if it was bad to do what Reese was doing, it was even worse to defend it. Amos Levine, after all, was Reese's boss. He had *that* much excuse. But for Esther to champion the cause of the shyster against a bamboozled old woman was little short of heresy. She smiled with a touch of bitterness as she walked home after lunch. It was curious to feel that she and Reese could still be allies. She had not altogether abandoned the idea that he might come back to her. His living away, in distant and novel surroundings, had invested him with some of the romantic aura that had made his wartime absences so heart-filling an experience.

Esther's fantasies, however, to give her any abiding satisfaction, had to have some basis, however tenuous, in the realm of possibility. When she considered more fully the news that Miss Street was coming again to Parmelee Cove, she had to concede that Reese did not appear to be heading towards reconciliation. And had she ever *really* believed, she asked herself bitterly now, that he was? Did she not know enough at this point of his stubbornness and consistency? Was she to let him ruin her life away from her as he had when with her? And that very afternoon she telephoned to Finny Coit and told him that she was going, after all, to be in town on Wednesday and would be glad to have dinner with him.

She and Finny had been thrown constantly together. In a society of younger married couples it was the task of each anxious Northfield hostess to find an "extra girl" for Finny, a task that was complicated by his unconcealed dislike of the few who were available. His partiality for Esther now seemed to have solved the problem permanently. She did not know whether to be more amused by the evident relief of the hostesses or by the cautiousness of Finny's approach. He had been obviously alarmed by her sudden reappearance in

Northfield as a divorced and hence marriageable woman, but she had taken immediate care to persuade him tactfully that the prospect of remarriage was actually repellent to her. After all, she was not above enjoying the enhancement of her local prestige which his attentiveness would bring or the strengthening of her position at Parmelee Cove. Without in the least contemplating a serious maneuver to catch her furtive admirer, she could still divert herself by mapping out the steps that could lead to his capture. And having mapped them out, it was only human to try a few, as an expert fisherman might practice his casts on a lawn.

It was a pity, of course, that his physical attractions were not greater. It would have made the game more fun. Finny gave the rather disconcerting impression of being two people at once. First was the big, roly-poly youngster with the egg-shaped face and thick, red hair. And second was the elderly man, dry, dogmatic, used to command, who seemed to have got inside the boy and was pushing to escape, so that the bulky figure was ungainly, as if always engaged in this curious struggle, the hips expanded, the gait awkward, the fluty voice occasionally bass. The boy and the older man, perhaps, were equidistant in age from Finny's thirty-seven years. But however lacking in charm, however positively mean Finny could be if he suspected that anyone was trying to get the better of him, there was a naïve and confiding, a "sweet" side to his nature that touched Esther. It was the side that was uppermost on the night that he took her out for dinner at the Colony, and insisted that she order all the most expensive things. If he added and readded the bill afterwards, it was not from stinginess but from the besetting fear that he might be "done." With the aid of cocktails and wine and of her smiling and comprehending silence, he talked without interruption of the frustrations of his childhood and of his present success.

"I never could wait to grow up," he told her. "I used to think those long years at St. Lawrence's would never end. I knew it wasn't the time for me. My time was coming later. What did *I* care about Latin and Greek? What did it matter to *me* that I was clumsy at hitting and catching balls? Let the others do that. Much good might it do them! I always had my eye on the thing that really counted: business. It was plain enough to any boy who cared to look around him. Who had built the school? Who gave the gymnasium and the hockey rink and the chapel? Who paid the scholarships? Business-men! Businessmen, all! But even at home they didn't seem to realize it. My grandfather would have, of course, for he started the stores. But he was dead, and Daddy was in charge. Daddy cared about all the things the boys in school cared about, swatting balls and so forth, and he almost ruined the business. I used to wake up at night, crying for fear he would dissipate the whole thing before I'd had my chance!"

"But he didn't."

"No." Finny's small dark eyes glittered with relief at the memory. "And one thing I'll say for Daddy, he knew when to move over. He had the guts to put me in charge when I was fresh out of college! Think of it, Esther! I told him I wanted to scrap the works, borrow from the banks and build new factories in the South where labor was cheap. It meant risking every cent the family had. Doubles or quits! God, you should have heard them howl! But Daddy backed me up to the hilt, and we did it. And won! I'm sure you've heard a lot of griping, Esther, from various members of my family at the way I run things, but damn it, I have to! They'd all be broke today if I'd listened to them!"

Esther found herself rather thrilled. To be able to gamble a family business on one throw of the dice and win — surely that was romantic. Surely it was more creative than spending one's days in a musty courtroom haggling over an old woman's legacy to her lawyer! Who was Reese to sneer at Finny?

The first dinner led to others, always in the most expensive restaurants. Finny liked to be where he was known and where the waiters could be counted on to make a fuss over him. Esther had no complaints. But from time to time she made him listen to her own problems and the difficulties of living so close to the Parmelees. It would never do to let him dominate the conversation altogether.

"Don't you worry about Reese's family," he would mutter. "You're worth three of every one of them."

Sometimes they went to his mother's. He had lived alone with Mrs. Coit, since his father's death and the marriage of his younger brother and sisters, in two great square red brick Georgian houses, one on upper Park Avenue and one in Northfield. The top floor of the town house had been converted into a penthouse apartment for him with a separate entrance and elevator, but he took all his meals downstairs with his mother. Mrs. Coit was a tall, thin woman, always dressed in black or white, with great dignity of bearing. She had a pale, lined, sadly smiling face with deep-sunk dark eyes that seemed to promise wells of intelligent sympathy. Yet Esther had never experienced so wide a discrepancy between appearance and character. Mrs. Coit's smile was the smile of total indifference; she was a gentle alcoholic whose only distraction from the bottle lay in cards. Without Finny she would have gone entirely to pieces, but he kept the fabric of grandeur tightly laced around her like a corset. In return for his care she gave him what vagrant affection she had, put all her interest in the company into his hands and refused even to listen to the complaints of her other children. With her stock added to his own, Finny's dominion over the business was absolute.

Mrs. Coit, though she did not much care about it, vaguely felt that her oldest son should marry, and she approved of Esther. It was a relief to have as a candidate a girl whom she already knew. The other Coits hoped that marriage might humanize Finny, or that it would at least provide an intermediary through whom he could be more closely approached. The family as a whole was thus inclined to favor Esther. Much to her amusement she found herself now cultivated by Finny's youngest sister, Cynthia Fearing. Their joint abandonment by Reese had not provided the basis for a very easy relationship, and after their divorces they had almost ceased to see each other. Now, however, Cynthia was all solicitude. She was very much taken up with an idle and handsome young man called George Wrexam for whom she hoped to find employment in the family business.

"You're not thinking of marrying him, are you?" Esther asked.

"Of course I'm thinking of marrying him," Cynthia retorted with a toss of her head. "Women are always thinking of marrying the men they talk about. Particularly divorced women." She looked at Esther darkly, but got no response. "What terrifies me is that *if* I married George and *if* he went into the business, Finny would send us out to Omaha to run the store there. That's Finny's way of doing things. He sent Mary's husband to Seattle. And that poor boy of Aunt May's has been lost somewhere in North Carolina for God knows how long!"

"I think Finny's quite right. How can you learn a business by sitting in New York night clubs?"

"Oh, Esther! You're as bad as he is. I might have known it!"

"Then why come to me?"

"Because *you* can talk to him. You can tell him that he

needs us right here in town. Honestly, Esther, I could give more parties and entertain more business people than —"

Esther cut her short. "That's not the way Finny sells furniture."

"Oh, God!" Cynthia groaned. "Even after Reno you're still a girl scout!"

With the attentions of Finny Coit and his family Esther found that she was spending more nights than usual in town where she always stayed at her mother's apartment. Mrs. Means was not only ecstatic to have her; she was even willing to go down herself to Parmelee Cove to spend the night with the children if the nurse wanted to go out. But when old Mrs. Parmelee began to decline, Esther felt obliged to spend more time with her, and her visits to the city became less frequent. There was no real reason, with so many children and grandchildren living so close by, that Esther should have had to undertake this, except that she wanted to. She rather fancied herself in the role of a trained nurse, moving silently and efficiently about a darkened room. Reese had always sneered at this, but was it so terrible to want to help? Mrs. Parmelee was subject to fits of childish petulance and to distressing illusions, and her children were firmly of the opinion that her grandchildren should be allowed "to remember Granny as she used to be." This drastically reduced the number of sickbed visitors, and Alfred Parmelee's refusal to do more than grunt "hello" to his mother from the bedroom door reduced it still further. The old lady's daughters and daughter-in-law were more than grateful, therefore, to Esther for her availability, particularly as she seemed to have such a soothing effect on the patient. Esther would send the nurse out for a walk and sit for a whole afternoon, knitting by the old lady's bed and giving quiet rational answers to loud, irrational questions. It mattered very little to her that Mrs. Parmelee's mind was largely gone. Reese's grandmother had been the head of the family all during the years of Esther's marriage; she had been the symbol of the life to which Esther had tried to adapt herself. If, at the end, the old lady submitted herself with more patience to Esther than to her own blood kin, was it not fair to take this as a token of how far she had succeeded at the Cove? Birth and death, growth and decay, were only parts of the same process. Each had its separate beauties and distinctions.

One Sunday afternoon when she was sitting with Mrs. Parmelee, the nurse came in, and said that "Mr. Parmelee" was outside to see her. As she stepped out into the long, dark upstairs hall, closing the bedroom door softly behind her, she was startled to see not Reese's father but Reese himself. He seemed as startled as she.

"How's Granny?"

"About the same. Do you want to see her?"

"Of course I want to see her. Is there any reason I shouldn't?"

"Well — she's sometimes a bit odd with people she's not used to."

"She's quite used to me."

"I mean, people she hasn't been seeing recently."

"Look here, Esther," he said impatiently, "I know all about Aunt Fanny's theories. It's just a way of excusing everybody's laziness. I blew Joan up when she told me she hadn't been to see Granny in a month!"

"But, Reese, it would be so distressing for her!"

"Well, who the hell is Joan not to be distressed? Letting her own grandmother die alone, a few hundred yards away, so she can preserve a lace valentine memory and you can play Florence Nightingale! Will this family *never* come to grips with reality?"

Esther's heart was beating violently, painfully. "They're not very realistic about old ladies' deathbeds, true," she half whispered in a panting voice. "They don't have your cool, clear head. Why don't you go in now and ask your grandmother to change her will? Maybe she'll write a codicil for Mr. Levine!"

Reese simply brushed past her and opened his grandmother's door. Esther stood in the corridor for a few moments after he had gone in, waiting. Then she suddenly heard the old lady's voice raised almost to a wail: "Why, Reese! Reese, my darling, darling boy! Where have you *been?*" And she heard the sound of Reese sitting down on the bed as he was probably embracing her and his voice answer: "Poor Granny, I've been all tied up in a lawsuit. But now I'm here, I'll stay for a good long visit."

Esther went downstairs without her knitting. She paused at the threshold of the living room and looked about it as if for the last time. Then she went out the door and across the lawn to her own house and telephoned Finny to say that she would be free, after all, to dine with him in town that night.

When she met him at the restaurant she had a small valise. Perhaps he would be kind enough to take her to the station after dinner? She was going back to Parmelee Cove for the night. Actually, she had made up her mind that she was going to stay in his apartment, but for this a nightgown and a toothbrush were absolutely essential. Any other prospect would have been bound to repel him. At dinner she allowed herself to appear a bit weary and discouraged, but not to the point of failing to enjoy his company. When he suggested afterwards that they go to a night club for a drink before her train, she said there was nothing she'd like better, but would he mind terribly — she *was* a bit tired — if they went up to his apartment instead where it was quiet?

Finny's apartment had been decorated by his Fifth Avenue store and looked like one of its show windows, bright and chintzy and new, a collection of wedding presents. Esther had the feeling that everything she used, whether a glass or ashtray, was being used for the first time. Finny mixed her a drink and then excused himself for several minutes. When she heard his step in the hall she picked up her handkerchief so that he could just see her daubing her eyes as he came in.

"You'll have to forgive me," she said, taking a deep breath as if she had just regained control. "It's idiotic of me, I know. And I was always brought up to believe that it was unpardonable to show emotion outside the home. But everything seems to have hit me at once today. First poor old Mrs. Parmelee being worse and then my being made to feel such an outsider. Don't worry, I'm over it now." She smiled with determination up at his troubled face.

"Don't go back to Northfield tonight, Esther."

"Don't go back? I've got to. Mummy's using my room in her apartment tonight for a friend."

"You could stay here. I mean, downstairs in the house."

"And bother your mother's maids at this time of night? I wouldn't think of it."

"Well, you could stay *here* then." He hesitated and began to flush. "I mean, in the guest bedroom. I have one in back. It's never been used."

Esther pretended to be suddenly struck with the idea. "Oh, do you think I really and truly could? Would it be decent? Of course, I'd be gone early in the morning, and you could tell the maid it was an old college friend." She clapped her hands together. "Oh, Finny, what a lark! I just can't seem to face the prospect of Parmelee Cove tonight!"

It was agreed, and she went back to inspect the room with a good deal of exclaiming and laughing. It turned out that there were no sheets on the bed, but these she found in a linen closet that he did not even know he had and spread them on with a competent hand that he clearly admired. When she had finished, and they were standing by the bed, he suddenly caught her hand and blurted out:

"Would you be furious if I asked you if I could spend the night in here too?"

She looked very startled for a moment, but then smiled. "I shouldn't be furious, Finny dear, no. I have no right to be furious after the bold way I agreed to stay here. A man's a man, after all. But may I refrain from being furious and still refrain from accepting? Do you mind, my dear, terribly? Do you feel I've led you on? I'm so sorry!"

"Forget it," he said briefly, and she could almost hear the exhalation of his sigh of relief. She pictured him lying happily alone in his own room that night, staring up at the ceiling like one of the heroes in Stendhal whom Reese had always been talking about, murmuring: "It's all right! I *asked* her! I asked her, and she refused!" If such were his exultations, she reflected dryly, he was exulting too soon. But she would give him something real to exult over.

"I tell you what I *will* do," she said, as if making a great concession to his manly insistence. "I'll get all ready for bed and let you come in and kiss me good night. Will you do that? That will take away some of the strangeness that I always feel in a new room. It will help me to sleep."

It was fortunate that the bed in the guest room was double. When she had combed her hair and put on her new blue silk nightgown, she got into bed, pulled up the covers neatly about her and called him. He was dressed in clean pajamas and a pink robe the color of his cheeks. As she had suspected, the limitation that she had placed on his manly commitment made him almost passionate in his embraces. He kissed her repeatedly on the lips and ran his hands up and down her back with little whimpering sounds. She drew her head back, as if overcome, so that he was kissing her neck.

"Please, darling," she murmured, her eyes closed, "do something for me. Just lie down beside me till I get to sleep. Just till I get to sleep, mind you. I've been feeling so alone, and you've been such a comfort. I'll never get to sleep if you leave me. Please!"

He switched off the light and lay down beside her, and she waited, motionless until she heard his snores. Then she, too, went to sleep. But when she woke up in the middle of the night, she moaned at first in a low tone and then shrilly, as if she were having a nightmare. He sat up suddenly, half asleep, and then reached down suddenly to take her in his arms. She had never had ecstasy in the sexual act, and this helped her to concentrate more effectively on assisting him. It was not a very fine experience for either, but for him the ecstasy was in accomplishment and for her in the knowledge that she had given him a reassurance that all his stores and factories could never give. She would make use, too, of this assurance, use for him and use for her. There was really no end of the things that she could do for him. Or of the things that he could do for her children.

7

THE SURROGATE'S opinion in "Matter of Howland" appeared in the *Law Journal* only a few weeks after the end of the trial. It was very brief for a case which had received so much publicity. After summarizing the evidence on both sides it concluded in rather grudging language:

> The testatrix must be deemed to have known what she was doing. She was aware of who were the natural objects of her bounty for she divided her residuary estate among her nephew and niece. The legacy to Levine was certainly a large one and perhaps out of proportion to the size of her estate, but when it is set against the background of her proven feelings of friendship and gratitude and the failure on the part of the objectants to show any evidence of incompetence beyond occasional eccentricity, I am obliged to sustain the codicil.

Levine was in court that day, but late in the afternoon he came into Reese's office and closed the door. He was not a demonstrative man, and his putting his feet up on Reese's desk went far to convey a sense of his jubilation. During the trial he had several times protested to Reese that he was fighting the Howlands purely as a matter of principle and that if he won he would turn the whole bequest over to charity in memory of their aunt. There was no further discussion now of this possibility.

"I suppose they'll appeal," Reese said bleakly.

"Of course, they'll appeal, but what good will that do them?" Nothing could dampen Amos's spirits. "Why should the Appellate Division reverse a jury? There's no question of law involved. Facts, my boy, simple facts. You've nailed them to the wall with your facts!"

"Well we were lucky, I guess."

"Lucky? What did luck have to do with it? We had the winning side, and we won! We were bound to win! Where you were so terrific was that you not only won, you crucified them! And that brings me to the point. You've done something for me. Now I want to do something for you."

"I didn't do anything." Reese shrugged. "That's my job, isn't it? You pay me for it." But he settled back in his chair and watched Amos narrowly. He was curious to see how much of a bonus a man so stingy would propose.

"I've been doing a lot of thinking about it," Amos continued. "Like how much I'd have had to pay outside counsel to do the same job. Twenty-five thousand?" He paused, smiled and suddenly wagged his finger reprovingly at Reese. "And then, too, I have to take into consideration that if you'd sent Miss Howland to a lawyer I *didn't* know, in the first place, instead of trying to talk her out of making any legacy, we mightn't have had all this fuss!"

It was a shrewd thrust, but Reese was suddenly too angry even to discuss it. "Damn it all, Amos, you don't have to look for mistakes on my part in order to cut down a bonus you have no intention of giving me! You don't owe me anything. I get my salary, and that's that!"

"Tsk, tsk, my boy, your temper, please!" Amos held up his

hands placatingly. "That's a terrible temper you have! Save it for the courtroom. We may need it there. And don't worry about bonuses. You're right. I have no intention of giving you one. I've decided to ask you to be my partner instead. And give you twenty-five per cent of the firm's take!"

Reese's temper fled away as he sat upright so suddenly that his tilted chair crashed to the floor. "Your partner?"

"Why not? I've never had one, and I figure it's time I began. I'm not getting any younger, and I need someone to take part of the load off me." Amos's tone was suddenly very soft. "I'm not kidding myself, Reese. If I'm going to hang on to a man as good as you, I'm going to have to pay. I'm going to have to make it worth your while. Very well, I'm willing. I'm not a man to quibble about the price. What about it? What about Levine & Parmelee?"

Reese closed his lips tightly, for he felt his breath coming in pants. Financially, the offer was dazzling. He knew enough of Amos's affairs to know that it would more than triple his income. But his habit of suspicion permitted him in the next moment to see the advantages to Amos of such an arrangement. In the first place, in Amos's tax bracket, it would cost him next to nothing. It would simply mean diverting to Reese money that would otherwise be paid to the Federal Treasury. In the second place, it would guarantee for the future a young and industrious assistant. And finally it would associate with a name that was currently something less than fragrant the respectability of the Parmelees. Oh, yes, one could be sure that under the garden of Amos's generosity lay the sturdy weeds of a good bargain!

"That's quite an offer, Amos. You've taken me a bit aback. Mind if I ask for a day to think it over?"

Amos was too shrewd himself not to approve the concealment of any elation that his offer might have brought. He smiled broadly. "That's right, my boy. Take your time. Take all the time in the world. And I'll tell Miss Nussbaum to open the firm books for your inspection. I don't expect you to buy a pig in a poke!"

It was obvious to Reese that he was not going to do any more work that day, and he left the office early. Rosina and Grace were giving a joint cocktail party that evening at Grace's mother's apartment; it was a very special affair at which Mrs. Doremus herself was expected. As he had an hour to kill before he was due, he went to his favorite bar in the Village. Sitting alone in an old, dark wood booth, he drank beer and pondered what he was almost sure would be his ultimate refusal to accept Amos's offer. But why? Was it because of the disloyalty of his attitude to Levine at the trial and his feeling that this could never be the basis for a happy partnership? Or was it because of his lingering distaste for Amos's cultivation of Miss Howland, a performance that repelled him, even assuming the motives to have been innocent? Yet if Amos was innocent of mercenary motives, what did his distaste for Amos's friendship with the old lady boil down to, except, as Rosina had put it, snobbishness? If Amos had innocently liked her and innocently written her those sentimental notes, if he had innocently believed their relationship to be a special one, then the moral reason for Reese's hostility collapsed, to be replaced perhaps by the unrootable prejudice of a St. Lawrence graduate against the author of that kind of slush. One could be the employee but never the partner of such a man: that would be the attitude of Parmelee Cove. Reese considered carefully the possibility that it might be his own attitude. Then he rejected it. He minded the tone of the notes to Miss Howland; he abominated their unctuousness, but he could have swallowed them. What he could not basically bring himself to accept was the threat to his liberty.

He had cut himself loose from his old ties at an agonizing price, and now it was done. He was free. It was as if he were swimming naked beneath the surface of a translucent bay, moving easily in the cool, clean water, only to become aware, below him, of the reaching tentacles that wanted again to snatch him. Was it not only sense to dart up and away? What were humans and their ceaseless yearning for commitments but so many octopuses? What did Amos want but to bind him forever to a partnership? And Rosina, for all her independence, for all her affectation of indifference, had she not betrayed herself the other night? Had he not seen the fury of her jealousy and peered into her basic female desire to own him? Could none of them leave him be? He brought his fist down so hard on the worn surface of the table, rugged with initials, that his beer spilled over. Startled, he looked up at the bar to see if people had turned around, but nobody had. He noticed, however, the round blond back of Duey Lispenard's head. He was talking, of all things, to a girl.

She was a young girl, dark haired and pretty, and was listening to Duey attentively. She had an air of never having been so far south on Manhattan before, and Reese remembered that Rosina had told him how Duey had been seen about with a debutante called Katie Fisher. Anstiss, it appeared, had been sponsoring their friendship in a desperate effort to force a wedge between Duey and Cliffie Suter. Reese quite forgot his own inner conflicts in his immediate absorption with the couple before him. It was obvious that the poor girl fancied herself admired by a genius. The spokesman for flaming youth had at last kindled a spark in the heart of a near contemporary! Duey suddenly turned and saw him and waved a hand, seeming pleased. Then he whispered something to the girl, and together they came over to Reese's booth.

"I say, Reese, old boy, I'd like you to meet my fiancée, Katie Fisher."

Reese jumped up. "Your fiancée!"

"It's going to be in the papers tomorrow," Duey said proudly as the girl smiled, shy and embarrassed. "Mrs. Fisher's giving a little party for us tonight. If you and Rosy are free, we'd love to have you drop in after dinner."

"Well, I'll be darned!" Reese looked in astonishment from one to the other. Then he recollected himself. "I certainly congratulate you. Only I'm afraid I can't make the party because I'm going to one Rosy's giving. It may run on too late."

"Oh, Rosy's party, I wanted to ask you about that," Duey continued with a frown. "Do you think she'd mind if I brought Katie? I'd like to take her in for a few minutes."

"Why, of course not!"

"I see." Duey nodded several times thoughtfully. Then he turned back to Katie. "You go sit at the bar a second, will you, sweetie? I want to ask old Reese here a question."

The girl went obediently back to her stool, and Duey and Reese sat down on opposite sides of the booth table. Duey rested his chin on his hands and stared straight into Reese's face. It was impossible to tell what went on behind that remote, arrogant stare.

"I haven't told Cliffie," he said at last. "Do you suppose he'll be there?"

"Yes."

The light grey eyes were unblinking. "And Anstiss?"

"Oh, certainly."

"It doesn't matter so much about Anstiss," Duey said with a shrug. "I expect Anstiss knows."

Reese began to comprehend what a sorry mess it all was. The poor girl at the bar was to be sacrificed because this little peacock wanted to boast himself a man, or because he needed her father's money for his wretched play, or possibly only because Anstiss Stranahan hoped that she would prove a weaker opponent than Cliffie Suter. Duey himself was sublimely unaware of his ultimate incapacity to satisfy either sex; he thought it was enough if he preened his feathers and waited for their inevitable attentions. This hardly mattered to Reese so long as only Anstiss was unaccountably infatuated, or even Cliffie, or even perhaps poor old Grace Chess. He was perfectly willing to let all the precious ridiculers continue indefinitely their grotesque strutting around this marble-hearted Pan. It was more than likely that they even derived a perverse pleasure in debasing themselves before this deity of youth. But the girl *had* to be saved. Her eyes had to be opened.

"Why don't we go to Rosy's now!" Reese exclaimed. "The three of us! I'll tell Cliffie myself when we get there. It's always better to do these things at parties. Then there can be no recrimination. The atmosphere operates as a kind of anesthetic. Believe me, it's the kinder way of doing it."

"Are you sure?"

"I'm sure. Leave it to me!"

At Mrs. Chess's apartment on Lexington Avenue the ladies from *A Woman's World* seemed like so many gaudy parrots on perches against the love seat, the framed embroideries, the horsehair sofa. The atmosphere was muted by the presence of old Mrs. Chess, so sweet and vague and hospitable, offering tea to people who felt they could not refuse it. Mrs. Doremus, in gold lamé, was seated by her hostess and making every gracious effort, but her graciousness crumbled away before the hard front of Mrs. Chess's near total deafness. Rosina, very nervous, in a new red dress that was not becoming, pulled Reese aside and coached him in a hurried whisper as to which corners of the party most needed attention. She barely noticed Duey and Miss Fisher. Reese promised to do as he was told and then went straight over to the bar table where he had spotted Cliffie Suter alone.

"Have you met Duey's fiancée?" he asked. He had a mo-mentary misgiving when he saw Cliffie's large white bulbous face congeal and felt the clutch of his hand on his arm.

"Is it true? Are you sure?" Cliffie asked desperately. "How do you know? Is that she, over there? Oh, no, Reese! *Is* it?"

"Certainly. Duey told me so himself. It's going to be in the papers tomorrow."

"Tomorrow!" Cliffie was actually panting. As different emotions began to glide over his face, like the reflected lights on a ceiling at night from cars moving outside, Reese was aware of the sudden rumble of his wrath. "Tomorrow!" he cried. "Why it's not even decent! That bitch, Anstiss, can't wait a minute to get him away from me, can she?"

"Now, Cliffie, old man, take hold of yourself."

"Take hold of myself!" Cliffie's big eyes bulged at him un-comprehendingly. "Take hold . . . !" He exuded a long sigh, and the danger of his attracting the attention of the room seemed momentarily to pass. "Which is the lucky girl?" he demanded in a tone of suddenly assumed enthusiasm. "Oh, over there, of course! I can see what a darling she is. Shall we go over and pay our respects to the happy pair?"

Reese followed him closely as he sauntered over to Duey and Katie. The girl looked at Cliffie wonderingly, and Duey stared at the floor as the high, squeaky congratulations issued forth:

"Well, well! Why don't you keep your old friends in-formed, Duey? Are you ashamed of us? Are you ashamed to let this beautiful child see the kind of riffraff you've been associating with? Don't believe everything he says about us, Miss Fisher. We're not *all* that bad. There are a few sad old souls among us who have felt a genuine affection for the lad and who have had a true understanding of his gifts. I speak not, mind you, of a certain she-vulture who tries vainly to conceal her somatic itchings under the feeble disguise of a matronly Maecenas, but rather of the older man's high serious affection for aspiring youth. And affection, as John Addington Symonds tells us, existed among the Greeks, however vilified by later critics. That was, in fact, a chief glory of Argos. Have you read John Addington Symonds, Miss Fisher?"

"I'm afraid not."

"I see there are many things in which you need instruction. Come, my dear, to the sofa with Uncle Cliffie and let him warn you of the Scyllas and Charybdises through which your frail and beautiful bark must pass. I sing, O Muse, of the perils of Stranahania! Come!"

Reese watched with misgiving as Cliffie led the bewildered Miss Fisher away, pausing at the bar to refill his glass to the brim with undiluted gin. He was about to warn Duey to follow them when his sleeve was plucked, and Rosina drew him aside.

"What's all this about?" she asked in a sharp whisper. "Are they really engaged?"

"Yes."

"And Cliffie just found out?" He nodded. "You told him? *Why*, for God's sake?"

"He had to find out some time."

"Yes, but why here? And why *now*? You know how light a head he has. He might do anything!"

"But you don't see it, Rosy!" he exclaimed with an attempt at enthusiasm. "It makes your party! All of Anstiss's little group have been warming their hands against the one small coal of Duey's youth. And now it's removed! Don't you see how dramatic it is? It's like *Rheingold* when the giants drag away Freia, and age descends over Valhalla. Usually with the help of a scrim."

Just then a particularly harsh laugh burst from Cliffie's corner, and Rosina glanced nervously around. "I happen to be giving a cocktail party," she retorted, "and not a performance of the *Ring*. You started this, and you'll have to keep an eye on him. If he ruins this party, I'll never forgive you, Reese!"

Reese hurried back to find Duey, but the latter was talking to Mrs. Doremus, keeping his eyes averted from the part of the room where Cliffie was lecturing his fiancée. Obviously, Duey was not going to be any help at all. And it was useless, of course, even to hope to induce any of the magazine people to do the smallest social favor. Grace Chess would normally oblige, but she was a co-hostess and could not be disturbed. There was no way that he could gather a group around Cliffie to act as an absorbent to the painter's increasing excitement, and so, with Rosina's admonitory eye still on him, he went over himself to try, as in a modern version of a Greek drama, to make an individual do the job of a whole chorus. Katie looked up gratefully as he joined them, but Cliffie, who had drained his glass and taken another from a passing tray, ignored him entirely. He was talking of the problems created by mothers, and in particular, by Duey's mother, a lady whom Reese had never met, but who had furnished the only subject on which he had ever heard Anstiss and Cliffie agree. She was, apparently, the origin of all poor Duey's problems.

"And yet, of course, for all her dim little bourgeois standards, Mother Lispenard is not a bad sort of woman," Cliffie conceded. "You will have no trouble with her if you assert yourself firmly at the start. Tell her: 'Mother Lispenard, let it be understood that you come to Duey and me only on invitation.' The old creature will whimper a bit and talk about what darling Duey owes her, but when she gives in, you'll have her trained for life. No, she's not your real problem. That, my dear, will be a certain tall cold drink of water, into which I observe Scotch is being ineffectively poured, over there talking to Rosina Street."

"You mean Mrs. Stranahan? But I *like* Mrs. Stranahan!"

"You like Mrs. Stranahan!" Cliffie repeated, mimicking her. He rolled his eyes at Reese. "Did you hear that, Reese, my boy? She *likes* Goody Stranahan. Do you like measles, my dear? And poison ivy?"

"Take it easy, Cliffie, will you?" Reese warned him.

Cliffie eyed him coldly. "First, I must take hold of myself, and now I must take it easy," he retorted. "My dear Reese, for a lawyer you have a most restricted vocabulary."

"Keep your voice down. Let's not have a scene."

"Are you afraid that the Stranahan will hear?" Cliffie demanded indignantly. "Let her hear! Why should I care? Because I might be excluded from the next meeting of her preciously ridiculous group? How would she dare? Am I not the only person who ever graced her drawing room who has been able to convert his own fantasies — for what is art but fantasy? — into hard cash? Do you think any of the others could market their sleazy little daydreams? Never! That is why they come waddling into Anstiss's, lowing like so many unmilked cows, to let it ooze out there. Phew! Small wonder that I have almost stifled there!"

"Nobody made you go," Reese pointed out.

"That's just where you're wrong! It was that dear boy over there whose presence drew me into the wasteland of Stranahania like a guiding star! Do you think if *he* hadn't been there —? But never mind." Cliffie leaned over her to give Katie's hand several small encouraging pats. "He will go no more, I am sure. He will have better things to do henceforth. He will have this sweet creature at home, and they will have many babies as beautiful as themselves. Won't you, my dear? Beautiful babies whom old Uncle Cliffie can beautifully paint? What have you to do with wastelands or sterility?"

Reese turned from poor Katie's furious blush to see Anstiss herself bear slowly down upon them.

"I'm warning her, Anstiss!" Cliffie cried shrilly. "I'm warning her against you and me! Against *age!* What have young people like Duey and her to do with age?"

Anstiss came to a stop before him. "I'm sure that Duey will give up many of his acquaintances when he marries," she said with a small, ominous smile. "Men usually have to. But I doubt if his criterion will be their age."

"Oh? And what do you not doubt it will be?"

"Well, it's customary, I believe, for the husband to give up old ties of a sentimental nature."

"Oh, what scorn, what Olympian scorn!" Cliffie threw back his head and emitted a scream of laughter. "I'm crushed! I'm pulverized! Nothing will raise me now from the gutters in which I beg." He suddenly dropped heavily to his knees on the rug. "Except your gold, O lady bountiful!" He held out two fat hands, cupped, to Anstiss. "Give a few farthings of your excess! It will not only relieve that stern mentor, your conscience. Better yet! It will provide a new topic for the ridiculers. Think, Anstiss! A *new* topic!"

Anstiss's face was livid with contempt and fury. "You're too cheap to be borne," she hissed. Jack Stranahan's bald head appeared suddenly over her shoulder, and his eyes bulged like Cliffie's as he took in the latter's kneeling figure.

"Is he bothering you, Anstiss?" he cried. Reese noticed that, when excited, his voice rose almost as high as Cliffie's.

"He's being thoroughly repellent. Come away, dear."

"For two cents I'd smash his fat pansy face in!"

Cliffie fell backwards against a sofa with a real scream of laughter. "Oh wondrous!" he cried. "Oh passing wondrous! So dirty a pot to malign so clean a kettle!"

At this everything happened. Jack Stranahan fell on Cliffie, and in a moment they were thrashing about the floor like two fighting squirrels fallen from a limb. A chair was knocked over and then a whole table of drinks with a tremendous roar. There were shrieks from several ladies and a general convergence of the room around the fighting pair. Reese swooped upon them and, catching Jack Stranahan by the shoulders, tried to tear him away, but because of the latter's weight he stumbled and another table with glasses turned over. The room was now pandemonium. Reese finally succeeded in dragging Stranahan off Cliffie, but the latter, staggering to his feet, shrieking: "Dirty faggot!" came after them again. Reese, holding Stranahan pinioned, saw a red figure glide suddenly in between him and the approaching Cliffie and heard a sharp slap.

"There!" cried Rosina in a loud, fierce voice. "Now, get out of here, Cliffie Suter, and stay out!"

In a very little while it was over. Cliffie left, sobbing. Anstiss and Jack Stranahan waited moodily by the door until he had gone down in the elevator and then followed him. Nobody apologized. Grace Chess took her mother to her bedroom and returned to whisper to everyone that the old lady had been upset by the noise, and would people mind terribly leaving now? There were murmured offers to help "clean up," and people drifted away. Mrs. Doremus said in a clear, smiling tone: "Well, girls, nobody can accuse you of giving dull parties, can they?" Duey Lispenard appeared from behind the piano to reclaim his fiancée who looked dazed. Reese noticed that she did not take the arm that Duey offered her as they left.

When everyone had gone and Grace had returned to sit for a few minutes with her mother, Rosina silently poured herself a drink.

"I think I need this," she said tonelessly, "before I clean up."

Reese was standing by the fireplace. He was disturbed by her calm. He had hoped that she would have one terrible burst of temper and that they would then go out for dinner. "*I'll* clean up," he said.

"No," she replied in the same tone, "I don't want you to. I want you to go now. I think you'll agree you've done enough damage for one day."

"Look, Rosy," he pleaded. "It's not as bad as you think. Really, it's not. There wasn't one person in this room, including Mrs. Doremus, who wouldn't rather have seen that rumpus than the best show in town!"

"Yes," she said nodding, "you *would* see it that way."

"But that's the way it was! They can dine out on it for months!"

"You mean they can dine out on *me*."

"Do you grudge them a little thing like that?"

"Of course I grudge them that. Because I care. I don't despise people the way you do."

"Oh, Rosy! Despise people?"

She nodded wearily, sitting down on a sofa. "All you want to do, basically, is make fun of people," she continued. "All you want out of life is a little perch from which you can sneer at the passing parade. You sneered at your family and Esther. You sneered at your old firm and now at Amos. You sneer at Anstiss and at Cliffie. Well, I'm tired of your sneers, that's all."

"Surely you don't think I sneer at you?"

"Of course you do. You sneer at my job and my friends."

"Rosy!"

"You do, Reese." She turned away now, but he could see that she was crying, and he started over to her. Her hand gestured him sharply away. "You knew what this party meant to me," she continued in a strangled voice. "You knew that I wanted everything to be nice for Mrs. Doremus. You knew how I'd worked on it. Yet you thought nothing of turning it into a shambles for the sake of one lousy joke! What was it to you but a cockfight?"

"Rosy, for God's sake, be reasonable! How was I to know they'd behave that way?"

"But you didn't *care!*" When he touched her arm, she jumped up and away from him. "Let me be!" she almost shouted. "Don't *touch* me! Get out out of my life before you hurt me as badly as you've hurt the others!"

"Why don't you go along now, Reese?" It was Grace Chess, standing in the doorway. "I'll look after her and give her a pill. I think she'd better have a quiet supper and spend the night here with me."

Reese walked all the way back downtown to the bar in the Village that he had left that afternoon. He had to keep moving to dull the sharpest stings of Rosina's last remark. He was even surprised at how sharp they were. For how could he have been caught off guard by the very stroke he had so long anticipated? Was all his proud rebellion to end in the bathos of surrender to anything as trite and obvious as a woman's tears? It seemed pitiful indeed that after kicking down the stable door, after leaping every stile and gate, he should now stand still, in a field of clover, placidly chewing his cud while Rosina tripped over to him and slipped a flowered harness about his neck. And yet that, he felt suddenly sure, was exactly the way it was going to be. For what alternative was there? Would he not be just as much a cap-

tive if he made himself turn his back on her, if he obliged himself to deny her his consolation? What if she gave up seeing
him? What if he no longer had the prospect of their arguments, of the sudden flare of her temper? What would his
days be like if he could no longer discuss them with Rosina?

By the time he was back at his booth with a drink in hand,
the prospect had become unthinkable. It was too late to give
up Rosina now. When he thought of the way she had turned
away from him and remembered her sudden sob, when he
considered the hours of her careful, meticulous planning for
that ridiculous party, when he remembered the passion which
she put into everything that he cared nothing about, he knew
that he was beaten. He was like a man lying on a beach, half
submerged in a receding wave, who has ceased to struggle
and feels the strong pull of the water turning him over, feels
the suck against his back and the swoosh of the sand on his
legs. After his second drink he was in a telephone booth.

"Amos," he said when the number answered, "I'll take it!"

"You'll take what?" came a sleepy, startled voice. "My
God, is that you, Reese? Do you know it's after midnight?
You've woken my wife up, too."

"Good night, partner. I'm sorry."

He hung up and rang the Chesses' apartment. He smiled as
he heard it ring and ring and thought how angry Rosina
would be. "I'm sorry, Grace," he said when she answered.
"I've got to speak to Rosy. I know it's late, but I've got to."

"Reese, she's asleep!"

"I tell you I've got to speak to her!" he exclaimed, his tone
quickening with anger. He felt a sudden panic that Grace
might hang up. "I tell you it's important!"

"All right, all right!"

A few minutes later he heard Rosina's voice, sleepy and
toneless. "What is it, Reese?"

"I've decided to marry you!" he cried. "To make up for what I did!" There was a long pause. "Are you there?"

"I suppose it's the least you can do," she said in the same flat voice.

He laughed in sudden sharp jubilation. "Can I come up now?"

"To Mrs. Chess's? Are you crazy?"

"Yes!"

"Oh, no, Reese." Rosina's tone was softer now. "I've had a sleeping pill, and I'm half out, and you wouldn't believe what my hair looks like. Go home and call me in the morning. First thing."

"I love you!"

"Try to remember that in the morning," she murmured. There was another pause, and this time it was she who laughed. "But if you don't, there's someone who will!" she exclaimed in almost her old, sharp tone. "And I think you may take a bit of reminding, too!"

8

He CALLED the next morning as soon as he was awake and asked Rosina if he could come up to Mrs. Chess's apartment. It was Saturday, and he was not going to work.

"Amos and I are partners now!" he boasted. "I didn't want to tell you last night. I was afraid you'd be after my money!"

"Oh, Reese, how wonderful!" She sounded confused and shy. "It all really happened, then, last night? I mean your phone call?"

"Don't try and get out of it!"

"Oh, darling." She gave a sudden laugh. "If you only knew!"

"Can I come up now?"

But she still didn't want him to come up to Mrs. Chess's. She was very firm about it. She needed more time, she insisted, to pull herself together, and she would meet him at the Greek's for an early lunch at noon. He had to be content with this and to go for a long walk until the appointed hour. At the restaurant, waiting for her, he wondered if she would be wearing the same red dress that she had worn at the cocktail party. But he immediately saw that she wasn't. She came over to his table in a blue dress that he had never seen before, and they held hands for a constrained moment of silence.

"I'm sorry about Cliffie," he murmured.

"Don't be."

"Did they break much?"

"No."

"Can't I pay Grace for it?"

"If it will make you feel any better."

The drinks that he had already ordered were put down on the table.

"To us," he said, picking up his glass.

"To us!"

"Did you really feel desperately about the party being broken up?"

"No, I thought it rather exhilarating."

"You say that now. But you looked sick at the time."

"Women can enjoy looking sick."

"Honestly?"

"Don't make me go on, or you'll think the whole thing was a trick."

"For what?"

"Why, to catch you, of course!"

"This is impossible," he exclaimed suddenly. "We can't just sit here and make chit-chat. Let's finish these and go to my apartment. What do you say?"

Rosina said nothing, but she nodded quickly, and they left the restaurant after swallowing their drinks in silence. They went to his apartment and stayed there until Sunday, by which time they were as much at ease as if they had been married a year. On Monday he went to the office and asked for the following week off, which was the most he could possibly expect in face of the trial calendar, and on Thursday he and Rosina were married in the chambers of a judge who was a friend of Amos's in the presence of Grace Chess and Andy Fearing. Reese could hardly believe that Rosina would not have preferred a larger wedding, but she seemed sincere in her denials. She would not even write her mother until the day before the ceremony. As for the Parmelees, Reese drove down to the Cove on the preceding Tuesday to explain his plans to them. His news was not wholly a surprise nor was it wholly unwelcome. His mother, at least, had liked Rosina. She was hurt and mortified that he wanted none of the family present at his wedding, but, like everyone else, she had learned that Reese had his own way of doing things.

Andy had obtained for the new couple the loan of a friend's house on an almost deserted island in the Caribbean — Reese swore never again to make mock of his "café society" world — and on Friday evening, when the little sea plane that had borne them from Puerto Rico set them down by a pier that led to the longest and whitest beach by the bluest sea Reese had ever seen, the speed of so many changes had carried them almost beyond exhilaration.

"My God!" Rosina cried. "What a cover it would make!"

The effect, however, in the following days, of the sea and air, was to stifle such comments. She seemed to put aside entirely her magazine and Anstiss's little group; she had scratched the immediate past as totally as she must have once scratched her childhood, and she clung now passionately, even greedily, to this little week that seemed so oddly outside of time and space. Reese had never felt loved in that way before. What had drawn him first to Rosina and what had proved her strongest hold on him had been her resentment of his own attraction for herself and the interruption that it had threatened to her scheme of existence. With the collapse of her opposition had been born a dependence of equal strength; the hands that had once beat him off so fiercely now dug nails into his back and shoulders in moments of passion. At night he would sometimes awaken to find her arms wound tightly about his neck and to hear her murmur in her sleep that he mustn't ever leave her there, that he mustn't go home alone, as if she already forecast herself as an abandoned Ariadne and saw their small isle as a Naxos. He would lie awake, stroking the huddled figure at his side and hoping that, having battered down the sturdy little walls that she had erected, with such seeming success, around her bustling life, he might not prove the one to make her suffer from her new vulnerability. In the battle between them he had been wrong in fancying that she had been the victor. He was the less changed of the two.

Yet he also was changed. When he got up early in the morning and went out in a glass-bottomed boat to peer down at the blue and green marine life by the little rocks at the point, the kind of occupation that at other times would have held him rapt for hours, he found himself impatient for the time when Rosina would be awake and he could return to breakfast with her. Or when he was collecting sea shells down the beach and came upon one of especial beauty, he had to take it back to where she was reading under an umbrella and show it to her, nor did it matter if her interest was only perfunctory. He had to communicate, perhaps for the first time in his life. He had never, that he could remember, even in the beginning, wanted to communicate anything very personal to Esther. On the contrary, he had wanted to keep things from her, as he had kept them from his family. But it was fun now to steal up behind Rosina and take her book out of her hands and start to tell her something, and if he couldn't express it, or if he found after he had started that it was the kind of thought that fled with articulation, they would simply smile and kiss and perhaps make love. For Rosina, unlike Esther, never tired of that. He had glimpses of the frustration that must have been her old bedfellow in the very violence of her love-making.

"If I had gone up to your apartment that first night you took me out," she asked him once, wide-eyed, "do you think we'd be married now?"

"I think we'd have been married months ago!"

"Fat chance!" she retorted. "I'd have been your mistress for three weeks, and you'd have left me flat!"

"Because I wouldn't have 'respected' you?"

"Yes!"

"But I respect people who do what they want."

"Oh!" she exclaimed. "You assume I wanted to! Even then?"

"Of course I do. And, after all, you *did* come up in the end."

"But that was different!" she insisted, slapping him on the shoulder. "We were practically married then. And I'm glad I waited as long as I did." She made a sweeping gesture towards the sea. "I'm glad I waited for this. Aren't you?"

"The site doesn't matter. It's the girl that counts."

Yet the site was more important than he admitted to her. It struck him that islands had played a curious role in his life. During the war he had made what he felt to be his closest approach to the reality beneath the fantasy of things with the vision of sudden death on tiny atolls, mere pinpoints in the enveloping sky and sea. Under the vast blue neutral smile of infinity, microbes of men had struck at each other in bloody and futile fray. And now, alone on a long beach by a sapphire Caribbean, with a light warm wind stroking their bare bodies, with the lapping of small waves in their ears, he and Rosina made love and lay back to look up at the terns that darted and the pelicans that wheeled above. Was it not an equal glimpse of reality? Did not one merge with the surrounding infinite as much in the quick nervous spasm of love as in that of death? But when he tried to explain this to Rosina, she murmured something about the third act of *Tristan*, and he was put off. What an ass he was to try to express such things! It was late in the afternoon of their last day, and it was beginning to be almost chilly. He put a coat around her and went to sleep with his head on her breast. When she awakened him by rubbing a sandy finger on his forehead he noticed that her expression was grave.

"Please, darling," she begged, "I don't want to go back to New York."

He blinked and sat up. "Ever?"

"Well, not for weeks, anyway. Couldn't you cable your office?"

"You don't understand. I have cases coming up. You can't just walk out on them. Not and have any practice left."

She scooped up a handful of sand and threw it away. "I don't seem to care about your practice," she said impatiently.

"You, who were always the practical one?"

"But don't you see? That's just it! I've been practical all my life. I was a cold little practical child. I could never enjoy the morning without planning to enjoy the afternoon more. And after that the evening. I had no present. That's what you've given me, the present! If I only could have a little more time, I think I could learn to love the present always, wherever I was. I could get used to it! And then, darling, I'd be so much a better wife!"

He studied her eyes carefully and saw that she was in earnest. He debated for a moment cabling Amos, but no, it was impossible. He was due to argue an appeal the following Wednesday. "I'm sorry," he muttered, "but we can't risk it now. Just as I've started to make good. I want all sorts of things for you. And I still have to look out for my children and Esther —"

"You don't!" she cried indignantly. "You've done too much for them already! You've stripped yourself for them! Your mother told me so. You and I deserve a little time to ourselves! Just a few days together on a beach!"

"But we'll be together at home," he protested. "And I'll take you back here again. I promise!"

"There'll be other things at home. Things that will come between us!"

"What?"

"Oh, I don't know." She was looking morosely at the sea, both hands buried in the sand. "My job. My friends. All my old, silly life."

"You don't have to go on with your job."

"Oh, but I do! Even if I hate it! How else could I stand it with you away all day in the office?"

He put his hands on her shoulders and turned her around to kiss her. "Hate it, my eye!" he retorted. "You know you adore it!"

"I adore no one but you!" she cried fiercely and threw her arms tightly around his neck. She clung to him in what seemed almost a panic, and when he drew his head back, he was startled to see tears in her eyes.

"Poor silly," he murmured, running his hands down her back, "you'll find you can adore me in New York just as well." Over her shoulder, far down the beach, he saw the tiny spot of their approaching houseboy. "Come on!" he exclaimed. "It's time to go back for supper! Get some clothes on before Vincente catches you!"

That night they drank champagne and were very gay. Rosina said nothing further about extending their honeymoon and seemed resigned when they departed the next day. Their plane stopped off in Miami, and she bought all the current fashion magazines and studied them intently on the trip to

New York. Once he took one out of her hand and turned her chin so that she had to look at him.

"Are you mad at me?"

"What on earth for?"

"For taking you home."

"Not in the least." She laughed, and for the first time in the seven days of their marriage he wondered if she were being entirely sincere. "Reading this stuff is like tightening a seat belt. It prepares one for the jolt of coming down to earth!"

PART III

The Cove
Revisited

I

ON A SATURDAY AFTERNOON in early spring Rosina Parmelee
pushed a baby carriage with gleaming wheels and a dark blue
hood matching her suit up a sloping path in Central Park
towards the eroded Cleopatra's Needle. Little Agnes, now
six months old, already had some of her father's stockiness
and even a bit of his air of reserved decision. Rosina smiled
as she contemplated the likeness. She liked the spring air and
the new carriage and the park; she liked the red brick and the
Cretan arches of the old west front of the Metropolitan Museum and even the dirty, strutting pigeons that walked but
never flew from her approaching wheels. She wondered that
other mothers ever complained of the park. There were
enough different shades of green and enough well dressed
children for her to see it as a Renoir; she could censor for
herself the old, unshaven, corpselike men on the benches and
the team of Puerto Rican boys, in shiny red polo caps and yellow jackets, who sprinted past, shouting things to each other
that she did not wish to hear. For Rosina was determined to
have her Renoir, and nothing that had happened to her in the
past fifteen months had caused her in any way to doubt the
strength of her determination. Things had worked out well,
incredibly well, and she was beginning at last to settle down,
albeit wearily, to the curious prospect of happiness.

First and foremost, of course, was Reese. During their

week's honeymoon she had seemed to step outside of herself. It was as if all the sensitive aching little pieces of her ego had been packed together tightly, like parts of an old porcelain set, into a crate stuffed with the rags and tissue paper of love. For seven days she had enjoyed a novel ecstasy, walking on the beach with her husband hand in hand, collecting sea shells, sitting with him in the evening to exchange stories of pasts so utterly different. He had been carefree with her, devoid of sullenness and at times almost childishly excited. She had feared only that it might be an anticlimax to come back to New York, and so, indeed, it had been — at least for him. Some of his old sullenness had returned after a single day at the office. But with her, new happiness seemed to have created new appetites. Back in the city, there was the magazine and her editorial work and the small brownstone house that Reese had purchased in the eighties near the East River and the fascination of a whole family of in-laws and, finally, little Agnes herself. Oh, yes, it was her year, and it was only common sense to take as many tricks as possible in a winning streak.

Reese's financial position had been greatly improved by his partnership with Amos and by his grandmother's death which had occurred just after their return from the Caribbean. His share of her estate had gone, it was true, to Esther, but it had relieved him of the obligation to pay alimony and support. His family had hoped that Esther, who could have bought and sold the Parmelees since her marriage to Finny Coit and who had, in fact, bought most of Parmelee Cove from the old lady's executors, would renounce her legacy, but Esther had not seen fit to do this. Still, by Rosina's standards, she and Reese were rich. They had a part-time maid and a full-time nurse, a house, a car, several abstract paintings and the superlative baby carriage that she was now wheeling.

The house — she could not get over actually owning a house. She paused now, on her return from the park, to admire its shabby, honest, brownstone look, like that of a faithful, waiting dog. It was only four stories high and eighteen feet wide, with two windows to a floor, but the rooms were well shaped and there was a back yard of infinite possibilities. Of course, she had to do it all little by little; even the living room was less than half finished, but the Chinese screen and the yellow curtains with the humming-birds were already a tremendous start. It would come in time, and she *had* time. That was the incredible thing that she had to keep telling herself over and over again.

The colored girl, who opened the door and took little Agnes upstairs, told her that Mrs. Doremus was waiting in the living room. Rosina found her standing at the french window, looking out at the bare little yard. Smoke from her cigarette filtered critically back over her shoulder.

"Oh, don't look out *there*, Gilda!" Rosina exclaimed. "I haven't even touched that yet!"

"There's a sale of garden things at Coit's, my dear," Gilda replied, turning back into the room, "with just the thing you need for it. A little pink French marble basin with two horses' heads and a riding Cupid. It's angelic. And you'll never in the world believe where it comes from."

"Parmelee Cove."

"Oh," said Gilda, disappointed, "you've seen it?"

"No. But Mr. Coit has bought the place, and I know his wife's doing over the garden. I suppose she uses the store as her dump."

"Well, take my word for it. It will *make* your yard."

"I'm afraid we have to do one thing at a time." Rosina sat down to examine the layout for the next issue which Gilda had brought while the latter wandered about the room, carefully scrutinizing the screen and curtains. When Rosina had finished, they settled down to work. They worked well together. Gilda cared only about competent, successful people, and she had been quick, after Rosina's marriage, to recognize her as one of these. Once within the circle of Gilda's elect, all her brusqueness and snobbishness seemed more like saltiness and humor. In the thin air of Parnassus equality reigned.

"I've been thinking that I need an executive editor," Gilda said later when they were having tea. Her tone, however, was more judicial than reflective. "Someone to represent me in all the departments of the magazine." She waved a hand. "A sort of alter ego."

"But isn't that what Grace is?"

"To a lesser extent. Grace could be feature editor."

"You mean you want *me* to take Grace's place?"

"No. I want you to take a *new* place." Gilda gave her a small, firm, encouraging nod, the one she used to forestall protest in subordinates. "I want you to be 'Executive Editor.'"

"It sounds wonderful!" Rosina exclaimed with sincere regret. "But you know what friends Grace and I are. Everyone would say I had done her out of a job. They'd all know you'd only invented the title to save her face."

"Face savers are not to be scorned. Even when people know they're face savers. They make up the record, and the record is what we stand on."

"But it would hurt Grace!"

"Look, Rosy." Gilda assumed her highest didactic tone. "There's no room for sentiment in a magazine. At least, in running it. I'm sorry about Grace, but she's losing her nerve. She worries too much and talks too much. When I have to demote somebody, I do it, and I do it fast. I can't abide the sort of people who whimper about hurting friends and then hide while somebody else does it for them." Gilda paused, the least bit ominously. "Don't be one of those people, Rosy."

"I was only thinking of all the years Grace had been with you!"

"Don't. You're doing well, dear. Keep your mind on that. As you move up in the world, your friends are bound to envy you. Well, let them! It's one of the compensations of failure to be able to call the winner high-hat."

"Grace would never do that."

"She never would," Gilda agreed triumphantly. "Which is just why you'll never lose her friendship! Because she's a saint! And you'll find that's one of two categories of friends you can always hang on to. Those who are saints and those who are just as successful as you are. Personally, I find it's quite enough."

Rosina looked up and saw Reese in the doorway. He came across the room and shook hands with Gilda with the quick little bow that she had learned was his way of greeting people whom he disliked. But he was very good and offered to make her a drink.

"Oh, no, I must be rushing," she said tactfully, getting up. "I was just congratulating your wife on becoming our new executive editor."

"Really?" He turned and looked doubtfully at Rosina. "I hope it won't mean more work."

"Heavens, no. It should mean less. A *good* executive, in my opinion, should be able to delegate. Now don't forget to tell him, Rosy, about the fountain from Parmelee Cove!"

As soon as Gilda had gone, Reese asked about this, and he seemed upset when Rosina explained. "You mean the little two-horse fountain? Esther's selling *that?*"

She saw immediately in his quickened interest her chance to

finish the back yard that year. "Oh, darling, let's get it, shall we!" she exclaimed, clapping her hands. "I think it would be so wonderful to have a bit of the family place right here in our garden!"

He paused, clearly tempted. But then he set his jaw. "No, we've spent too much this year. It's out of the question."

"But, supposing we give up a trip this summer? Supposing we just stay here with the baby? I'd much rather work on the house. And you *know* you want that fountain!"

He agreed finally to meet her at Coit's on Monday and at least to look at it. When he had gone to the pantry to mix the cocktails, she stepped through the french window into the bare yard and hugged her shoulders in the cool spring air as she visualized what she would make of it: a gravel border, a tiny rose garden, a rhododendron on either side of the fountain. They would give cocktail parties there; she even saw it as a cover for *A Woman's World*. But was she going too fast? Wasn't it madness to yearn for things when she already had so much? And once again she had that funny little feeling about Reese, half a fear, that if he should ever decide to go back to his old way of living in the Village, he would do it, and nothing would stop him. She had a momentary vision of his suddenly saying: "No, this is it, Rosy. I'm not going to spend another cent on this house. Ever!" When he was that way, he was unbudgeable, the way he had been when her younger sister had come up from Roanoke to look for a job in New York. Rosina, who had not seen the girl for years, had thought it quite adequate to ask her for dinner and take her to a musical, but Reese had insisted that she stay in the house and be encouraged to invite her friends there. Happily there had been no job, and the girl had returned to Roanoke, but the visit had been a great trial to Rosina. Her sister had been noisy and inconsiderate, and the friends worse, and it had been impossible to impress upon Reese that there was a difference of obligation in families like hers, where she had had to make her own life from an early age, and families like his where love and money were lavished on the children from birth. Had *she* been brought up in Parmelee Cove, how willingly would she have entertained her relations! But to be expected to do as much for the Streets was simply an imposition. It wasn't snobbishness, was it, if one *sincerely* disliked one's family? She turned back to the house with a little shudder, for the air was growing cold, and she heard Reese in the living room shaking the cocktails. Was she being selfish about the garden? But wasn't it for him, too? Wasn't it *their* home?

At Coit's on Monday, when she walked down the main floor to meet Reese in the garden section where fountains plopped amid glass tables set for dinner by candlelight and umbrellas on paper grass protected shoppers from an imagined sun, she found him silently contemplating the fountain. Gilda was right; it was perfect for the yard.

"Do you like it, darling?"

"Of course I like it," he said gruffly. "But it ought to have been left where it was. It's so like Esther to have to change everything! To show who's boss!"

It pained him to have to buy something from his birthplace, and he was abrupt with the salesman to whom he gave the order. While he was doing this, Rosina's attention was diverted by two ladies who were standing by the center fountain, a very elaborate one, with many fish and seals around a Neptune. The taller of the two was pregnant, but pregnancy became her. She had a fine clear skin and was tall with broad shoulders. She pointed as she talked, and there was a note of authority in her tone. The other lady, blond and very thin, was listening. They must have been important customers, for they were accompanied by the floorwalker who bowed and smiled as the pregnant lady talked. Suddenly she turned and saw the Parmelees.

"Why, Reese!" she cried. "What are *you* doing here?" She walked over to them slowly, with a confident, easy smile. "I never thought you'd set foot inside Coit's. And *this* must be the famous Rosina. So I'm finally to meet Rosina! I *am*, aren't I?"

Rosina had never seen her husband so confused and inarticulate. "Rosy, this is Esther," he mumbled and actually turned his back on them to go on talking to the salesman. Nothing, however, seemed to disconcert Esther.

"He's embarrassed, the poor darling," she said soothingly. "Men always are. But you and I needn't be, need we, Rosina? I may call you Rosina, may I not? It's *too* absurd for me to say 'Mrs. Parmelee.' And here's someone else you may remember, Reese," she continued firmly, nudging his elbow and obliging him to turn. "My sister-in-law," she explained to Rosina, "Cynthia Wrexam. An *old* friend of Reese's."

Once again, Reese barely acknowledged her. Rosina tried to make her smile of greeting cover her amusement. Poor Reese, she thought, for he had told her about Cynthia. To be trapped on the ground floor of Coit's in the middle of a supposedly safe, masculine working day by two wives and an ex-mistress!

"What brings you two to Coit's?" Esther continued with indestructible good humor, but just then she took in the fountain, and her eyes became vividly regretful. "Ah, the fountain, of course. I should have known." She shook her head, several times quickly. "Reese, you must believe me when I say I never dreamed you'd want it. But now, of course, you must take it. It's yours! Salesman," she continued to the man who was still making notes in his book, "never mind that now. Put it on my account. It's Mrs. Coit. Tell him, Mr. Barnes."

The floorwalker hurried to the salesman's side to whisper instructions, but Reese interrupted him sharply: "I've bought that fountain, and I mean to pay for it."

"But, Reese! Can't I make you a little present?"

"Not of Granny's fountain, you can't," he retorted, very red now, and turned back abruptly to the flustered salesman.

Cynthia Wrexam made her first comment. "Same old Reese," she observed in a sour tone.

Esther, however, seemed unperturbed. "Men are so funny, aren't they?" she asked Rosina with a high laugh. "But, of course, we all know that when Reese once makes up his mind, there's no changing him. Let him buy his old fountain, then. I'm sure Coit's can use the money. What *I* want to find out is whether you and I can't lunch together one day. Don't you think we ought to get acquainted? After all, you're my children's stepmother, aren't you?"

"Why, I'd like it very much," Rosina replied, startled.

"Shall we say next week, then? I don't like to put things off *too* long in my condition." Esther smiled and named a day. "I think we'll make it at my apartment. Then we can have a real talk. Goodbye, Reese!"

Reese looked darkly after the retreating backs of Esther and Cynthia. "Are you really going to lunch with her?"

"But, darling, why not?"

"Don't trust her, that's all."

"What can she do to me?" Rosina was determined not to miss this chance to satisfy what she considered a perfectly natural curiosity about her predecessor. "She says it's for the children's sakes. After all, that *has* been a bit awkward. Maybe I can calm her down a bit."

It was an unanswerable argument. Esther had been guarding the children even more closely since Reese's remarriage. When they came to see their father in the city it was always in the company of a Coit chauffeur or tutor, and they were never, under any circumstances, allowed to spend the night. Reese did not complain, but Rosina knew how bitterly he resented it.

"All right," he said reluctantly. "But I hate to have you mixed up in it."

They spoke no more about Esther, and when, on the morning of the proposed lunch, Rosina received a telephone call from Mr. Coit's secretary to inform her that Mrs. Coit would be unable to keep her engagement because she had been delivered the night before of a nine-pound boy, she sent her congratulations and expected to hear no more of the matter. In this she underestimated Esther. Only a day later she had another call, this time from the happy mother herself, and was asked if she would call at the hospital in the late afternoon. There was obviously no refusing this, and Rosina even went so far as to send flowers in advance of her visit.

She wondered, as she came into Esther's big white room with its immense view of the East River, that there had been any flowers left in the city for her to buy. Everywhere, on tables, in baskets on the floor, on the window sills were bunches of roses, irises, lilies, carnations, tulips. Esther, radiant in pink, pointed to Rosina's little bunch by her telephone and cried:

"My dear, do you know you're the only soul who's sent me violets? How did you guess they're my favorite flower? Did Reese tell you?"

"Can you imagine Reese remembering anyone's favorite flower?"

"Ah, how true. Sit down, sit down. Will you have a drink?" Esther pointed to a small white icebox almost secreted behind a bank of lilies. "You'll find a little pitcher of martinis in there. I'll have one, too, but just a tiny one. I don't want the son and heir of the Coits to be drunk in the first week of his life!"

Rosina decided that she might need a drink and carried out her instructions. When she was seated, and both had raised their glasses to the health of the new child, Esther proceeded, with an easy assurance, to the point of their meeting.

"There isn't any reason, you know, that you and I shouldn't be friends. After all, there's no issue between *us*. You and Reese didn't even meet until after he and I had parted. But I confess I was a bit worried when I first heard he had married you. You'll forgive me, dear, won't you? I'm afraid I'm awfully stuffy and cautious, but your magazine — well, you see what I might have visualized. Someone terrifyingly worldly and elegant. I saw my poor children being scared to death. So you see, I was put off. But then everyone began to tell me how lovely and sweet you really were, and I said to myself: 'Now, Esther, remember your rule. When you're wrong, admit it. And try to be the first to make it up!' So here we are, and here I am telling you I was wrong!"

Rosina felt thoroughly uncomfortable under that benign stare and half-smile. "I think it was only natural for you to be suspicious," she said. "There are plenty of women in the magazine world who would make terrible stepmothers."

"Ah, you *do* see it, don't you!" Esther exclaimed. "I knew from the moment I saw you that we'd get on." She clapped her hands together suddenly. "How perfect! Now I want to tell you my little proposition. But mind you, you're not to give me your answer now. I want you to promise me to think it over for a few days and discuss it with Reese. Do you promise?"

"Certainly," replied Rosina, bewildered.

"Well, here we go." Esther took a sip of her drink as if to encourage herself. "I thought the perfect time for Alfred and Eunice to catch up with their father would be this summer. I'm going to be at Parmelee Cove the whole time. We're not going away because of the baby. But I've moved, you know, into Reese's grandmother's house. That leaves Reese's old house entirely free. What I'd like to do is give it to you for the summer. It's in perfect shape, all equipped. You wouldn't even have to bring down a towel or a piece of soap. I guarantee it will be cleaned and painted and repaired within an inch of its life!"

"It's — it's very generous of you."

"Now wait!" Esther held up a warning hand. "I haven't finished. Of course, you'd be entirely independent. You wouldn't even have to lay eyes on Finny and myself, though we hope, of course, you would. And I want you to tell Reese that we'd all be eternally grateful to him if he'd take over the children's game classes at the Cove. They've been in the doldrums without him! Oh, Alfred and Eunice would be *so* proud to have their daddy back!"

"I'm really overwhelmed. I —"

"And another thing!" Again Esther's hand was up. "Oh, very important! Reese always hated the big gateposts that were attached to the back of that house. Tell him I've pulled them down! And now that's all." Esther put a cautioning finger to her lips. "Remember, not a word. I want you to think it over. That's all!"

They were interrupted, at any rate, by the arrival of Esther's mother, Mrs. Means, and of her sister-in-law, Cynthia Wrexam. Rosina found herself excluded from the conversation between Cynthia and Esther which dealt entirely with people of whom she had never heard, and Esther did not make it easier by constantly turning to supply her with little footnotes of the persons discussed. Mrs. Means said almost nothing, but kept hurrying out of the room to see if it was time to see her new grandson behind the glass partition. She gave Rosina an occasional furtive, half-frightened look. She evidently regarded it as an unaccountable, if not morbid taste in her daughter to seek the society of her successor. But after the first minutes of constraint had worn off, Rosina, determined to show the good manners of staying at least until she could catch a glimpse of the young Coit, began to feel her customary sense of ease in the role of observer. She had always been ready to accept new worlds, a willingness born of her childhood need to take leave of her own. In listening to the easy exchange of chatter between Esther and Mrs. Wrexam, she was struck by the prevalence of the theme of money. It was not that they talked so much of money itself — though it was, indeed, mentioned — but there seemed to be a remarkable number of references to things that cost a lot of money or things that could not be done or acquired without a lot of money, or to people who had a lot of money, more perhaps even than the Coits. It might have been that these subjects were simply second nature to them and struck Rosina as pecuniary because of her own associations. But she doubted this. She suspected that their associations were the same. She had once imagined that people like the Coits were freed by their money to think of other things. But it seemed, on the contrary, that the increased emphasis on security in the modern world had hit the rich as well as everyone else, and they could no longer live without constantly reaching a hand behind their back to give a reassuring pat to their little pillows of gold. She was thinking that she could do a piece on the subject, when she heard Esther telling Cynthia of the summer project. The latter turned to Rosina and laughed in candid surprise.

"Well, it will really be like old times again, won't it?"

But Rosina was not put off by this. She felt that she could handle worse than Cynthia. She felt indeed that she could handle all of Parmelee Cove. And she was quite clear now that she wanted to. Whatever the merits or demerits of Esther's world, she wanted to study it at closer quarters. She had no illusions that she would find it a particularly gay or fascinating world. But these were qualities that she had always believed one had to supply oneself, rather than find, in other people's worlds. The fun of discovery lay in moving forward more than in what one discovered. To limit one's social life to what was stimulating or kind or comfortable or even just friendly was by just so much to limit one's horizon. And, besides, was not Parmelee Cove Reese's old world and a part of her own daughter's heritage? Did it not behoove her to become acquainted with it? Circles of life intersected with others as one grew up; it was unnatural to deny the process. It was part of the constant, necessary re-embellishment of one's existence. One had to redecorate a life, from time to time, as one had to redecorate a living room.

Reese, of course, did not see it in that way. He was very quiet that evening after dinner while she told him of Esther's proposal. She tried to put it entirely on the basis of what was good for the children, but it was difficult to conceal things from him, and she felt in his sullen glance that he regarded her as the promoter as well as the communicator of the idea. This was evident in his first remark, delivered as he paced the room.

"You've all ganged up on me, haven't you? Esther knows I can't turn her down. If I do, she'll say I don't give a damn about the children! She might refuse to let me see them at all. I can just hear her, too." He mimicked Esther's tone of concern. "'But I did everything I *could*, didn't I? I practically *thrust* them at him. A free house and everything!'"

"I don't see why you distrust her so," Rosina protested. "You act as if she had something to get out of it. Why isn't it an act of simple good will on her part?"

"Because it's not! Because Esther likes to manipulate people. We're so many little marionettes to her. She likes to pull the strings and cluck over us. You watch! Little Agnes will become her child, too. Esther, the great earth mother!"

Rosina was shocked at the survival of so much prejudice. It even made her faintly jealous. "Don't you think you're exaggerating just a bit? I still think the poor woman's only trying to be nice."

"You don't know her!" he retorted fiercely. "She wants nothing better than to sit up there in Granny's big house and queen it over the Parmelees! Why do you think she bought that old shingle pile, anyway? Can't you hear her saying to Alfred and Eunice: 'Come now, children. It's time for you to run down to the *little* house and see Daddy. Be sure to be *very* polite about everything. You mustn't forget that Daddy isn't in a position to give us all the things that Uncle Finny can!' "

Rosina jumped up. "Darling, we won't go, then! It's not worth it if you feel that way!"

"No, no, we've got to do it," he insisted, shaking his head, disgusted now with himself. "And, of course, you want to — why shouldn't you? Why should you be cooped up in the hot city with little Agnes all summer when there's a cool, well equipped house standing free in the country? No, I see it. I'm not blaming you. Obviously, we have to go."

"Oh, Reese, sweetie!" She stopped his pacing by catching his shoulders and trying to look into his stubbornly averted eyes. "Don't you know there isn't anything I wouldn't give up for you? Don't you know that basically you're all I want? Oh, I go on about trifles, but they *are* trifles."

"It's all right, Rosy," he said brusquely, moving away, embarrassed. "I'll call Esther in the morning and tell her we'll take the house."

But that night, after their lights were out, he turned away from her, and she knew that he was lying awake, brooding. She dared not talk about it any more. She had got her way, but there was very little pleasure in it. And yet she had been perfectly sincere in saying that she would have given up anything for him. But did that have to mean that she should start giving up things before it was necessary, as if to keep in practice for a crisis that might never come? It was difficult to know how much to lead him in things, how much to impose her own desires. If she did nothing to broaden or vary their life, she suspected that his inertia would keep them in the same narrow groove in which he seemed content to lie. Yet whenever she made a move towards change she had the uneasy feeling that she was being selfish and contributing to his moody sense of encircling female conspiracy. The tears came to her eyes as she considered how hard a task it still was to be happy.

2

Reese had known very well that he was paying the price of his freedom for Rosina, and it was a price that he had been quite willing to pay. He had even begun to suspect that, deep down, his nature must have always been fundamentally uxorious. But if he loved Rosina, it did not mean that he had to love *A Woman's World*. If the days were few when he came home, tired from the office, to find that he had to mix cocktails for Gilda Doremus, they nonetheless stuck in his mind. He tried not to blame Rosina for being herself, but it was sometimes difficult. All her small, passionately conceived plans lost some of their charm from the viewpoint of a husband. Happiness, which he was certainly glad to have brought her, seemed merely to have widened the arena of her relentless curiosity. If he had nursed the illusion that motherhood would have concentrated her on the fundamentals, if he had pictured her holding little Agnes like a brooding Rodin figure, he had now to face the fact that their daughter's arrival had opened up to Rosina a whole new world of baby clothes and nursery wallpaper and schools and friends and summer places. He had created still another ally against himself.

It was much the same in his office. Partnership, after all, was itself a kind of marriage, and Amos, too, had a different look under the domestic light. He took less trouble now to conceal aspects of his law practice that Reese found objectionable. He seemed to assume, with a grin and a shrug, that such objections were a mere hangover from the salad days of his clerkship. It was all very well to be holy on a small salary. It was not, of course, that Amos did anything that contravened the law. He was far too successful for that. They were small things, all the more galling to Reese for being so small. For example, Amos grossly exaggerated to clients the difficulties of winning cases when he was taking a contingent fee. And in matrimonial disputes, when he represented the wife, he did not hesitate to tell the most flagrant lies about her feelings of loneliness and desertion, her perhaps fatally declining health, even when he knew that she was waiting only for her decree before flying to the arms of an already selected next spouse. But worst of all was the unhesitating way that he bought and sold stock on the basis of private information obtained from corporate clients. He would come into Reese's office with his tips and merely smile when the latter refused to act on them. He clearly took for granted that Reese's highmindedness was only an act and that he would call his broker as soon as the door was closed behind his informant. For Amos was totally incapable of seizing Reese's distinction between tactics inside and outside the courtroom. To Reese a jury trial was like a battlefield where one could use anything but poisoned gas. It was a question of killing or being killed. Once in that arena all doubts about the justice of one's cause had to be repressed. But outside the courtroom his normal scruples operated to make him ultra-sensitive on questions of ethics. To Amos this was a matter of the rankest hypocrisy. What was life itself but a jury trial? And it irked Reese that he sometimes found himself wondering if Amos were not simply more realistic than he, if his own splitting of the practice of law into different moral categories was not the very error that had bred the smugness in Stillman which he had always so deplored.

It was not the least of his exasperations that there was nothing in his new life about which he could take a definitive stand. It was perfectly natural for Rosina to want a house and then a back yard and then a place in the country so that little Agnes could escape the summer heat. It was entirely understandable that she should want to see her friends and that on occasion her boss should be asked to the house. And could he claim that there was really anything about Amos's way of conducting his practice that was not in accordance with Amos's character as he had known it from the beginning? Even the latter's habit of throwing most of the work on his junior partner had been anticipatable. Such, anyway, were the reasons behind Reese's objections to Esther's proposal. For here at last was something that he could coherently resent. Here at last was a real grievance.

But it appeared that even this was to be snatched from him. One morning, only a few weeks after he had been maneuvered into accepting the hospitality of his former spouse, he found Esther herself in the waiting room of his office. She put down her magazine as he stopped before her and smiled up at him as if her being there were the most natural thing in the world.

"Good morning, Reese!"

"What can I do for you?" he asked abruptly. "Shall we go into my office?"

"Well, actually, I didn't come to see *you*. I came to see your partner."

"Amos? What on earth for?"

She smiled archly. "Isn't that perhaps my business?"

"Oh, come off it, Esther. What's up?"

"Well, as a matter of fact, I have no objection to telling

you." She crossed her legs calmly and straightened her dress. "I have become more conscious of money problems since little Finny was born."

"I didn't think you had any. Since you married big Finny."

"That's where you're wrong," she retorted, but with implacable good will. "I want to be sure that none of the money your grandmother left me goes to my baby. After all, he's not a Parmelee."

"It's your money," he said tersely. "You can leave it to anyone you want."

"That's not the way I look on it. I look on it as a trust. Besides, little Finny will have so much more than Alfred and Eunice, anyway. So I decided that I would put your grandmother's legacy in a trust for *our* children."

Her serene stare seemed to challenge him to resent this, and he shifted uncomfortably from one foot to the other. "That's very handsome of you," he admitted finally.

"Not at all, I consider it simply my duty. The only question was selecting a lawyer to draw the instrument. I didn't see why the children's father shouldn't get the fee, but I thought it might be a bit tricky for you and me to work together. So I'm doing the next best thing. I'm taking it to your partner."

Reese thought that it was hard indeed that he should now have to churn the sour milk of his anger into the sweet butter of gratitude. How could he tell her in the face of this that he did not trust her? But he was suddenly spared by the receptionist's nasal politeness: "Excuse *me*, Mr. Parmelee. But Mr. Levine can see Mrs. Coit now." And Esther, with a quick smile reached for her pocketbook and walked down the corridor after the office boy in her long stride.

Reese knew that Amos would come to see him as soon as the interview was over, and so he did, all smiles and puffing at a cigar which he had just lit.

"A charming woman, your former wife," he said, "a very charming woman. I think we got on very well together."

"I'm sure you did. Esther knows how to manage people."

"Why should she want to manage me?" Amos raised his eyebrows. "It's much more the other way round. Coit Stores. Just imagine! Do you think if I charged no fee in this matter, she'd tell her husband, and he'd remember it?"

"It wouldn't do you the slightest good. I know Finny. He's the kind who likes to farm out small family matters to different law firms. Each firm does it for a nominal fee, hoping the big stuff will follow. It never does."

"Still, you never can tell."

"If you don't mind, Amos, I'd rather not see us chasing after my ex-wife's husband!"

"Now, now, Reese," Amos said soothingly. "Don't get on your high horse. A client's a client, after all."

"Have it your way then. But don't say I didn't warn you!" He turned back to his work and refused to have any further discussion about the Coits. When Amos's secretary, a few days later, brought in drafts of his children's trusts he declined even to read them. "Mrs. Coit is *not* my client," he scribbled on the margin and sent them back to Amos. If Esther insisted on being his hostess all summer, she could at least keep out of his office. Her infiltration had to be stopped somewhere.

As it turned out, Amos was not able to continue his pursuit of Finny Coit's business because the following week he suffered a heart attack. It was termed a light one by his doctor, but he looked very white and scared and somehow smaller in the oxygen tent at the hospital where Reese went to see him. He kept repeating that it was unfair, that he was only fifty-six. Reese would have limited his visit to a few minutes, but Amos begged him to stay.

"Tell me something, Reese," he asked in a funny, small

voice. "Something I've been meaning to ask you. Do you believe in an afterlife?"

"Now, don't worry about that, old man. You're going to be okay. The doctor said so."

"Sure, sure. But I still want to know. It makes you feel awfully funny when you think any second you may go — poof! I've never been much of a believer. Maybe I've been too busy. Or maybe that's why I *was* busy, to keep from thinking about it."

"That's true of most of us."

"Yes, I know. But I want to know about you. You were brought up in a church school. You're always talking about how you should do this or how you shouldn't do that. And you've got some kind of strength, too. I feel it, I tell you!" Amos would have sat up in his sudden excitement, but he remembered his condition and kept his mouth closed for several seconds as he forced himself to relax. "Tell me, Reese, is it faith? Do you believe in an afterlife?"

"I can't believe that anything would stop you from litigating," Reese answered, smiling. "Even dying, which you're not going to do. Heaven help Saint Peter if he ever tried to keep you out!"

But Amos gave him no answering smile. "I want to be serious, Reese. I've asked you a serious question."

"Yes, of course, you have." Reese paused a moment to add conviction to his lie. "Certainly I believe in an afterlife, Amos. I do now, and I always have."

Amos stared at him for a second and then closed his eyes. "Thank you" was all he said, and Reese walked quietly out of the room.

At the office he was inundated with work. Amos, the doctor had informed him, could not work at the earliest before six weeks were over, and then he would have to be on a much lighter program. Reese had to postpone some of Amos's trials and take over the ones that could not be postponed, and he spent several evenings reading through his partner's files. This took particularly long because of Amos's fondness for office memoranda, filled with insignificant and often irrelevant details. But there was one memorandum which contained a minute that he read with a sudden, sharp intake of breath.

"Conference suspended from 11:25 to 11:50 while Mr. Levine stepped outside to speak to Mr. Shea."

The date of the conference was a date that Reese had already remarked, for it was not a date that he would soon forget. It was the date on which Miss Howland had signed the codicil to her will giving Amos his big bequest. And that same day Pat Shea had called on Levine! Well, of course, it could have been another Shea, or it could have been Pat calling on another matter, but once again Reese's mind teemed with suspicion. He was so moody that night when he came home that Rosina hardly dared talk to him.

"You've got to work less hard, darling!" she exclaimed finally. "Or the same thing will happen to you that happened to Amos!"

"He'll be back in a few weeks," he answered grimly, "And then I can ease up."

Obviously, he could ask no questions of Amos while the latter was sick. The matter would have to wait. But he gained some new information on the subject from a most unexpected quarter a few days later at a dinner meeting of his committee at the Bar Association. This quarter was none other than his former boss. Stillman was always at his most affable in the dark, dank congenial atmosphere of a lawyers' building; he picked up what was certainly not his first cocktail and took Reese to stand under two gentle seascapes hung in the "weekend painters'" exhibition. Reese's success in the law was not the kind that his old firm much admired, but it was still success, and Stillman recognized it.

"I was sorry to hear about your partner," he said. "Was it a bad attack?" He shook his head as Reese shrugged. "Well, it can happen to any of us, that's certainly true. This pace we live at, this killing pace. Still, whatever happens, I'm sure you can run that firm."

"I'm not that worried about Amos," Reese said, somewhat taken aback by the speed with which Stillman dispatched his partner. "But, anyway, you're wrong. I have no name in the law, and Amos has. Besides, all the clients are his."

"I would say, on the contrary, that the big name was yours!" Stillman exclaimed, and Reese remembered with a smile that his grandfather's name was still in Clark, Day & Parmelee. "And as for the clients, if it ever came to a tussle, I'm not so sure that Mr. Levine would be the one to prevail. That Howland case did a lot more for you than it did for him, my boy!"

"How did it?"

"A magnificent job of advocacy. Magnificent! But you don't think you fooled anyone, do you?" Stillman took a long sip of his drink, as if to warm himself into a state of indiscretion. "You don't think for a moment you pulled the wool over *my* eyes as to what old Levine was really up to?"

Reese became very tense and still. "What was he up to?"

"Oh, come, Reese, you weren't born yesterday!"

Evidently Stillman hoped to communicate his intelligence by repeating that it was as well known to Reese as to himself. In this way, anyway, he could always excuse himself if he ended by telling.

"If you're implying that there was any funny business about that codicil," Reese said sternly, "I give you my word I don't know of any."

"Funny business!" Stillman appeared to gape and then to snicker at the inadequacy of the term. "My dear Reese, I don't know what you mean by funny business, but if you think I don't know the whole thing was cooked up by Levine and Shea from the beginning, you must think I'm as wet behind the ears as Parsifal himself!"

"All right, Parsifal," Reese said grimly. "Let's have it. What do you know?"

Stillman was sobered now by Reese's expression. He turned and pointed to a group of men headed towards the stairway. "Isn't that your committee going down for dinner?"

Reese did not even look. "Let them go."

"You really don't know?" Stillman eyed him now with what seemed a sincere curiosity. "Maybe I should tell you, then, for your own good."

"I'm waiting."

"You won't fly off the handle?"

"Oh, come on, Stillman, out with it!"

"Sit down then." But even seated, Stillman hesitated, staring at the floor for several moments in a judicial pose. At last he looked up and coughed. "All right. You've asked for it. Here it is. After we lost the appeal in the Howland case, I decided to have Levine watched. I don't mean shadowed, exactly, but I wanted to find out about any dealings that he might have with Shea. You see, I can't give up easily on things, Reese. I'm a bit of a bulldog. I *knew* that sooner or later Levine would have to pay Shea off for what he'd done for him, and I wanted to know when that happened. Well, it happened."

For a moment the two men stared at each other. Stillman had recovered the offensive to which he was accustomed, and his manner was once again assured.

"Are you going to tell me what happened?"

"If you want." Stillman shrugged. "The knowledge can't help *me* now."

"Isn't it your duty to keep it for your clients?"

"Ah, but that's it, my boy, they're not my clients any more. As far as I'm concerned, they'd be the last people I'd tell it to now. I'd rather have Levine keep the damn money than see them get a penny of it!" Stillman's little eyes glittered with a perfervid dislike. "Would you believe it, Reese, they refused to pay my bill! Mrs. Anthon had the gall to tell me I'd lost the case by cross-examining that switchboard woman!"

Reese smiled thinly. "I hope you're suing her. You ought to collect easily enough!"

"You seem to forget," Stillman reminded him with dignity, "that Clark, Day & Parmelee has never in its history sued a client for a fee!"

"It's a luxury not everyone can afford," Reese retorted. "But what was it you found out about Amos?"

"Some time after my disagreement with the Howlands," Stillman proceeded, refusing to be hurried, "*after*, you understand, the relationship of attorney and client had ceased to exist, the man whom I had hired on their account and whose employment I had continued purely to satisfy my *own* curiosity, brought me two very interesting pieces of information." Stillman paused for emphasis and held up one finger. "First: on the death of one Mrs. Seumas Gayley, widow of a wealthy Brooklyn real estate operator, it appeared that Amos Levine had been named one of her three executors. His commissions would have amounted to some thirty thousand dollars, with substantially no work entailed. Yet for no apparent reason he refused to qualify, and the successor executor named in the will took his place. It should not surprise you to learn that the successor executor was none other than our old friend Shea." Stillman now held up two fingers. "Second: you may remember the collapse of the roof in that store in Manhasset? One man was killed and two injured. An open-and-shut case of negligence. Yet Amos Levine refused the case and turned it over to Pat Shea. You will admit that the coincidence is interesting?"

"I'm sure there's a perfectly good explanation. Amos was cutting down on his work load, even before his heart attack."

"I see. But you will forgive me if it still strikes me as singular. If I were to cut down on *my* work load, I should try to steer it to my partners. *Not* to my competitors."

"I'll ask Amos about it," Reese retorted with smothered anger. "And I'll let you know what he says."

"Please do. I shall be intensely interested."

When Reese left the building that night he was tingling with exasperation. To have to sit by in silence while Stillman, of all people, condescended to enlighten him on his own partner's little tricks, had been a deeply mortifying experience. He spent that night alone in his house, for Rosina and the baby had gone to Parmelee Cove, and decided, after several sleepless hours, that none of the success that Amos had brought him in the law could compensate for the discomfort of that interview.

The following evening he went down by train to Long Island and drove from the Northfield Station to Parmelee Cove. In his present mood he found it peculiarly galling, on entering the drive, to pass the large black sign with gold letters that announced Esther's possession of his grandmother's acres. It did no good to reflect that she had saved the place. The big house, newly painted white with blue shutters and huge new windows facing the sound to let in, as never before, the light and sea, had certainly been improved, but it dominated the lawns and garden now in a way that struck Reese as offensive. Similarly the extension of the new colors to all the subsidiary buildings on the place, including the one now occupied by himself and Rosina, made him feel that his family had donned Esther's livery. Only his father's house and those of his two aunts, which had been excluded from Esther's deed, maintained their original hues, but even they seemed to be hiding now behind their trees, as if to escape the notice of further raiders from the big house, armed with pots and brushes.

He found Rosina in the kitchen, preparing a casserole, and she gave him a happy look that immediately tore at his heart. He kissed her on the cheek and hurried upstairs to see Agnes who was having her bottle. Through the open window he could hear young Alfred and his cousins playing baseball. He was supposed to join them, but he went downstairs and mixed the cocktails instead.

"A drink already?" Rosina asked cheerfully as she came into the living room. "You're not going to play with the boys?"

"No. I've got something to tell you. You'd better take this."

He handed her a drink which she took immediately and then sat down, watching him intently. "What's it about?"

"Miss Howland's will."

He heard the sharp, impatient intake of her breath. "I always knew that chicken would come back to roost," she said impatiently. "It's your nemesis, that case." Then she was silent and listened, grave and motionless, while he told her the whole story.

"Very well," she said after a pause, looking away from him, her eyes unsympathetic. "What does it all prove?"

"You don't think it looks as if Amos were paying Shea off?"

"What for?"

"Why for putting that bequest in the codicil, of course!"

"I really don't know or care how it looks," she said in an

irritated tone. "It seems to me that Amos has his own peculiar way of doing things and always will have. What does it matter? Obviously, it's never going to be your way. He can't corrupt you, if that's what you're worried about."

"Can't he? You seem to forget we're partners."

"That doesn't mean you have to share *everything*, does it?"

"Perhaps not. But I think it means we have to share this."

"You'd better tell me what's on your mind, Reese," she said sharply. "If you're waiting to hear me say I'm shocked at Amos, you're waiting in vain. I don't give a hoot what Amos does. And as for taking sides between him and those grasping relatives of old Miss Howland's, I say it's a case of dog-eat-dog."

"I wish I could share your detachment."

"What are you going to do about it?"

He was suddenly glad of her defiance. It made it easier to say what he had to say. "As soon as Amos is well enough," he told her firmly, "I shall ask him to explain why he has done what he has done for Shea. If he cannot give me a satisfactory answer, I shall resign from the firm."

Rosina's expression did not change; she did not even blink. "And what will that mean? To us?"

"It will mean starting over, I'm afraid. Or pretty much so. The practice is ninety per cent Amos's. Oh, I'm not saying I won't be able to grab off a client here and there, but basically I'll be on my own."

"And how long," Rosina continued in the same level tone, "will it take you to get back to where you are now?"

"I don't know. It was quite a break when Amos took me in. That kind of thing doesn't happen every day."

"No!" she cried, suddenly bitter. "Of course it doesn't! If it did, it wouldn't be nearly so much fun to throw it away, would it? Will we have to sell the house in New York?"

"I guess maybe."

Rosina at this threw herself down on the sofa, and he was shocked by her sudden hoarse, strangled sobs. "My own darling house!" she cried. "The only home I've ever had!" She plunged her face in a pillow, and her shoulders heaved.

Reese, watching her, felt his stomach turn over in a tumult of disgust and pity. That she could *care* so was as heartrending as it was absurd. "Rosy," he managed to say. "Rosy, please. Don't go on that way. I'll find a way of keeping the house. I'll borrow the money from Dad. I'll do *some*thing!"

"No, sell it!" she exclaimed, sitting up now and glaring at him. "Sell everything we have! You're only doing it to punish me, anyway! Punish me for daring to like anything in the world except *you!* For liking my house or my furniture or a summer in the country! Even for liking your own friends and relations! You think it's all trivial and foolish, and you want me to go straight back where I came from!"

"Rosy, will you listen to me, *please!*"

"No!" Her breath was coming in pants. "You think I ought to be happy being simple and highminded like you. But I wasn't brought up the way you were brought up. I didn't have the things you had. I haven't learned that they're trivial and foolish!" Her voice rose to a wail. "I *like* them!"

"Listen!" He took her by the shoulders now and shook her until she stared at him, shocked. "You talk about the things *you* like. Well, I want you to have them. I mean you to have them, too. It's only a question of time. But do you want them so much that you'd have me go on working in an office where I'm miserable?"

"Oh, no," she said quickly, her whole expression changing. "Oh, no. I'd hate that."

"Well, that's what you'd be asking. If what I suspect about Amos turns out to be true."

She hesitated. "It would really make you so miserable?"

"It would." He put his arm around her shoulders. "I know it's asking a lot of you, but you told me once you'd give up anything for me."

She turned suddenly and flung her arms around his neck. "Oh, darling, of course I did, and I meant it, too!" She burrowed her head down violently into his chest. "You've got to help me! You've got to make me understand that you really *are* different. I know you are, darling, but it's so easy to forget. You see, it's almost incomprehensible to someone like me that you could really mind about Amos. I mean *really* mind. Oh, disapprove of him, deplore him, even be angry with him, yes, of course. But to be actually *unhappy* about him! We have to live in this world, don't we?"

"No," he said with sudden dryness, "we can choose our own. It's what I've tried to do ever since I left Esther. It's the only thing that justifies me."

She raised her head at this. "But if Amos *could* explain? Everything would be all right?"

"As all right as it ever was."

She sighed and rested her head on his shoulder. "Well, at least I have you. As long as that's true, I can make out somehow."

Reese, stroking her hair, smiled wryly as he considered how ridiculous his scruples must seem to her. Nothing that a man did in the business world would have given her the least discomfort. She would have asked no more questions than a cave woman of the mate who was returning with a slab of bison. But it was solacing to his male ego, after the frustrations of his week, that she should at least admit the sincerity of his motives. He wanted to make her happy, but not at the price of violating what integrity he still claimed. Was that not where he had failed with Esther? Had he not surrendered to her, in one way or another, almost to the end?

3

Until the night when Reese told her of his suspicions of Amos, Rosina had found Parmelee Cove a haven of peace. Gilda had agreed to let her take her vacation by working only three days a week in July and August, and so she had time to herself, while Reese was in the city, to stroll about the place and become acquainted with her various in-laws. She liked them all, and after a while she felt they liked her. She had only to overcome the lurking doubt that she would prove too "smart" for them, and this to a person of her basic simplicity was no difficult matter. She spent a whole morning in the kennels with Aunt Fanny Talcott and learned almost enough about poodles to consider doing an article on them. She went out sailing with her father-in-law and acted as a respectful and obedient crew and even allowed Reese's sister Joan to give her tennis lessons. They were all of them well enough disposed, but not one ever asked her a question about her own work or interests, associating such things, as they undoubtedly did, with people who lived in the city and took no exercise. Rosina would as soon have expected it of them as a newly conscripted private would have expected it of his platoon sergeant. It was their world, after all, and she had always taken it for granted that it was her job to adapt herself to other people's worlds. Nor was there any sense of inferiority in this. It was simply that as a child she

had taken no interest in her own home and could not therefore expect anyone else to. She even took something of an
artist's pride in being able to adapt herself to the exigencies
of a family quite as different from her own as the Parmelees.
There were certain things, however, about which she had to
be firm, and nothing is more successful than the sudden firm-
ness of those who have been generally compliant. When her
mother-in-law, for example, showed signs of distress at the
discovery of Rosina's first marriage, of which Reese, quite
simply, had forgotten to inform her, Rosina took the position
that it was not to be discussed.

"I never speak of it," she told Mrs. Parmelee who looked
abashed. "I will just say this, because you have a right to
know. I do not consider it a marriage. It was annulled.
There is no trace of it left for me."

Mrs. Parmelee was surprised, but after a bit she was satisfied. She was beginning to be comfortable with her new
daughter-in-law which made her in turn more at ease with
Reese. Rosina had realized immediately that what the Parmelees most dreaded was any kind of personal approach, any
kind of prying intimacy. It was as if they believed that
human affection must vanish as completely as Cinderella's
coach at the first efforts of articulation. She had also sensed
that Esther had never divined this and had been accordingly
considered, in Joan's scornful monosyllable, "damp." Indeed, Rosina had come to realize that one of the cardinal
points in her own favor was the contrast which her predecessor so vividly afforded. It was a contrast, too, that was kept
alive by the proximity, deeply resented by all the family, of
Esther in the big house. It was true, of course, that Esther
had saved the place from becoming a housing development
and that she had proved a good neighbor to the older Parmelees and a good landlady to those of the grandchildren who

still occupied some of the buildings which she had purchased. She was indisputably generous in urging them all to continue using the pier, the tennis court and the swimming pool. But a nation occupied for its own protection is nonetheless occupied. The Parmelees could never quite forgive Esther for saving their home.

Rosina, who might have been considered the member of the family least likely to be congenial with her predecessor, was actually the one who saw the most of her. Esther was unremittingly hospitable, at least when Reese was in the city. He had made it very clear that he would not be entertained in his grandmother's house by Finny Coit. But there was no reason that Rosina should not go there for lunch during the week, and she did, even on occasion bringing a friend, at Esther's persuasion. Anstiss and Jack Stranahan had taken a house in Northfield for the summer, and Duey Lispenard was staying with them. Neither his engagement nor his friendship with Cliffie Suter had survived the famous scene at Rosina's cocktail party. Since then Anstiss had taken him over entirely, and Rosina suspected that the main purpose of her move to Northfield had been to provide Duey with a site in which he could revise his play and from which he could not easily be lured. There were none of the little group available, except those who could come for a weekend, and Anstiss was glad to be able to bring Duey over on a hot afternoon to swim in Esther's pool. She had long had to concede that Reese was, after all, the right kind of Parmelee, but she had done it as ungraciously as possible, yielding the Parmelee world to Rosina as if it were only a minor appanage of the greater territories which she herself had abandoned.

"You'll get used to your in-laws," she assured Rosina. "I know you've heard me poke fun at that Long Island world, but there's not a bit of harm in them, really."

Duey was much nicer about it. He seemed to enjoy country life more than Rosina would have expected and even qualified for men's doubles with Reese and the Talcott brothers on weekends. He adored Parmelee Cove with its old, ugly buildings, its unexpected statues and fountains, its heavy, Edwardian comfort.

"But it's just where you belong, Rosy!" he had cried after his first enthusiastic tour of the grounds. "It's so *you!*"

Rosina forgave him all his sarcasms of the past for this remark. It was so exactly what she felt herself, but had not ventured to say. She *did* belong there. It was why it was so terrible that everything should now be threatened. For although they paid no rent for their cottage, she knew that Reese would never accept it from Esther unless he were in a position to pay the rent if asked. Otherwise it would be charity. That was the way his mind worked. She felt that she could not bear to give up their new life now. The summer was working out so perfectly for everyone, even for Reese. Young Alfred had made great strides in baseball and tennis under his father's tutelage, and the gradual, shy renewal of intimacy and understanding between the two had been beautiful to watch. Little Eunice was still inclined to cling to her mother in the big house, but even her wide-eyed reserve was being overcome. Reese had been restored to the Parmelees, and everyone was the better for it. And was all this to be interrupted now because Amos Levine had swindled some money out of an old woman whom none of them even knew? It was not as if Reese had had anything to do with it or even received any of the money. What sort of a world was it where the guilty were allowed to keep their loot and the innocent had to atone? It was more than flesh and blood could bear.

There was no member of Reese's family in whom she

could confide. They would have taken it for granted that any partner of Amos Levine must have had to swallow far worse things than Miss Howland's codicil, so why make an issue of it now? The subtleties of Reese's conscience would have baffled them entirely. She dared not seek counsel from Anstiss or Duey, whose discretion she could not trust, and the people of the neighborhood were still bare acquaintances. There remained only Esther, and to Esther her need for communication steadily drew her. In favor of Esther was her friendliness, her stake through her children in Reese's life and, above all, her understanding of him. Against her was the prospect of Reese's anger should he ever learn that he had been the object of such a discussion between his two wives. But then Reese need never learn it.

It all came out one hot morning when she was sitting before lunch by the pool with Esther. They were alone, and Esther had ordered gin and tonic. The sun and the effect of a drink so early in the day finally elicited the whole story from Rosina. Esther listened quietly, her eyes directed over the sound, a detached half-smile on her lips. But Rosina had the impression nonetheless that she had not missed a word of the narration. When she had finished, there was a long pause.

"It sounds so *like* Reese," Esther said finally, in a dreamy tone. "So extraordinarily like him. I feel for you, my dear. I really feel for you."

"You don't think I'm wrong to mind?"

"But of course not. Men are such children about their little rules. They have to be handled with such subtlety. I even have trouble with Finny, and he's a good deal more sensible about that kind of thing than Reese ever was."

Rosina, now that she had told, was troubled by the feeling that she had been disloyal. "Of course, I suppose it was a pretty shabby thing of Amos to do. *If* he did it?"

"But, my dear, of course he did it!" Esther exclaimed with more animation. "What possible doubt can there be after what you've just told me? A man like Levine never gives something for nothing."

"But you don't think it's the kind of thing one should worry about?"

"One should *worry* about it, yes. But one shouldn't go around busting up perfectly good law firms because of it. That's where men simply can't be trusted!"

"But is there anything *I* can do?"

"Naturally! Why, it's as clear as the nose on your face!"

Rosina began to feel that Esther was being a trifle condescending. She reached down and ran a hand through the water. "What shall I do?" she asked almost sullenly. "Shall I make a scene?"

Esther smiled. "Not unless Reese has changed rather drastically since my day. That would be fatal."

"What then?"

"Go to Amos!" Esther exclaimed, as if it were the simplest thing in the world. "Go to Amos and tell him everything! You have time, that's the great thing. Reese won't take this up with him until he's out of the hospital. But we needn't wait. *We* don't have to be gentlemen!"

"What good will it do to tell Amos?"

"Why, you darling goose, it will give him time to prepare his answer! It will prevent Reese from taking him by surprise!"

"But what answer can there be?" Rosina asked gloomily. "If he did this thing, he did it. If he paid Shea off, he paid him off."

"My dear, you're being naïve! A man like Levine could explain the blood on his hands if you caught him walking out of the room where his murdered wife lay. If he had five minutes he could make you believe you'd killed her yourself. Well, we're giving him five minutes!"

Rosina held her breath as the idea began to sprout in her mind. "If Reese should ever find out!" she murmured doubtfully.

"Reese never will."

It was just what Rosina had told herself about the very discussion they were now having. And having embarked on a dangerous course of action, was it not paltry to turn back at the first faint rumble of thunder? She was only trying to save Reese from his own folly. Would there be any real happiness for either of them without some risk? When she left Esther, she pondered the scheme for the rest of the day. The more she pondered, the better it seemed. She began to be excited at the idea of putting it into execution. She had never been one to brook delay.

The next day, in New York, she left her office, as if for an early lunch, and went uptown in a taxi to Amos's hospital. She had not dared to call ahead, but by good fortune, she found him alone.

The last time she had been in a hospital room had been to see Esther. Amos's room gave much the same triumphant impression. It was filled with flowers and games, and Amos, in a red robe and yellow silk pajamas, was working on an enormous picture puzzle with the intensity of a child. The part done showed a cavalcade of men in armor emerging over a drawbridge from a castle. Rosina noted the titles of the books on the table: *Be Glad of Your Heart Attack!* and *Coronary: The Friendly Warning*. Amos, who was showing none of the depression that Reese had described, greeted her with a cheerful smile.

"Well, Rosy! If this isn't the nicest thing!"

She sat down, and he gave her a detailed and complacent

account of his illness. He had more than assimilated it; he had made of it a prize possession. Rosina was not bored because she did not listen. She was wondering nervously if she would be doing a terrible thing in telling him what Reese had told her. Suppose he should die in front of her? But, of course, no one would then have to know that her visit had not been a purely social one. She blushed at the thought. She was being not only bad but silly. Amos would not die. With a man like him there was no danger in shock or surprise. Such things were the daily texture of his life.

"You know, Reese has a habit of getting bees in his bonnet," she said abruptly when he had finished, despairing of any better opening for her news. "I thought I'd better warn you of one that he seems to be nursing now."

Amos's eyes slightly narrowed. "A bee in his bonnet? What about?"

"Well, this time it seems to be that old Howland case again," she said with a rather tinkling laugh. "Honestly, you can't imagine what a worrier he is. I really ought to apologize for bringing up such trifles."

Amos's stare, however, did not change. "What is it about the Howland case that's worrying him?"

"Well, he seems to have some crazy idea that you're engaged in 'paying off' Mr. Shea."

"I think you'd better tell me everything, Rosy," he said quietly. While she did so, haltingly, at times almost incoherently, but without ever the least prompting from him, he continued to work on his puzzle. Even when she had finished he did not look up, but fitted in the final piece of a corner and smoothed the other pieces down with both hands.

"Why are you telling me this?"

"So it won't come as a shock to you!" she exclaimed. "So you'll be able to explain it all to him easily and calmly."

He glanced up at her. "Don't you mean so that I'll have time to make up a story?"

"Of course not!"

"Come now, Rosy. You and Reese both think me a crook, don't you? Only *you* don't care."

"I don't think anything," she protested. "All I know is that I don't want Reese to break up the firm. He's worked too hard to get where he's gotten. I don't pretend to understand the ins and outs of legal ethics. But if there's something that's worrying Reese, and you can calm him down, why isn't that to everybody's advantage?"

"Very practical, my dear," Amos said with a reassuring smile. "Very practical indeed. And very like a woman. Only I'm not sure you don't know quite a bit about legal ethics. It must be a favorite topic of Reese's. However, there is one thing you and I can both agree on. We don't want Reese to leave the firm. I'm not sure of your reasons, but I can suspect them. As for mine, they're pretty obvious. When I get back to work, I'm going to have to lean on him more than ever."

"I know he's basically happy with you."

"Do you, my dear? Do you, indeed? It's more than I do. But to business. Let us consider what explanation there may be of my conduct that will satisfy your husband's exacting conscience." Once more Amos paused for several moments over his puzzle before supplying another piece. "Well, now," he continued, "suppose we consider Mrs. Gayley's will first. How would this sound to you?" He looked up as if he were piecing their problem together, like another puzzle, on the ceiling. "Let us say that the Gayley children thought I was being adequately compensated as counsel for the estate without being an executor as well. Let us say there was talk about objecting to my appointment. Could I afford to go into court again in another suit involving an old lady's will? So soon after the Howland case? How would that have looked?" He lowered his eyes towards her and raised his eyebrows as she had seen him do in court.

"Bad, certainly."

"Bad, indeed." He nodded and directed his gaze back again to the ceiling. "So what must I do? I must bow out. Is it *my* fault, then, that Pat Shea happens to be the successor named in the will? Is it *my* fault that he married old Ma Gayley's niece? I think that sounds rather convincing, don't you?"

"Most convincing."

"Let us turn then to my sending Pat the case against the store in Manhasset. That looks a bit worse, doesn't it?" He touched the tips of his fingers together and pursed his lips. "But let me see, let me see. Supposing it turned out that the furniture store in Manhasset was a subsidiary of Coit Stores in New York? Or at least partially owned or controlled? Could I not remind my scrupulous junior partner that Mrs. Phineas Coit, your own predecessor, my dear, had recently retained my services in connection with two trusts and that I had made no secret of my anxiety to secure the good will of her husband? Would I be ingratiating myself with him if I started by leaping at his throat in Manhasset? Hardly. That is Pat's affair. Altogether Pat's affair. And if I then could show that Pat and I have referred such cases back and forth to each other for years — well, I think it would fit, don't you?"

"Oh, Amos!" she cried, in sudden compunction. "You're pretending to make it all up, and it's all perfectly true! I'm so sorry!"

"Now what was the third point?" he asked, holding up a hand to check her. "Oh, yes, Pat's calling on me the very day Miss Howland signed the famous codicil. Well, that's harder, isn't it? Let me see." But after a moment he simply shrugged and smiled. "I guess we'll have to rest on the frequency of Pat's visits. That he was always in and out of the office. Will that do, do you think?"

"Oh, Amos," she said humbly, "forgive me. Please forgive me!"

"Nonsense, my dear. How do you know I'm not making it all up?"

She stared at him, bewildered. "But you're not, are you?"

"I'm having far too much fun to give you a simple yes or no. Who would want to break up so fine a game?"

"Reese would," she said dismally. "Reese would hate it. You must never tell him I even came to see you. Will you promise me that?"

"Promise? Oh, come, Rosy? Must we be so serious?"

"Yes!" she cried, and the tears jumped into her eyes. "You have my marriage completely in your hands. He'd leave me if he ever knew. He'd leave me flat!"

"Well, well, then I must be *most* discreet." Amos continued to fix his gentle stare on her. "I tell you what I'll do, my dear. I will keep our little secret filed away. Up here." He tapped his temple. "Where nobody can ever come across it. But files are useful. Who can tell? Maybe someday you'll be an old lady living alone in a hotel. God forbid, but maybe. And maybe I'll still be around at the age of a hundred because this coronary will have taught me to take such good care of myself. And then maybe I'll come and call on you in that hotel and remind you of that file I've kept such a secret all through the years. Just maybe. And then maybe you'll add a codicil to your will and leave me a hundred and fifty grand!"

She stared at him for a moment and then burst into almost hysterical laughter. "Oh, Amos, you old darling!" she cried and hurried over to give him a hug.

She knew in the weeks that followed that Reese had not spoken to Amos. Obviously, he would have told her, either of his reassurance or of his resignation. It was so like him, she reflected guiltily, to restrain his curiosity until there could no longer be the least danger of causing a shock to Amos. But then she also suspected that his curiosity was not so great as hers. Now that they had agreed in principle to his resignation if he were unsatisfied about Amos, his mind seemed to be entirely at rest and his spirits even high. He loved playing baseball with Alfred and the other children at the Cove; he loved to take them sailing and fishing. He loved their picnics on the beach and the swimming late at night. He admired Rosina's fresh color and her cooking and told her that at heart she was just a country girl.

"It took a bulldozer like Gilda Doremus to make a slick editor out of a rosy-cheeked peasant like you," he would say. "I always told you she was your bad fairy!"

It made Rosina uncomfortable to reflect that his good mood must have sprung so largely from a misinterpretation of her own. He must have believed, after all, that she had accepted his decision and that she was being philosophic at the prospect of any temporary privations which it might entail. If he had known that her philosophy was based instead on the private assurance that they would not be necessary! She tried to console herself by remembering that what she had discovered about Amos really made everything all right, that he was, in fact, innocent. It was true that Esther had not been convinced, that she had merely shrugged, on hearing Rosina's explanation, and said airily: "I told you, didn't I? That he could bamboozle the devil himself?" But then Esther had taken a strong position on the issue of Amos's culpability, and Esther was not one lightly to reverse herself. Rosina decided finally that she could not worry about everything in the world. She had to build her house on the twin founda-

tion stones of Amos's vindication and Reese's reassurance.
That left only the shifting sand of what Reese might think
of her own role in the case. It was not agreeable for her to
consider that the happiness of her marriage might depend on
something that she had hidden from him, but had that not
always been the case in her life? Had not the money that
had sent her to college depended on her grandfather's mis-
conception of her religious beliefs? Would Anstiss have ever
admitted her to the little group had she known her true
opinion of it? And would Gilda have even hired her had
she not lied about her previous editorial experience? It was
the way life was; few, if any, human beings ever deserved,
by their own sympathy and self-control, true frankness from
their neighbors.

Nevertheless she was nervous, particularly at having confided her secret to Esther. Esther, it was true, seemed serene
and successful in the prosperity of her second marriage.
Surely she had no interest in jeopardizing that of her successor. Yet there was something faintly sinister in the broad
coverage of Esther's smile, as if she were trying to collect
under its protective aegis as many human beings as she
could. Just what Esther wanted to protect them against was
far from clear, and Rosina uneasily suspected that it was a
decision that Esther would not announce until her human
collection was complete. Reese, of course, had warned her,
and she had not listened. Her anxiety now took the form of
spending more and more time with Esther. Like a naval
officer who relaxes only at nighttime on the bridge, scanning
the murky horizon with his glasses, so she relaxed in the
morning by Esther's pool, listening to the latter discuss the
events and plans of her day. Anstiss Stranahan frequently
joined them; the leader of the little group herself seemed to
be swinging gently on an outer thread of Esther's web, not
yet aware that she had been caught.

"I adore Esther," she told Rosina. "She's such a *real* person."

Rosina began to suspect that Anstiss was ready to return to her old world. Jack Stranahan had always secretly yearned for it, and his wife might have felt, having won her long struggle with Cliffie Suter over Duey, that she could afford now to return from her raid into enemy territory, bearing the prize specimen whose capture had been the purpose of the expedition. Yet in returning she did not want anyone of her old world to undervalue the broadening nature of the experiences to which she had subjected herself. Anstiss now posed as an authority on the left, and Rosina reflected with astonishment that it must have been from such dangerous radicals as Grace Chess and herself that she had gleaned her information.

"The tragedy of America today is that the left has disappeared," Anstiss told Esther and Rosina one morning at the pool. "There's no real bohemian society any more. If there were, I believe I should know it. I don't suppose many people have had Jack's and my opportunity to know writers and painters. But writers and painters are no longer any fun to know. They've become middle-class. Like everyone else."

But with Esther she could no longer get away with such superiority. Esther had been impressed with Anstiss, but she had now assessed the latter's exact need for the hospitality of Parmelee Cove and knew that she could afford to take a stronger line with her. She adopted, therefore, the suave knowingness of Finny Coit's political tone. "I wonder if the fun in knowing people like that wasn't *always* rather exaggerated," she suggested. "And I wonder if I quite agree with you, Anstiss, that the decline of the left is a tragedy. Hasn't our left always been a bit whiny? And doesn't it really resent that we are conquering poverty without it? We are told there is nothing left for youth to die for. I wonder if it's really so great a hardship for youth to learn to live?"

Anstiss was effectively silenced, and Esther, having cleared the air of politics, told them of the dance that she was planning at the big house for a Saturday night in August.

"It's to be a house warming," she explained. "I know we've been living here for some time now, but we haven't had a real house warming. I wanted to wait until the alterations were finished. Now, Rosy, I want you to promise me to bring Reese. No, don't shake your head like that. I know all about his little resolutions. What I want you to tell him is that this is the only thing I'm going to ask of him *all* summer. I want everyone at Parmelee Cove to be at my party. The children are going to be allowed to stay up, and I think it would be so nice if, just *once*, they were given a picture of family solidarity and family affection. Now there it is, Rosy. I'm counting on you. I honestly don't think it's too much to ask."

"I'll try, Esther. That's all I can do."

She was going to ask Reese that night at cocktails while Grace Chess, who had come down for the weekend, was still upstairs in her bath. But Reese, with a rather sheepish smile, told her a piece of news that drove other projects momentarily from sight.

"I guess it looks as if Levine & Parmelee was going to stick for a while," he said as he brought in the cocktail shaker.

She stared at him for a moment and then jumped up. "Oh, darling! You've spoken to Amos!"

"Yes, he came to the office this morning, and he seemed so well I thought I could risk asking him. Well, he explained everything." Reese shrugged. "At least, I guess he did. He laughed at me. I must say, I felt rather a fool."

"Oh, sweetie, I'm so glad!"

"Do you want to hear what he said?"

Rosina suddenly knew that she would never be able to bear it. She might betray herself; anything might happen. "No, I don't understand those things. Anyway, what does it matter, as long as you're satisfied? Oh, darling, I'm so happy! Shall we open a bottle of champagne for dinner?"

"How do we explain it to Grace? That we've just discovered my partner isn't a crook?"

"We can say it's a private anniversary!"

"Does it really make all that difference to you?" he asked, a bit ruefully. "Frankly, I had rather looked forward to being on my own again. Not having to worry about Amos's little tricks. And I had just started to believe that you weren't going to mind."

"But you don't understand!" she exclaimed in dismay. "I didn't mind! It's been one of the wonderful things about this summer, knowing how little it *would* matter, giving up the house for something you really cared about!" She stopped, aghast at the lengths to which this sudden burst of emotion had carried her. But it was true, she thought with vehemence; it was perfectly true! That she had tried to stave off disaster did not mean that she would not have behaved well had disaster fallen. Nor did it mean that she would not have found a certain exaltation in it. "But it's still nicer not to have to make sacrifices, isn't it? It's nicer to be able to go on living in a house we're proud of. Is it so *wrong* to enjoy these things?"

"No, dear, of course not," he said, but his voice was just a bit gruff.

At dinner she found herself in a tense, excited state. She could hardly follow what Reese and Grace were saying. When the latter inquired about Anstiss, she was suddenly put in mind of Esther's party and asked Reese a bit shrilly, if he would go. He looked down the table at her in surprise.

"But, Rosy, you know I won't."

"Not even for my sake?"

"Why should you ask me to?"

"Because she's done so much for us!" Rosina cried. It suddenly seemed to her that everything was again in jeopardy if Reese wouldn't go to that dance, that Esther would tell all if she failed to produce him. She sat for a moment, pale and quiet, her heart pounding. "I've been swimming there *every* day. And taking friends there, too. And this is the only thing she's asked of us!"

"I told you when we moved down here," Reese said firmly, "that I was *not* going to the big house. I think I made that entirely clear. If you have put yourself under obligations to Esther, it was with full knowledge of my position. *You* can go to the dance if you want, but I'm staying right here." He turned now to poor Grace who was nervously anticipating a family quarrel. "This is my ex-wife," he explained acidulously, "who has bought my grandmother's house and wants to play Queen of the May. You can't conceive of the passion for money among the girls who've been brought up near it, but without ever quite having it. I tell you, it's frightening. When they finally get their hands on a fortune, like Esther, they make the worst parvenu seem positively refined. Finny Coit was very smart to let my ex-wife pick him. If an ordinary girl had married him for his money, she'd have left him when she got tired of it. But Esther will *never* tire of it! Not while she breathes!"

"You know that's unfair, Reese!" Rosina exclaimed. "All Esther thinks of is what she can do for people!"

"She may have taken *you* in, my dear. But please don't forget I was married to her."

"Reese, I beg you to go to this party! For one hour, at least. I beg you!" She saw Grace and Reese exchange glances of astonishment.

"Rosy, what's got into you?"

"I don't know. I don't know." To her humiliation she started to sob. "But please. I *promised* Esther!"

"All right!" He slammed down his napkin and got up from the table. Rosina dared not look at him, but his tone was furious. "I'll go to the stupid party if you're going to have hysterics about it! But for God's sake, pull yourself together! We're giving poor Grace here a fine weekend!" He stamped out of the room, and they heard the loud slam of the screen door in the hall. Rosina thought dully that he would go to the beach. Esther had told her of his way of working off anger in Parmelee Cove by walking for miles down the beach.

"Rosy, dear," she heard Grace's appalled voice, "why do you do it? How can you ask a man to go to his former wife's party? It's not like you, my dear. It's not like your usual tact."

"I know, Grace." Her tears were coming more easily now, and she made no effort to stop them. "I'm in a rather emotional state just now. Maybe it's the weather. It's been so humid."

"It has, hasn't it?" Grace said soothingly. "And now that you see what it is, dear, don't you think, when Reese comes back, it would be a nice thing to tell him that you've changed your mind? And that, of course, you don't care about his going to that silly dance?"

"But I do!" Rosina cried suddenly, sitting up and staring at her astonished friend. "I care passionately! And you heard him say he would, didn't you? You're my witness!"

4

THE SUMMER had not been working out for Esther. It was particularly hard, because she had expected so much of it. She had meant it to be a harmonious blend of her two lives; she had fancied herself as bringing together in happy fusion the Coits and the Parmelees with the big house, so beautifully redecorated, as a kind of community center. If she was herself to preside over that center, if it was to be an opportunity to show the Coits how good a Parmelee she had been and the Parmelees how good a Coit she was, this was simply a minor, if agreeable consequence of a plan that was, quite simply, the best plan for *everybody's* summer. If one had things, one should share them, and Esther had things. To check the impulse of generosity because the act of giving might expose one to the charge of condescension, or might underline too strongly the fact of one's superior riches, would have been a base surrender to the neurotic conventionalism of the times. One had to have the courage to affirm the old principle that responsibility and leadership were the handmaidens of wealth and not be like the modern counterpart of the man with the single talent who buried it in the sand to conceal it from his neighbors. This was the reason that despite all Finny's objections, she had persisted in her plan of taking over Parmelee Cove.

Yet nobody had seemed to appreciate her motives. Take

Cynthia, for example. When she had married George Wrexam and asked Finny to place him in the family business, Finny had stipulated, as Cynthia herself had anticipated, that his new brother-in-law should spend two years in the Omaha store. Who had intervened to save the Wrexams from their dreaded exile but Esther? And if, in return, she expected Cynthia to turn up from time to time and help out at some of her less lively dinner parties, had she deserved the latter's muttered reproach that she might have paid too high a price for her deliverance? Maybe Cynthia had better go to Omaha, after all. Maybe it was just what she and George needed.

And then there was Reese. She had rather visualized a series of talks with him, on the days when he came to fetch or deliver the children for sports, tending gradually, over a drink or so, to a friendly reperusal of the past. She had seen him saying some rather handsome things about how well she had done with their children, even congratulating her on her beautiful baby and perhaps coming as close to an apology for his past conduct as one could imagine from Reese. She had seen herself waiving old bygones with the smile of one who has found a happiness before undreamed of, with even a hint of something like gratitude to him for a desertion that had proved, however painful at the time, the open sesame of such a wonderful new life. And, of course, he would have had problems with a new wife of so little social background or experience; it would have been up to Esther to give her a helping hand. Well, it was true that she had been able to do a few things for Rosina. But as far as Reese was concerned, he might as well have been spending the summer at the other end of Long Island. Not once had he set foot inside her house, nor would he even join her Sunday night picnics. He had actually behaved as if he were the wronged party of their divorce! And when he had, after an invitation that was almost an entreaty (she blushed to think of it), condescended to accept, Rosina had announced the news over the telephone as if it had been a triumph of persuasion!

It was as if the flag of Reese's independence had spread rebellion through Parmelee Cove. The young Fred Talcotts had announced that they were buying a house on the next point and would soon release their cottage. Aunt Fanny, Fred's mother, instead of offering her place next door to Esther who had, after all, saved its value for her, had sold it, without so much as a by-your-leave, for a thumping price to a builder of ranch houses. Esther could only feel that she was being treated with a proper respect by what Reese used to describe sneeringly as Finny's "court," the various young couples in Northfield who worked for Coit Stores. And even there she knew the respect was really all for Finny and not for herself. She had hoped in the beginning to have a hand in the business, at least to be a consultant as to the arrangement of the big store windows on Fifth Avenue, but Finny had been quite unpleasantly adamant about this. "Stick to your charities and committees," he had warned her. "That's a woman's work." Esther, much hurt, had learned that her powers of persuasion were confined to domestic matters. She had then thought that she might console herself with an intellectual life, that she might found a kind of salon, and she had been interested in her new friend, Anstiss Stranahan, who had done this very thing in New York, but even here her enthusiasm had been dampened by the reflection that Reese, aloof in his cottage, would have the satisfaction of knowing that she owed Anstiss to his wife.

Yet of all the disappointments of the summer, there was none to equal the defection of her own son. Alfred, now twelve, was Esther's particular pride; she liked to show her independence of the vulgar modern fear of phrases not suggestive of masculinity by describing him as a "beautiful" boy. It gave her great satisfaction that he did not favor the Parmelees. He had her large brown eyes, her steady smile and some of her equanimity of temper; he was a quiet, undemanding child who usually fitted in with her plans. He could be stubborn, however, almost as stubborn as Reese, in a few small matters about which he seemed passionately to care. One of these, she suspected, was involved on the morning when he came to sit in her bedroom while she was having breakfast. He was silent and restless.

"Now, Alfred, what is it?" she asked, looking up from her paper as he ran a wet finger around the rim of a glass. "Or if you've come to be social, be social."

"Mummy, is it all settled that I'm to go to St. Lawrence's in the fall? I mean, completely settled?"

Esther contemplated him with admiring eyes. She would have liked to have had him painted in just such a concentrated pose, and for a moment she indulged herself in a little fantasy of Alfred as a Velasquez prince, all pale intensity and staring eyes against a background of red velvet. What a pity that it was no longer permitted to dress children attractively. "But, darling, you know it's all been arranged. You wanted to go yourself. You told me so."

"Yes, I know, but I was just thinking that if I waited a year and went in the second form, I could go at the same time as Peter Talcott." He still did not look up, and Esther knew at once that he was more concerned than he cared to reveal. "Besides, more than half the boys now wait to go in the second form."

"Well, of course, that's true," she said doubtfully. "But we've given up your place in Woodbury Day, and I'm not absolutely sure we could get it back." When she had married

Finny and bought Parmelee Cove, it had been decided that
the children would remain in their schools in Northfield.
Finny's apartment in the city was to be considered a "pied-
à-terre" for her and him to spend weekday nights, free of
responsibility for the young. "The schools are all so crowded,
now, darling. It's very difficult to drop in and out just because you've decided it might be fun to wait another year
for Peter Talcott."

Alfred looked up at her brightly, as though he had just
been struck by an idea. "Oh, but that would be all right!
Daddy says he could always get me into Branford in New
York!"

Esther felt a sudden dryness in her throat. "Oh, he does,
does he? And would you mind telling me where you expect
to live in town? Uncle Finny's flat, you know, is not adapted
for the whole family."

"But why couldn't I stay with Daddy and Rosy? They
have a whole house!"

The boy quailed before her startled stare. He was evidently not as innocent as he wished to appear. He knew
perfectly well that he had just tossed a hand grenade into the
very pink center of her double bed. "Was that Daddy's suggestion?" she demanded, after a pause to drain some of the
temper from her tone. "Did he invite you?"

"Well, he said I could always come. He said he had a
spare room."

"I see." She paused to push away her tray. "And you'd
be willing to leave Mummy?"

"But it wouldn't be like going to St. Lawrence's," he
pointed out in the tone of one who has anticipated this
argument. "I'd come home for weekends. And that's all I
see you in the winter, anyway!"

This argument was quite inconsistent with Esther's picture

of herself as a mother, and she did not like it at all. "Do you think I neglect you, Alfred?" she asked in a reproachful tone.

"Oh, no, never!" Alfred seemed genuinely upset by such an interpretation. "Oh, Mummy, no!" He got up and came over to the bed to kiss her awkwardly. "I just thought you wouldn't mind, that's all."

"I think your father might have spoken to me himself about this."

"Oh, but he's going to!"

"He is, is he?"

"Yes." Alfred was eager now to justify his other parent. "As a matter of fact, I wasn't to have said anything about it yet. I mean about staying with him."

"I see," Esther said dryly. "It all sounds rather like a conspiracy against poor Mummy."

"No!" exclaimed the boy, bewildered at the depth of the mire into which he seemed to be slipping. "It's just as you said, that it was up to Daddy to speak about it first."

"I meant, before telling *you*," she retorted, but then immediately caught herself. She was itching to tell Alfred how badly his father had treated him, how little until now he had been concerned with his son's education. But she had pledged herself against any such tactics. Such would never be *her* way. "All right, darling, we'll think it over," she continued in a lighter tone. "If you want another year at Woodbury Day, I daresay it can be arranged. They've been trying to get Uncle Finny on the board for years."

"Oh, but I'm tired of that old school!"

"Really? You seem hard to suit this morning. Well, maybe if you'd like to go to Branford, I can persuade Uncle Finny to get a larger apartment. Then we can all be together in the city. Wouldn't you like that?"

Alfred looked perplexed. Clearly, she had outmaneuvered him. But she was not prepared for the sharpness of his disappointment. "Oh, I guess it's all too much trouble," he said brusquely. "Let's skip the whole thing. I'll go to St. Lawrence's!" And he abruptly quitted the room, leaving Esther with the unpleasant reflection that the only thing he really wanted was to stay with his father that winter. She would not have believed that a child normally so affectionate would have been capable of hurting her so.

She was just about to get up to go to her mother's room when the latter appeared in the doorway. Mrs. Means, as always on her visits to Parmelee Cove, was dressed as for a day in town. Esther would have liked to have her come in her dressing gown and breakfast with her cozily alone, but her mother would never do this, rising early and going down instead to the dining room to sit with Finny. She struck a dark, neat, rather puritan note in the lacy pinkness of Esther's great bedroom, standing out a bit starkly from the poodles, the cushions, the silver breakfast things, the semi-Oriental, courtlike atmosphere of her daughter's early morning hours. But if she struck a dissident note, it was only in her appearance. No Eastern amah could have tried harder to blend into Esther's scene.

She sat now on the sofa by the bed, her fidgeting hands resting uneasily on her knees, while she listened to her daughter's account of what little Alfred had said. Gradually the uneasiness of her hands seemed to mount to her features, which Esther recognized as the nervous symptom that she always betrayed on the rare occasions when she felt it her duty to disagree with her daughter.

"It may surprise you to hear me say so, dear," Mrs. Means began when Esther had finished, "but it doesn't seem to me that it would be such a terribly bad thing for Alfred to be a little more with his father. He strikes me as being a bit too shy and quiet. It might help him to spend a winter with Reese before going off to boarding school."

"Mother! After what I've heard you say about Reese! How *can* you?"

"Reese behaved very badly to you, my dear." Mrs. Means shook her head sorrowfully. "Nobody knows that better than your mother. And I can never forgive him for it. Never! But I'm an old woman, and it doesn't matter whom I forgive and whom I don't. There's no point cluttering up young Alfred's life with old resentments. I've watched Reese conduct those children's classes this summer, and he's changed. I think he's settled down."

"That's what people said when he married *me!*"

"I know, dear. But he's older now."

"Older and cleverer!" Esther retorted in a tone that trembled with bitterness. "Clever enough to have won over my own mother!"

"Ah, my dear." Mrs. Means's look of pain would have satisfied any but a daughter. "You ought to know how little *I* could be won over. You ought to know whose side I'm always on."

"But that's precisely what I'm trying to find out!"

To this Mrs. Means could respond only by again shaking her head. Esther knew that she had not entirely succeeded in working her mother into her new life. In the period before her remarriage their relationship had been closer than ever before. Mrs. Means had been able to devote herself, body and soul, to the consolation of her abandoned child. But in the splendor surrounding Mrs. Phineas Coit there was little function for a parent but to make small exclamations in the background, to raise her arms up and down in a constant gesture of admiration, like a Hollywood mother whose little girl, erupting with new hair, new teeth and new eyelashes, has become overnight a great star. Except, Esther reminded herself quickly, unlike the Hollywood star, *she* could never be in the least ashamed of her parents. On the contrary, was she not bursting with pride about them? Had she not offered them their choice of any cottage at Parmelee Cove? But then, as in the past, always when she least expected it, she had run into one of her mother's odd, brisk little moods of independence. No, it would appear that her father did not want to move to Parmelee Cove, that he was perfectly happy in the house that he had now occupied for twenty years, that he was old and set in his ways, and that her mother did, after all, have obligations towards him. Esther could not openly decry a deference to the wishes of her own father, but she could certainly allow it to swell her justified indignation at this brazen transfer of loyalty to her own ex-husband, and she now became almost shrill. "I suppose I should turn over little Eunice, also, to her father's care!" she exclaimed. "Maybe I should move out of my house altogether and let Reese move in. Is that what you recommend, Mother?"

"I'm sorry, dear," Mrs. Means said heavily. "I'm sorry that loving you as I love you should mean sometimes going against you. But it can't be helped. What sort of a mother would I be otherwise? I still think Alfred is too young to go to boarding school."

"He happens to be six months older than the average boy in his class!"

"Maybe he's a bit immature, then. Maybe he needs a father for a while."

"Finny's been absolutely angelic with him!"

Mrs. Means's silence was pregnant with dissent. When she answered, however, she was mild enough. "Finny's been very good, of course," she agreed. "But a father's still a father."

"I suppose it's *my* fault he hasn't had a father!"

"I didn't say that, my dear. I'm only saying that he has one available now."

"And one who can twist his former mother-in-law around his little finger!"

But Mrs. Means would not be backed down. She was looking away from Esther, across the room, still monotonously shaking her head. "I haven't even talked to Reese," she said stubbornly. "I've done no more than nod to him when he drives by. And that's all I care to do. I have nothing to say to Reese, nor he to me, I'm sure. But I *have* talked to his mother."

"A fine, impartial judge!"

"I think Agnes Parmelee *is* impartial," her mother said reprovingly. "After all, when you and Reese separated —"

"Separated! You mean, when he deserted me!"

"Yes, dear, when he deserted you. Agnes took your side entirely. Against her own son. I think you must give her credit for that. And I think, by like token, you should give her credit for thinking only of little Alfred's best good. If Agnes thinks he would do well with his father this winter, it seems to me you should at least consider it."

"This is fine!" Esther cried, giving vent altogether now to her irritation. "This is perfect! I am left high and dry, with two small children. I spend all my time loving them, caring for them, trying to be gay and cheerful so they won't grow up to resent their father. I marry again to give them everything in the world their hearts could desire. And what is my reward? The moment Alfred is big enough to be an attractive companion — and who made him that? — the moment the dirty work, so to speak, has all been done, in barges Reese, cool as a cucumber, to reassert his abandoned rights! Well, if he thinks he can get away with that, he has another think coming! If I had brought those children up as any other girl would have done, they wouldn't even be speaking to him now!"

"Oh, my dear," her mother protested, "you've done marvelously with them. Everyone knows that."

"Everyone? Does my own mother know it? What will *she* do if he goes to court to regain custody of Alfred? If he gets that shyster partner of his to invent some dirt about me? Will you testify for him?"

"Oh, Esther, darling!" Mrs. Means cried in anguish. "How can you *say* such things?" She raised her hands to her eyes and was silent for several moments. When she spoke, her tone was very low and sad. "I sometimes think you've changed, my child."

"*How* have I changed?"

"I don't know," Mrs. Means said, sighing as she rose to her feet. "I don't know," she repeated. "Maybe we all have. I'm going to walk in the garden now. I hope it will steady my nerves. And I hope it will give you a chance to reflect that you've been very unfair to me. I love you, my child. Probably I love you too much."

Esther, however, left alone, made a brave and ultimately successful effort to stamp out the incipient flames of remorse. When she felt some degree of calm again, she telephoned to Anstiss Stranahan and asked her to come over that morning to swim.

It was a hot morning, but there was nobody else at the pool except two of the Talcott children whom Esther dispatched to swim in the sound. She then ordered lemonade to be sent down from the big house, and she and Anstiss settled themselves on the patio for a morning's chat. It was not difficult for Esther to lead her guest to the subject of the Reese Parmelees' social life in New York.

"I suppose they see mostly the people on her magazine and the remnants of my little group," Anstiss speculated. "How could it be otherwise? Rosy didn't know a soul when Grace Chess first brought her to my house. I can't imagine that she met many people through Reese. He's so anti-social. Certainly not any women, anyway."

"Why not any women?"

"Well, the women Reese knew, my dear, were all of one kind."

Esther smiled. "But he knew *you*."

"Well, of course. But that was different. Rosy brought him to our house." Anstiss shrugged as she rubbed sun-tan oil on her long, white arms. "As a matter of fact, I imagine Rosina will take my place with the group if Jack and I decide to stay out here this winter. She has a house and likes to entertain, and my poor old precious ridiculers will do till she catches bigger fish."

"What sort of people did your group consist of?"

"Oh, good enough souls. Artistic in their inclinations. Sentimental in their politics. Occasionally talented. Duey was the best of the lot."

"You're like a great collector," Esther said with a small laugh. "From time to time you sell out the works, keeping one perfect thing. You've kept Duey."

Anstiss was struck and pleased with this analogy, as Esther had intended that she should be. "Well, I'm sure there's still a respectable amount of talent left. Enough, anyway, for Rosina to start on. She'll sell out herself in time. When she feels strong enough to do it. In some ways Rosina may do better than I did." Anstiss squinted at the sun, as if pausing to make a really detached appraisal. "Yes, I think with artists she really may. She can put up with more than I can."

"You mean heavy drinking, rough talk, that sort of thing?"

"Well — yes." Anstiss's shrug seemed to discount such things. "But more importantly she doesn't have some of my prejudices." Here she turned suddenly to Esther as if to make a disarming confession. "I have to admit that, try as I will, I can't learn to tolerate the big, shrieking type of fairy that's so much the rage today."

"Good heavens!" Esther exclaimed, shocked. "Can Rosina?"

Anstiss shrugged again. "Gives her no trouble at all. Reese neither, oddly enough."

"They have a lot of — *those* people around?"

"Well, I don't know about a lot. But there's one in particular they're very keen about, though they have sense enough not to ask *me* when he's there. He's that painter, Cliffie Suter. You've probably heard of him. Does small things of children?"

"Oh, yes." Esther was surprised to realize, after she had said this, that she *had* heard of him. "As matter of fact, I was thinking of getting him to do Alfred and Eunice."

"Well, Eunice, fine. But I wouldn't leave him alone too long with little Alfred, if I were you."

"Oh, I *see*."

They discussed for some time the other individuals who composed Anstiss's little group. It was a subject on which the latter liked to declaim. Esther listened closely for further depravities, but none were forthcoming. The group as a whole, it appeared, was innocuous enough. Nevertheless, she had what she needed.

Alfred went down to the cottage that evening before dinner, as he did every evening now, to pass a football with Reese when the latter arrived from the city. Esther guessed that he would tell his father of the morning's conversation,

and she waited in her own room for the telephone call that she knew must be forthcoming.

"Why, Reese!" she exclaimed pleasantly when it came. "How nice to hear your voice! I was afraid the whole summer was going by without our meeting. Now don't tell me you're not coming to my dance tomorrow night. I shall be *too* disappointed!"

"No, it's not that," he said in his old abrupt tone. "It's about what Al asked you this morning. Could I come over tonight and talk to you about it?"

"Oh, Reese, I'm afraid *not* tonight. My parents are here, and Mrs. Coit is coming for dinner. You know how those things are."

"What about tomorrow morning? I could stop in early before I take my train."

"But it's the day of my party! I'll be up to my ears!"

"I think Al's welfare is more important than a party," he retorted gruffly. "I'd appreciate it if you'd see me. Just for a few minutes."

"Well, I'm delighted you're taking such a sudden interest in Alfred's welfare," she said with a slight edge in her tone. "Come then tomorrow, before you catch your train."

It was very early, indeed, when he came, but Esther was ready for him. She met him in the garden and allowed him to follow her restlessly about for a few minutes while she directed the men who were already hanging the Japanese lanterns. When she turned to him at last, she surprised him by opening the discussion herself.

"Let me say right off, Reese, that I think you should have come to me before making any proposals to Alfred about next winter."

"It didn't come up that way," he answered, reddening. "We simply happened to be talking about St. Lawrence's —"

"Which I'm sure you told him was a terrible school!"

"Let me finish, please, Esther. I did no such thing. He said quite voluntarily that he didn't want to go next year. He said he'd like to go to a school in New York if he could still get in."

"Which you told him you could arrange!" she said with a snort.

"Well, I think I might. Andy is on the board of Branford."

"You, who used to be so against any kind of pull!"

"I don't mind doing something for Al."

"*Now!*"

They had been strolling, but they stopped at this, before the Roman temple, and faced each other. She saw how hard he was struggling to keep his temper. Well, let him! Who held the high trump?

"I see no point in recrimination," he said at last, taking a deep breath. "The simple question is not what I've done in the past that's right or wrong, but what's the best thing for Al now. I think he needs to be with a father for a while."

"My Finny's been more of a father to him than you ever were!"

He looked straight at her in his old bold way. "I don't think he likes Finny."

"You say that because you want to think it!" she cried, furious. "Finny's paid more attention to that boy in a year than you have in his whole life!"

"I haven't come here to quarrel with you, Esther."

"Oh, no! Saying that about Finny!"

"I haven't said anything about Finny," he insisted coolly. "I'm only saying what Al feels about him."

"How do you know what Al feels?"

"I don't. But I have a darned good idea. Would you like to know what it's based on?"

But Esther did not. She had no wish to dwell in any specific detail on Alfred's feelings towards his stepfather. She had a suspicion that these might not constitute her strongest argument. "Let's keep to the point," she said with dignity. "The point is that *I*, and nobody else, must be the judge of what is best for Alfred. I know you and Mother both feel he's not ready for boarding school. As a matter of fact, I've been coming to the same conclusion myself. I shall write St. Lawrence's today to enter him in the second form a year from this fall."

He turned sharply away from her, tense. "And in the meanwhile?"

"In the meanwhile he will stay right here and go on with Woodbury Day. Why should he change?"

Reese swung back to her now, openly angry. "Can you really believe you're not doing this to spite me?" he demanded. "To get back at me?"

"Of course I can!"

"Why, then, should you grudge me one winter of Al's company? It isn't as if you wanted him for yourself. Do you think I don't know your schedule? Do you think I don't know that you and Finny are in town all week while the children are out here with a governess? If he comes to me I'll promise to have supper with him every night. And breakfast with him every morning! Why be a dog in the manger, Esther?"

Esther's temples throbbed until she felt actually dizzy. She had to sit down on a marble bench to collect herself. She was still panting with the outrage when she was able at last to murmur: "*You!* You have the unmitigated gall to teach *me* about responsibility!"

"By God, I have!"

"All right," she said, taking a quick breath. "All right,

then. I was hoping I wouldn't have to go into this, but now, apparently, I must. Let me tell you, then," she said, looking up at him boldly, "that it's not simply a question of my wanting the boy here, though I most emphatically do. It's also a question of my not wishing to expose him to a certain kind of atmosphere."

"What kind of atmosphere? Are you talking about Rosy? What's wrong with our atmosphere?"

"Well, it's not exactly a question of being wrong." Even she hesitated before his angry stare. "I mean it's perfectly all right except where children are concerned. Naturally, I expect you and Rosina to select your own friends. And, generally speaking, I admire tolerance."

"Get to the point, Esther," he said impatiently. "Who do we tolerate that you don't?"

"Well, I hear, for example, that you have homosexuals in the house."

He gave a little yelp of scorn. "Who doesn't?"

"I don't." She turned away as he gave that offensive yelp again. "Not knowingly, anyway."

"Who have you been talking to, anyway?" The pause that followed his question was suddenly filled with his snort of disgust. "Oh, of course! It's that bitch, Anstiss! Cliffie Suter. That's the man, isn't it? The only reason she has it in for him is that her precious little Duey had a crush on him!"

"I don't care to go into that. The fact remains that I will not have my son living in a house where he might meet men like Mr. Suter."

"Very well, then," he retorted. "Supposing I give you my word of honor that he will never meet Suter? Or any other man whom I have reason to suspect of such propensities?"

"It isn't only that," she said, uncomfortable again. "It's not really so much the individuals as the atmosphere. An easygoing, liberal atmosphere, a magazine world —"

"Are you implying," he interrupted sarcastically, "that there's anything *liberal* about *A Woman's World?*"

"I won't be tripped up, Reese. You know perfectly well what I mean."

"I'm damned if I do!"

"Anyway, my decision is final."

"I congratulate you!" he exclaimed, abandoning now the last hope of winning her over. "Is it really conceivable that you can imagine that you have Al's welfare at heart? Yes, I suppose it really is. You just might! Who can follow you up to those dizzy peaks of intellectual dishonesty where you sniff the thin air like a contented mountain goat?"

Esther jumped to her feet, ready for anything now. "Better than the peaks of *actual* dishonesty!" she cried.

"What?"

"Better than being the partner of a shyster lawyer who swindled an innocent old lady out of her money! As *everyone* knows!"

But he simply snorted again in derision. "Everyone, apparently, but me."

"Exactly!" she exclaimed reckless. "Everyone but you! And the only reason *you* don't know is that your wife has kept you from knowing!"

This time his expression was all that she could have asked for. The anger in his eyes was clouded with his sudden confusion. "Explain yourself!"

"She and Levine hatched up the story he told you! In the hospital. If you don't believe me, ask her!"

He left her without another word, and her anger dwindled rapidly into fear as she watched his broad back retreat down the path. What would he do? And would Rosina come over with cries and lamentations to reproach her? Or even wait to do it publicly at the party that night? Esther trembled at the thought of what she might have stirred up, but as she started slowly back to the house past all the men who were hanging the decorations, as she saw ahead of her the butler consulting with the caterer on the porch, as she reflected on the number of people in Finny's employ, both at home and in all his stores, was she not adequately protected? Could she not summon help and ask that Mrs. Parmelee, even Mr. Parmelee, be expelled from her presence? It was no longer the heroine of Louisa May Alcott who walked now over the wide lawn to the terrace. It was Isabella of Castile, riding with her priests into fallen Granada at the head of the army of God.

5

REESE went straight from his meeting with Esther to the station. He did not even buy a paper, but sat moodily all the way into the city, staring bleakly out of the train window and piecing things together. When he got to the office he went directly to Amos's room. He found his partner, as always in the early morning, reading the stock market news.

"Amos!" he blurted out. "Did Rosina go to see you in the hospital?"

Amos smiled easily and broadly. "Yes, she did, God bless her!"

"And did you and she cook up that story for me of why you passed the business on to Shea?"

Amos continued to smile imperturbably. "No, I did that. It was a bit legal for Rosy, don't you think? Not, of course, that she's not a smart girl."

"Don't you think you owe it to me *now* to tell me what happened about Miss Howland's codicil?"

"If you wish."

Reese sat down, taken aback, in the chair opposite Amos's desk. "Were you expecting me to ask you this today?" he demanded.

"I've been expecting it for weeks!"

"Then I would appreciate your telling me."

"It's hard to know how to tell you things, Reese," Amos

answered as he calmly and slowly filled his pipe. "You have such a stiff, ramrod idea of what the truth is. There's even a bit of a suggestion that the truth has to be something unpleasant. Or else it couldn't be the truth, could it? I think your Rosy feels about it the way I do. She's trying to make the world fit into your concept of truth. And it's quite a job. She and I, we're the kind who try to get along with facts. Our only trouble is finding reasons for the things we do that you will accept as the real reasons. Often we don't know. We can't follow you up into the clouds of principle."

"Maybe I can make it easier for you," Reese retorted. "Maybe I can break it down into a few simple questions. Did you or did you not send Miss Howland to Pat Shea?"

"I did not."

"But did you know she'd gone to him?"

"Yes, Pat told me. That's why he came to the office the day she signed her codicil. To tell me she had left me a legacy. A large legacy. He didn't tell me how much."

"But you told me yourself that the first you knew of it was the day she died!"

"Pat had no business telling me," Amos replied, unruffled. "It was a breach of professional confidence. I wasn't going to give him away, even to you, Reese."

Reese began again to feel some of the same sense of frustration that he had felt at the trial. "Why did he tell you, then?"

"That's the way Pat is. He'd written a codicil that was going to mean a lot of money to me. He wanted me to know it, that's all."

"So you'd do something for him one day?"

Amos shrugged. "So I'd keep him in mind."

"Which it appears you have done. But if Miss Howland wanted to leave you a legacy, what possible favor did Shea do you? He was simply her agent, wasn't he? For which he was paid?"

"Yes, but he was a prompt agent," Amos pointed out. "If he'd delayed a few days, as most lawyers might have, she'd have been dead!"

"It was a simple one-page document. There would have been no excuse for delay."

"Look, Reese," Amos said patiently, "why be complicated about it? Pat did his job, and I got my legacy. Is it a crime for me to remember something like that?"

"To remember it, no. But to reward it? And what were you really rewarding him for? I suggest it was for what he did *not* do. For *not* making her think it over. For *not* looking carefully into what she was doing. For *not* suggesting that the legacy was out of all proportion to her fortune!"

Amos puffed at his pipe silently for several moments as he contemplated Reese without the least apparent resentment. "Of course, you would see it that way, wouldn't you?" He nodded his head several times. "And who is to say to what extent such considerations may have entered my subconscious or even my conscious thinking? I don't know, and I certainly don't care. That's where I'm not like you. And thank heavens I'm not. It must make for a tortured life. I prefer to think of other aspects of the picture. Aspects that would never occur to you. I prefer to consider that Pat Shea, in return for a small fee, had to undergo the public insults of the Howland family. To sustain a codicil which profited me greatly and him not at all, he had to be hauled over the coals by every newspaper in town. *That's* the kind of thing I choose to remember! And now, Mr. Reese Parmelee, great and impartial investigator, grand inquisitor of the conscience of Amos Levine, if you don't mind, I've said my last word on the subject!"

Reese got up immediately. "That's all then?"

"That is all. I take it I have not satisfied you?"

"No!"

"Well, you must make your decision on the basis of what I've told you. For I've told you all!"

Reese had started for the door, but now he turned around. "My decision?"

Amos smiled benignly. "Why, obviously, my dear boy, the decision of whether or not you're going to continue as a partner of Beelzebub!"

"I'll let you know," Reese said tersely. He walked quickly down the corridor to his own room where he heard his telephone ringing. It was Rosina.

"Darling, I had to call you," she began in an anxious tone. "What happened in your talk with Esther? Will she let Al come to us?"

"No."

"Oh, sweetie, I'm so sorry. Did she give you any reasons?"

"I'll tell you later."

"Tell me now!"

"No."

"Oh, Reese, something's happened. I know it! What's the matter? Will you be home early? It's Esther's dance, you know."

"I'm afraid I can't make it. I have to work tonight. You go on without me. I'll meet you there later if I can."

"Reese!"

"I'm sorry, dear," he said gruffly. "I've got people with me." And he hung up.

He left the office and spent his working day in Central Park. It was hot and humid; the greenery was almost tropical in its lushness. In the zoo before the placid, swaying elephants, the stretched out tigers, the peeling camels, in the Mall with its rows of empty chairs arranged for the evening concert, by the pond with its fleet of empty, moored rowboats, everything was inert, everything turned a glazed eye and a drooping eyelid on his problem. The park in summer seemed to repudiate distinctions. If he was to have help with Amos, it was not even to be from the usually active seals who lay like crumpled bags on the brown rocks before the Armory. For like them, like everything else, Amos had done nothing. He had simply reached out his hand to the universe. As Reese saw it now, he had to concede that Amos had never discussed his legacy with Miss Howland and had had nothing to do with her going to Shea. What the latter might have done, of course, was another thing. Reese could visualize Shea, sitting as quietly as one of the sleeping lizards while the old lady talked. And then moving, how swiftly, to implement her vague little plan, to catch, as with a darting tongue, the one-day butterfly of her fluttering generosity, so that the codicil was typed and ready with its hard little case for her rambling sentiment! And with what proud pleasure, a copy in his pocket, had he not hurried to Amos that very morning! *This* was the man whom Amos had not scrupled to reward!

But Amos himself had not done it. Amos had not even known of it until it was done. This was what Reese, sitting on a bench and flinging popcorn to aggressive pigeons, could not get away from. Amos had his own rules and yardsticks, but he applied them only to himself. He did not judge others. If he received a legacy, he did not question its source. It showed a lack of moral delicacy that Reese found offensive, but was it a reason for breaking with a man? Was it a reason for breaking up a firm? If it was, it was the last chance to do so. He faced that, too. For with Amos ill, it was up to him to assume the leadership of the firm, and having once done so, he would owe it to the staff as well as to Amos to remain. And Rosina, more unscrupulous than Esther, would have shackled him to her way of life more securely than Esther had ever dreamed of doing!

When he got home that night it was late, and Rosina had

gone to the dance. There was a half-moon over the big house, and he could make out the colored orbs of the Japanese lanterns in the garden. The sound of an orchestra floated faintly down the lawn, and the headlights of car after car moved slowly up the drive, into the big turn-around and were blotted out under the porte-cochere. Going outside he crossed the grass and went around to the terrace in back of the house. There were already people talking and drinking there, but the terrace was large and in the darkness he was able to stand by a column, puffing at his pipe almost unobserved, and gaze in the great window that Esther had cut in the side of the house. It provided a perfect view of the hall.

She had made the hall and living room into one vast chamber with the old Jacobean stairway spirally descending at one end. An orchestra was playing at the other, and the floor was filled with couples. The dark paneling had been painted a light tan and the sofas, pushed against the walls, were gaily covered in pink and yellow. Reese had a feeling that the poor old house was being made to smile and that all the Parmelees, collected again under its roof, were being made to like it. He was glad that he was outside.

It was striking how much of his past was there. He saw Esther sitting with his mother on a sofa, magnificent in a gold dress, half turned away from her other guests as she gracefully gave her primary attention to the senior member of the family which she had bought out. His mother was nodding vaguely and watching his sister Joan on the dance floor. Reese felt sure that she was instinctively worrying about Joan's partners, forgetting that she had been married for ten years and had a family of her own. He saw Rosina dancing with Freddy Talcott. She was wearing a new white dress that he had not seen before and seemed very animated and gay. Anstiss Stranahan was dancing with Duey. She had her head tilted way back and was laughing the silent laugh, her lips taut and parted, that she thought so engaging. He saw Cynthia Wrexam leave the floor and walk towards the bar, and he knew by the jerky way in which she moved her shoulders that she ought not to have the drink that she was about to have. He saw Andy Fearing in the stag line, but Andy had spotted him first and was waving. Reese only stepped back further into the darkness. They would all be waving to him if he stayed there, crying to him to join them, to dance and drink at Esther's. People no longer waited for the prodigal to return; they chased him, shaking sticks and rattling pans. The old stockade was too tottery to afford a single deserter; they were always engaged now in calling musters and checking rolls. Prodigal? *They* were the prodigals, spending their tiny capital of integrity in the endless task of adapting themselves cheerfully to the new, anything new.

As he was turning away in disgust, he felt a hand on his shoulder. Andy had come out to join him. For a moment neither spoke, and they continued to gaze at the dance floor.

"Rosy's told me the whole thing," Andy said at last. "Levine called her this morning."

"Everybody's told everybody," Reese said dryly.

"Go on in and dance with her, Reese. She's feeling sick about the whole thing."

"Why don't you mind your own business?"

"Oh, come on." Andy laid hold of Reese's arm, but the latter shook him roughly off. "You can't hold a little thing like that against her. She loves you, damn it!"

"Go home, Pandarus. Scat!"

But even this could not quench the determination of Andy's smile. "You never need anyone but Reese Parmelee, do you? You just want to be left alone, is that it?"

"It seems a simple request."

"It's always simple to be a heel."

Reese said nothing, and Andy, shrugging, turned back to the house. "I'll send her out."

Reese watched Andy cross the floor and cut in on Rosina. He saw her glance quickly at the window and then start towards the door. Outside, she came up swiftly behind him.

"Reese," she said pleadingly.

"Shall we walk?" he asked without turning.

They went silently down a gravel path towards the sound. At a turn by a wall, he paused, feeling dry and bitter.

"I'm not just angry," he said. "It's not that simple. But I'm wondering very seriously if you and I want the same lives. It's not just the house and the decorating and all the parties. It's not even your friendship with Esther and the revival of everything down here at the Cove that I tried to get away from. All that and more I could take. But when I find you trying to hoodwink me into thinking that everything in my office is on the up and up, I begin to ask myself if you will stop at anything."

"I'll never do it again," she said in a small voice.

"But how could you have done it *once?* Unless my standards are a farce to you? Unless I'm nothing but a silly joke!"

"Please, Reese! Tell Amos you'll resign! I don't care any more. Let's start over again. In another city if you want. I'll never interfere again!"

"But I can't be sure," he insisted grimly, shaking his head. "I can't ever again be sure!"

In the dim moonlight he saw her expression change. The pleading, the solicitude suddenly vanished; she seemed to go as dry and bitter as he. She turned away to the water.

"What will you do then?"

"I think I want to go away for a while."

She gave a deep sigh and shrugged her shoulders, but remained looking across the sound. "Will you drive out west?" she asked. "The way you did when you left Esther?"

"I might."

"I suppose it's not given to many men to make two escapes from the same prison," she said in a more grating tone. "Do you plan to do it a third time?"

"I have no plans."

"It's almost a relief, I suppose," she continued in the same tone, leaning now against the stone balustrade. "Ever since we've been married, I've been waiting for this. Waiting for the moment when you would get your wanderlust again. I've tried to distract you with little fireworks. I suppose they only had the effect of exasperating you. Maybe I'll have peace when you've gone. Anything is better than this uncertainty." Even in the semi-darkness he could see that her fists were suddenly clenched. "Anything!"

"Were you really thinking of *me* when you went to see Amos in the hospital?"

"Of course I was!" she exclaimed passionately. "Everything I've done has been for you! I've been a fool, but it's been for your sake. I've been running about like a mad thing trying to tie you down. So you wouldn't blow away in the first storm. Trying to distract myself from the truth. When I'm alone again, maybe it'll be better. It's *got* to be better than now!"

"But, Rosy, suppose *I* had gone to Gilda Doremus and hatched up a plot —"

"I know, I know!" she retorted furiously. "You want to put me in the wrong. You want to stick to the facts. But I know there's no answer for *me* in your facts. You didn't care about that old lady's will, any more than you care what I said to Amos. Not basically. All you care is that you find yourself stuck again. As you were with Esther. As you were with your old firm. But you won't be honest as you were in those days and just walk out! Oh, no! You've learned to be sly. Amos has taught you that much!" She stood up and walked closer to him, and he could see that she was trembling all over. "This time you've got to be in the right! You've got to have an excuse. And old Miss Howland has given you one. That's why you've been so fascinated by that situation from the beginning. How you've nursed it and how beautifully it's turned out!" She threw back her head suddenly and laughed a bit wildly. "Now you can walk out on your partner because he's a crook and on your wife because she sided with him. Bravo, Reese!"

"Well, if that isn't the most perverse twisting of a simple fact, I've ever heard — !"

"Perverse!" she cried. "You're the one who's perverse! *You're* the one who has to do the twisting. Because otherwise how would you look to yourself? Leaving Amos just as he's had a heart attack and me with a baby? It would never do, would it? We have to be thoroughly smeared first, don't we?" Her breath was coming in pants now. "But I don't think much of this new, cautious Reese. This 'respectable' deserter. This 'injured' goody-goody. I confess I rather admired the old Reese who had the guts to spit in the eye of his faithful Esther and of his assembled family, and just walk out!"

"Do you really believe all that?"

"Of course I believe it! Because it's true!"

"You're the one who should be the lawyer!" He even laughed, in sheer admiration of how completely she had taken the offensive.

"Amos and I try to live in the world, that's all," she said with a snort. "We don't try to be too good for it. We don't turn our backs on it at the first hint of compromise! But then we *like* the world. We don't need an excuse for running away from it!"

"Keep talking. You might even convince yourself."

"I'm not going to keep talking. I'm through!" She turned abruptly back to the house. "I'm going back to the party, and I'm going to have several drinks, and I'm going to dance till dawn! And when I get home, I expect I shall find you gone!" She paused, and he could hear the deep intake of her breath. "I hope so, anyway. I've got to get on with my life! I've *got* to!"

He reached out to take her hand, but she suddenly broke into a run, and he stood and watched her white figure retreat quickly across the lawn and merge with the figures on the terrace. Then he turned and walked down to the beach to skip small stones on the water.

6

WHEN Rosina came home from the party late that night, she found that Reese had gone. There was a note on the front hall table to tell her that he had put enough cash in their joint account to cover her expenses for three months. He had to "get away for a while," the note announced, and "hash things out" in his own mind. Rosina tore it into small pieces as she walked slowly upstairs to go to bed. The money did not interest her. She had always known that Reese would support her. It was the only thing, indeed, that he could be counted on to do. Because she knew that she would need all her energy for the following day, she took two sleeping pills, and the first night of her abandonment passed without restlessness or dreams.

The next morning she closed the cottage and moved with Agnes and the nurse back to the city. Reese, of course, had left her the car; he had taken nothing, in fact, but a couple of suits. The packing and moving kept her so busy that she had almost no time for reflection, and the following night she again had her pills. But more importantly she had her resentment. It was not that she really believed that Reese was never coming back. But she clung to her resentment as the only hope that she would not crawl on her knees to welcome him when he did.

It worked. Barely, but it worked. She would thrust his

image into the bottom of her mind, and when it popped back until she was too tired to resist it further, she would review with a grim deliberation the record of his summer misdeeds: his ugly temper at going to the Cove, his refusal to call on Esther, his sullen preoccupation with poor Amos's morals. If he had only been willing to leave things to her, how well everything might have worked out! She might even have succeeded in getting young Alfred away from Esther for the winter. But could Reese have borne this? Of course not! He had to handle the situation in his own peculiar way to guarantee the failure of his scheme, to insure the continued custody of his son by a now implacable mother. He had, it seemed, to stir the rubble of his first marriage with one hand while the other lit a fuse to his second. Oh, how right she had been that night in Grace Chess's apartment when she had begged him to get out of her life before he had hurt her as he had hurt the others! Sometimes she wondered if she did not want him back only to tell him all the things that she had stored up to his account.

Slowly in the ensuing weeks, with all the pumps of her energy desperately operating, the bark of life began to right itself. She worked with a frenetic zeal at the magazine and made herself go out in the evenings. Little Agnes had to be left entirely to the nurse, but it would be only for the initial period of readjustment. Rosina began to find that she could concentrate on her articles again. In fact, she was surprised at her own powers of recuperation. If there were seconds still in every hour when she would clutch her hands and feel the damp of her own panic, she knew now that they would pass. There was even relief in the simplicity of a life where she no longer had to feel apologetic to a husband for the deflection of her energies, or where, if invited to dinner by Gilda Doremus or Anstiss, she no longer had to consider his

reluctance to go. If she was lonelier, she was also more
efficient. She knew, of course, how Reese would sneer at
such a life. She could imagine the gibes that he would make.
It would not be, she thought with a sniff, what he called
"living." But if living had quite so many aches and pains,
perhaps it was better simply to exist and enjoy the memory
of what living had been. Even if such a memory should be
the only difference between herself and a woman like Grace
Chess.

Poor Grace at the office eyed her in a frightened way and
murmured little invitations to "talk it over." But Rosina had
never been one to confide greatly in friends, and now the
prospect was actually repellent to her.

"I'm sorry, Grace," she said firmly. "I know you only
want to help me, but talking doesn't help. There's something
shameful about a failure. It's better to pretend it hasn't happened."

"But, Rosy dear, you look so badly!"

"At least I'll get over *that*."

Gilda Doremus was the perfect friend for Rosina's mood.
She accepted Reese's defection without surprise and without
commiseration. Her only comment was:

"Keep in with his family, my dear. Remember how well
the first wife did. Keep in with your in-laws."

Rosina was more grateful for the briefness than the quality
of the advice. Actually, she had no intention of "keeping
in" with her in-laws, except in a normal, friendly way. Little
Agnes should obviously be brought up to be on good terms
with her grandparents, but Rosina had no intention of becoming a second Esther. When Mrs. Parmelee came into the
city to see her, filled with solicitude and even a bit tearful,
Rosina was careful to behave as if the separation had been a
matter of mutual consent. She was very definite about not
going back to Northfield.

"But how can you live here in the city all alone?" her mother-in-law protested. "With a small baby and a nurse! My dear, it's not safe!"

"I'm sorry, Mrs. Parmelee, but without Reese I don't really belong in Northfield."

"Ah, but my child, we'd change all that! We'd make you feel entirely at home. Everyone wants you there!"

"I'm afraid you don't understand," Rosina insisted. "Without Reese I don't *want* to belong in Northfield."

This effectively put an end to the suggestion. Rosina was sorry to hurt her feelings, but the Parmelees had never made the smallest effort to understand her, and with such people a jolt was necessary. She had been perfectly happy to take them as they were and to be a Parmelee herself. Now, however, it appeared that her life was to be led in a different pattern. Whatever she became, she would never consent to be a half-Parmelee.

Amos called her several times to be sure that she had enough money. He was very kind, but he upset her with his easy assurance that Reese was coming back. It was just what she could not afford to face. It was only the nursed illusion of a permanent abandonment that sustained her at all. It sometimes seemed that there was no possible acceptable form which the future could take. The present was bitter, but there it was, and she was making do with it. How was she to handle Amos's final call?

"He was in the office today!" he exclaimed. "But he left before I came in. He stopped in to check on a trial calendar date."

At least, however, it prepared her for the following morning. She was not taken by surprise, coming out of the front door, to find Reese waiting for her at the bottom of the stoop. Although it was a chilly fall day that threatened rain, he was wearing no overcoat, and the collar of his jacket was rolled up. He looked tired, and he had not shaved; his stare was enigmatic, perhaps defiant. Her heart pounded behind the tight wall of her instant irritation.

"You look like a bum," she said curtly. "Do you want some coffee?"

"Please."

He followed her back into the house and sat in the living room while she got the percolator out of the pantry where she had just left it. He drank his coffee silently while she stood, one arm on the mantel, and looked bleakly down at him.

"Have you been far?"

"Just up to Canada with Andy. To the camp of a friend of his."

"The deep woods. How appropriate for deep thoughts. Do you mind if I say you don't look it? What did you and Andy do? Fly up a plane load of whiskey?"

"No. But I've been back a few days. I've been on a bender."

"A reaction, no doubt, to simple living."

He took her meaning literally. "In a way it was. Up there I felt all smoothed out. I seemed to see what I basically was." He shrugged, as if sneering at himself. "A lone wolf, that was all. And a lone wolf has only one duty, hasn't he? To keep to himself?"

"Which you very sensibly decided to do?"

"Which I decided to do," he agreed, nodding. "But then I came back." He looked up to fix his earnest eyes on hers, but she looked sharply away. "Since then I've been going through something like hell."

"I suppose even a man can learn about hell."

"Everything went back on me. When I thought of Esther and what a bitch she was, all I could think of was who had made her that way? Who had made her so hard and ambitious? And when I thought of you —"

"Oh, you thought of *me!*"

"Yes, Rosy, damn it all, I thought of you!" He jumped up angrily, and she wondered if he was going to come across the room to shake her by the shoulders. But he turned instead to the window. "I thought of what I was doing to you," he continued moodily. "I kept seeing you turning into another Gilda Doremus. I began to wonder what furies they were that made me treat people the way I did. As if it were some kind of hideous duty that I couldn't escape from. When I thought how happy I'd been in this house, I wondered if I wasn't really going crazy!" He snorted in disgust. "It seemed to me that all my life I'd been nothing but a small angry child splashing in a mud puddle."

"Do you really think I'm interested any longer in *why* you behave the way you behave?" she demanded in a voice that trembled with anger. "Do you think a woman cares for the *reason* she's been deserted? You have a monumental arrogance, Reese. And a monumental cheek. You'd better go along now. I have to get to my office. I have to get on with my life!"

"Rosy," he said, turning around, "you don't understand. I want to come back."

Of all the emotions that suddenly tightened their coils around her heart, it seemed that exasperation was at least the most articulate. There he stood, unshaven, unapologetic, actually sullen, blocking the bright doorway of her busy day. It was as if he were stretching forth a dirty hand to tear off the tinsel trimmings of her desperately decorated life, as if one brutal masculine gesture was all that was needed to bring her to her knees. Did a man even have to shave to defeat Gilda Doremus? Did he have to do more than grunt?

"Oh, Reese!" she cried in a wail. "How can you say that? Is it just because you think you're doing the same thing you did to Esther? And that you're afraid if you leave me, you'll leave someone else later? Is it just because you think there's no end to it? So you might as well stop now?"

"No. If you were Esther, I'd leave you all over again."

"*Would* you?"

"A thousand times if necessary!"

"Oh, Reese, I don't know. I honestly don't know!"

"I'm too late, is that it?" he demanded, flushing suddenly. "You've learned to get on without me in a month? Not that I'd blame you. Not that I'd blame you worth a damn!"

When she looked up and saw the old truculent expression in his eyes, she knew that her suspicion was correct. He *didn't* have to shave to defeat Gilda. But it was all so unfair that she sat down suddenly on the sofa and beat the cushions with her fists.

"Won't you even tell me that you love me?" she cried. "Don't I even rate that? Or must I be content with the beautiful picture of you sacrificing yourself to keep me from turning into a worse bitch than Esther!"

"You know I love you, Rosy," he said gravely. "You know it's what makes the whole difference."

She gave him a long, doubtful look. "*Do* you? *Do* I? How can anyone tell with you? How do I know if I take you back, that you won't walk out again in a few months? I can't go through this again, Reese. I really can't. If you're going to come back, I've got to have some kind of guarantee that you won't leave me again. Some kind of hostage!"

"What?"

"I don't know!" She looked up at him beseechingly. "A promise maybe. Will you give me a promise?"

"But I gave you a promise when I married you."

"Yes, but that was to a judge. You don't believe in judges. Promise it to *me!*" She got up and went over to take his hands in hers. Even now he begrudged her the least thing that did not sit with his canons of honesty. But this much he would have to concede. This much she had to insist on.

"Is this the girl who used to boast that she could take the world as it came?" he demanded.

"Promise!"

"Very well, I promise," he said at last, but he could not stop there. Perhaps it was too much to expect him to change the habits of a lifetime in a single morning. He had to add: "Of course, I should warn you that I promised Esther. And in a church, too!"

"You're a heel!" she cried and suddenly burst out laughing.

"I've always been a heel."

"And proud of it!"

Suddenly everything was much better. Suddenly the tight red balloon of her resentment seemed to have exploded, as with the pop of her laughter. She turned away to hide the ensuing tears; he had had enough of triumph for one day. Through the window she looked out at the little back yard, bare except for the pink marble fountain from Parmelee Cove with its two horses' heads. It was beginning to rain, but nothing could alter the complacency of those reared necks and neighing mouths.

"It was at the fountain that I first met Esther," she murmured. "Think how many things that led to! We must always keep those horses to remind us of the past glories of Parmelee Cove. And of what can happen if I don't learn to be happy." She hurried back to him and threw her arms around his neck. "You have to *tell* me more. You have to tell me every time you don't like something! You mustn't just sit there and brood!" She felt his arms grip her closely, and then his hands moved slowly up her back. But over his shoulder she could still see the horses at the fountain, and it was possible even then to visualize how much better they would look with a bank of rhododendrons on either side. "Oh, darling," she cried, almost in panic, tightening her hold around his neck, "You must help me! You must promise! It's such a *job* to be happy!"